D1525027

# They Only

# Wear

# Black Hats

A Novel

By
**Edward Izzi**

# THEY ONLY WEAR BLACK HATS

Paperback ISBN -979-876-483-1244
Hardcover ISBN – 979-876-488-6060

# Author's Disclaimer

"They Only Wear Black Hats" is a complete work of fiction. All names, characters, businesses, places, events, references, and incidents are the products of the author's imagination or are fictitious to tell the story.

Any references to real-life characters or events are used purely to recite a narrative for enjoyment purposes.

For Peter Cataldi

A beautiful soul with a wonderful heart who watched us all grow up with a twinkle in his eye. Always there, always smiling, always looking after us with pride.

"I'm like a bad nickel," he used to say. "You'll never get rid of me," he used to tell us as kids.

Having him in our lives was worth all the nickels in the world.

## ABOUT THE AUTHOR

Edward Izzi is a native of Detroit, Michigan, and is a Certified Public Accountant with a successful accounting firm in suburban Chicago, Illinois.

He is the father of four grown children and two beautiful grandchildren, Brianna and newborn Theodore.

He currently lives in the Windy City, where he seldom wears hats, especially black ones.

## They Only Wear Black Hats

*The angels of heaven have expanded wings.*
*They carry harps of gold and silver.*
*Their glorious voices fill magnificent clouds,*
*Their psalms chant loud without a quiver.*

*But also in heaven are the holy seraphs,*
*Seeking justice as God's diplomats.*
*When the demons of evil draw innocent blood,*
*...their avengers will be wearing black hats.*

# CHAPTER ONE

On that early Friday evening, the brisk fall wind and crisp autumn air carried the sounds and scents of a high school football game. The odors of fast food from the concession stands were abundant, as students and parents got in line for soft drinks, hot dogs, burgers, pretzels, and slices of delicious pepperoni pizza.

It was the annual girl's powder puff football game at the Denby High School football field. The home team, Dominican High School, an all-girls school located on Detroit's East Side, was playing their archrivals, Regina High School from Warren.

Seventeen-year-old Yvonne Basilisco was with three of her girlfriends on that Friday evening as they excitedly climbed up the steel bleachers to watch the powder-puff football game between her school and their infamous rival.

She had just gotten a car for her seventeenth birthday, a 2016 Nissan Rogue, and was excited to go out with her friends and experience one of the many activities she would enjoy as a senior in high school. Many of the Dominican football players were her friends from school, and the four girls sat on top of the bleachers and began to enjoy the game.

Yvonne was a very pretty high school senior with light brown hair, big blue eyes, and a smile that could make anyone take notice. She had a strong resemblance to Jennifer Aniston of 'Friends' fame and had a memorable giggle that one could only laugh along with. Yvonne was a straight-A student, always made the honor role, and was involved in volleyball and student government. Her parents were incredibly proud of her, and she was the model daughter, always looking after her two younger brothers. She had just applied to the

University of Michigan and was planning on pursuing a pre-med program.

To say that Yvonne had a lot of boyfriends and high school admirers was an understatement, as boys from all of the surrounding high schools had been taking notice of the talented, intelligent Dominican senior. But she wasn't in a relationship with any of them. They were all friends, she would say to her parents.

Yvonne was raised in a very strict, Italian Catholic family, and she knew the rules. She wasn't allowed to date and could only go out with her girlfriends when adults were around to watch and chaperone her and her friends. As a typical seventeen-year-old, she was looking forward to going away to college and pursuing her dreams without the constraints of her strict, old-school parents.

Being such a pretty, beautiful teenager, it was admirable that her parents and family wanted to protect her. Yvonne was such a bubbly, happy student and always had a joke or a smile for every one of her teachers and friends.

On that Friday night, Yvonne was wearing her black and yellow Dominican letter jacket that she earned from volleyball and stood out from the crowd of other young girls sitting together at the top of the bleachers. They were all laughing and joking, and the high school friends took turns going to the concession stand for fresh hot pizza slices, sodas, and other goodies.

After half-time, it was Yvonne's turn to go to the concession stand. She collected five-dollar bills from each of her three other friends. She ascended down the steel bleachers to the crowded concession stand near the edge of the football field. She walked over to the line of people waiting to be served, then realized that she needed to go to the restroom.

The ladies' bathroom located on the side of the concession stand was dark and without lights. As

9

the autumn dusk was starting to turn black and murky, Yvonne was all alone as she went into the ladies' bathroom. As she entered, she realized that no one else was in the girl's restroom, and she was all alone.

As soon as she exited the bathroom, someone approached her from behind. A large burly man with tattoos on each arm quickly put his hand over her mouth while tightly grabbing her left arm. He was a very stocky, older man in his late thirties, with a thick graying beard and earring.

"Don't say a fucking word," he sternly warned the teenager as he quickly escorted her towards the back of the bleachers from the back of the football field, where it was dark and desolate.

As he was manhandling her, he quickly handcuffed her hands behind her back and duct-taped her mouth. He incapacitated her within less than three minutes and threw her onto the barren, grassless ground underneath the stands. He then began to remove her clothing, pulling her blue jeans down to her ankles. He then began to rape and molest her, pushing himself onto her while the noise from the football field drowned out her muffled screams.

After five minutes of brutally molesting and raping the young teenager, the large, balding stranger went into his right pocket and pulled out his boxcutter switchblade.

Thirty minutes had passed, and the high school friends became curious about where Yvonne had gone and why she hadn't returned from the concession stand. Her best friend, Susan D'Amico, began to get worried. She dialed Yvonne's cell phone.

There was no answer.

Susan then convinced the other girls to accompany her and go looking for Yvonne together. They went to the concession stand and asked several other students if they had seen her, which they had not. They looked in the girl's bathroom and started to search around the parking lot, but there was no sign of her.

After another thirty minutes had passed, they informed a policeman sitting in a patrol car in the parking lot of Denby High School that their girlfriend was missing. He was with the Detroit Police Department. He immediately called for backup patrol cars as he began to assist the girls in looking for their friend.

After another hour of searching for the young girl, one of the patrolmen began searching under the football stands, shining his flashlight on the ground.

Covered under some garbage and wood debris underneath the stands was the lifeless body of Yvonne Basilisco. Her clothing had been torn off, and her blue jeans had been pulled down to her ankles. There was blood splattered across her topless chest, exposing the knife lacerations on her breasts. The crimson red was still spewing from her neck wound. The teenager's hands were still cuffed behind her back. Her neck had been slit open from the boxcutter blade that the rapist had savagely used, and the girl's dead body was still warm.

By ten-thirty, two EMS trucks and several more Detroit patrol cars surrounded the football field. Several other students, including Yvonne's girlfriends, were interrogated extensively by the detectives. But no one had seen Yvonne when she had left them in the football stands, and no one noticed anyone looking suspicious.

Later that Friday evening, at 11:50 pm, Detroit Police Detective Michael Palazzola made that dreaded phone call that no parent ever wishes to receive.

11

# CHAPTER TWO
EIGHT MILE ROAD-SUMMER 2020

Manny's Party and Liquor Store on Detroit's East Side was filled with patrons on that late Friday night, as customers were coming in and out of the party store with their brown paper bags filled with goodies. It was just after one o'clock in the morning, and all of the late-night bars and strip clubs were letting out their customers for the remainder of the weekend.

It was an unusually warm evening for a late Friday night in the Motor City, as the odorous smell from the nearby garbage dumpsters perpetuated the hot, inner-city odors of the surrounding buildings. The popular party store was a twilight staple on Eight Mile and Van Dyke Roads because it had a liquor license that allowed them to stay open and sell liquor until four o'clock in the morning. The store had an extensive deli and pizza oven in the back, providing submarine sandwiches and freshly made cheese pizza slices to all of its customers who had the late-night munchies.

A black 2005 Chevrolet Malibu, displaying several dents in the rear quarter panel, pulled up into the parking lot, its bright lights shining onto the glass front door of the party store. A stocky, white male, balding with a long greying beard and wearing a sleeveless black shirt, entered the party store. He had several tattoos on each arm and a long chain attached to his wallet from his belt as he slowly walked to the liquor section of the party store. He was there to purchase a bottle of Chivas Regal for that evening.

Derek Johnson was excited to continue his celebrations that Friday night. He had just left the Crazy Horse Lounge on Eight Mile Road and needed to buy some liquor before returning to the strip club's parking lot. One of the exotic dancers who had been giving him lap dances throughout most of the night had agreed to meet him in the parking lot of the strip club after her shift was over at two o'clock in the morning. Derek knew he had to return with a bottle of Chivas Regal, along with two plastic glasses that 'Veronique' had explicitly requested. She had told him that she would not accept a ride home from him after her night shift unless he returned with her favorite alcoholic beverage.

With his large, six-foot, five-inch frame, Johnson exited his vehicle as he walked into the party store, leaving his car doors unlocked as usual. Besides his being excited to party with his new friend, Derek had another reason to celebrate. He had been released from Jackson State Prison two weeks prior, where he was being held without bail on a murder charge. He had been accused of raping and murdering a seventeen-year-old girl from Dominican High School in October 2019. After spending nine months in jail, he was abruptly released. The high school teenager had been found dead under the bleachers of the Denby football field, with her neck slit open from what appeared to be a boxcutter switchblade. She had been accosted during the football game and had been brutally raped and murdered. Her lifeless body was found under a large pile of garbage and debris underneath the school's football field bleachers.

The boxcutter switchblade was obtained at his home by an inexperienced Detroit police officer without a search warrant. Although the EMT technicians had used the rape kit at the crime scene, the DNA evidence had been mishandled and tainted by the Detroit Police crime lab.

Because there was no other evidence linking him to the murdered teenager, Johnson was suddenly released from jail, and the prosecutor dropped the murder charges. The Wayne County Prosecutor's office was highly frustrated with that murder case and had no other choice but to release the accused killer back onto the streets. None of the other DNA tests performed by the crime labs directly connected Johnson to the young, murdered victim.

A gray Toyota Camry pulled up next to the older Chevy Malibu as Johnson entered the party store. A well-dressed man wearing a black bowler hat with a dark suitcoat and tie exited his vehicle and stood outside for several long seconds. He then began trying to open the passenger doors of the older car. The stranger immediately discovered that the doors of Johnson's car were unlocked. The well-dressed man had been following the acquitted killer most of the evening, biding his time and waiting for the right opportunity to confront the accused murderer. He then quickly climbed into the vehicle and hid behind the back seat of the car.

After fifteen minutes had passed, Derek Johnson exited the party store. He got back into his car, not noticing a strange passenger hiding in the back seat. Putting his bottle of whiskey, plastic cups, and a bag of potato chips in the front seat, Johnson started his car and began to drive back to the Crazy Horse Lounge. Within five minutes, he was back in the parking lot, his radio loudly blaring AC/DC music as he waited for his exotic dancer date to come out of the lounge.

Opening the large Better Made potato chips bag, he snacked on them while looking at his old Timex watch. He was excited, knowing that 'Veronique' would soon be exiting the strip club, and they both would be enjoying their snacks and beverages in the front seat of his car. Johnson had not been with a woman for a very long time, and he knew that she would be taking care of his sexual needs in the back of the parking lot after her shift.

Suddenly, a well-dressed man, still wearing his black bowler hat, abruptly sat up from the back seat of the car.

"Good evening, scumbag," said a stranger calling himself Gabriel in a deep, low voice.

Before Johnson could even make a move, the intruder quickly wrapped a thick, quarter-inch rope tightly around Johnson's neck. Derek Johnson began

14

making loud gurgling noises, his body being pulled back towards the back seat of the Chevy Malibu. Grasping the rope around his neck, both of Johnson's feet began kicking out the front windshield of his car.

With blood and saliva protruding from his mouth, Johnson was now suffocating and struggling to breathe. While taking his last breath, the 'black angel' in the back seat with the black bowler hat softly whispered into his victim's ear:

"Die a thousand deaths, you fucking bastard."

# CHAPTER THREE
## GRATIOT BAR & GRILL

The drab, darkened tavern of the Gratiot Bar & Grill clad the front window with lighted, fluorescent beer signs. Vintage antique displays of 'Pabst Blue Ribbon,' 'Old Milwaukee,' and a classic 'Drink Stroh's Beer' signs were flashing brightly, even though none of those beers are any longer available. Several patrons were sitting at the long, overly varnished bar on that Saturday afternoon. They enjoyed their beverages while the seven or more television sets were strategically placed around the old lounge.

The blaring sounds of the jukebox in the back of the lounge seemed to conflict with the volume of the various scattered television sets. Someone had selected several Bruce Springsteen songs that seemed to be playing continuously, as the afternoon sunshine of the Motor City overshadowed its entrance doorway.

I had parallel parked my unmarked patrol car into the front parking space on Gratiot Avenue. I walked exhaustedly into the dark shadow forecasted doorway. I was more than familiar with what I would see once inside the entrance, as I could hear loud sounds and noises coming from all directions. Even though there was no smoking in the bar, the old tavern smelled like stale cigar smoke. The saloon walls were in dire need of a fresh coat of paint, which had well absorbed the tobacco and nicotine smoke from years past. The Detroit Tigers baseball game was playing above the bar as the older, blonde bartender approached me with her familiar smile.

"Detective Palazzola," she enthusiastically greeted me as I found an old, leather-bound stool to sit down at the bar.

"What will it be? The usual?"

Gina, the Bartender, broadly smiled at me. I couldn't help but notice her bright, curly, bleach blonde hair that didn't do a very good job hiding her extensive greys. Her right arm was covered with various tattoos as she grabbed a white, terrycloth rag to wipe down the long bar.

"Yeah," I nodded my head. "Jack on the Rocks with a splash of water," I smiled, looking up at the ball game and trying to get the baseball score. The Detroit Tigers were playing the Chicago White Sox that afternoon. I quickly realized that our home team was now losing, as usual.

"What's the score, Gina?"

"Twelve, zip...bottom of the eighth. 'The Boys' are getting killed."

"That figures."

The bartender still used the famous reference to the hometown baseball team, which started in 1984 when the Detroit 'Bless You Boys' Tigers last won the World Series.

"Off duty?"

"Just got off.... a twelve-hour shift. Been at it since five o'clock this morning," I replied, motioning her to hand me a small bag of Better Made potato chips hanging next to the cash register.

"It sucks working on Saturdays."

I had stopped off at my favorite watering hole after my weekend shift at the Third Precinct. My long day included two rape investigations, several car thefts, and a home burglary on Seven Mile Road. I usually stopped off when I finished my long shifts at the precinct before going home to my two teenage daughters and figuring out which pizzeria I would be calling up for carry-out.

I was enjoying my drink and watching the Tigers finish up the ninth inning. After ten minutes had passed, I was almost finished with my bag of chips when the six

17

o'clock news came blaring out from all of the TV sets in unison:

*"This is Joanne Spada, Channel Six Eyewitness News. There has been a gruesome murder in the parking lot of the Crazy Horse Lounge on Eight Mile Road very early this morning. The victim appears to have been strangled last night, and police are trying to put together the events that occurred in the parking lot of this exotic dancers club on the East Side of Detroit. The victim has been identified as Derek Johnson, a thirty-six-year-old white male who resides on Detroit's East Side on Chalmers Avenue. As you may recall, Mr. Johnson had just been released from prison two weeks ago after being acquitted on the murder charges of a Denby High School teenager back in October of 2019. The Detroit Police detectives here at this investigation mentioned a long, thick rope and a black bowler hat were left at the crime scene. This parking lot has been roped off with yellow crime scene tape, pending the investigation by the Detroit Police Department."*

I looked at the TV, shaking my head at the news report. I had not heard anything about this murder while at my shift at the Third Precinct.

I had faintly recalled the name of Derek Johnson, the scumbag felon who had raped and killed that beautiful young teenager at Denby High School. The young victim, Yvonne Basilisco, was a senior high school student from Dominican High. It was the same school that my two daughters, Adrianna and Sara, attended. Although my kids didn't know the victim, she was a very popular student with a bright future ahead of her. I had been called to that crime scene on that Friday evening last fall, and I had the horrific duty of calling the young victim's parents, informing them of her violent death.

"Did you hear about this?" Gina looked at me, thinking that I may have more information to report.

"To tell you the truth, no...I hadn't."

18

Truth be told, I was shocked by the news. I worked on those rape investigations and other crimes in my office cubicle all day, and I didn't hear about any other crimes occurring the night before.

"This guy was strangled, and the killer left the rope and one of those derby hats in the back seat of the car," the bartender commented, still wiping down the bar with her wet dishrag.

"Unreal. Hopefully, the detectives assigned to this case will be able to pull the DNA from the evidence left at the crime scene," I remarked, noting that I didn't know enough about that crime scene to make any comment at all.

At that moment, another familiar face walked into the Gratiot Bar and Grill. He sat right next to me while ordering his drink.

"Seven-Up, Gina...on the rocks. Throw in a few limes."

"Well, hello, Detective Valentino. Are we having a police convention at my bar this afternoon?"

"No, Gina. If we decide to have a convention at your bar, we'll be sure to bring along the warrants," he replied with a smile, tongue in cheek.

The bartender smiled back at him flirtatiously as she put down her dish rag and stood at attention for the new patron.

"And you're still not drinking? I'm so proud of you, Johnny," she mentioned, quickly filling up his glass of soda with several ice cubes and some freshly cut limes.

"Thanks. I've got to be careful when I go into a bar these days. Those Nazis from A-A are lurking everywhere," he smiled, grasping his soda drink with his left hand while shaking my hand with his right.

19

"Be careful of those spies," she smiled as she looked at herself in the mirror behind the bar.

"So…what's up, Mikie? I haven't seen you around lately."

Detective Johnny Valentino was my partner from the Third Precinct. He had been working the streets on a stake out for a potential drug bust in the Corktown neighborhood and had been primarily out of the office. He had been a life-long alcoholic and regularly attended Alcoholics Anonymous meetings every other Wednesday at some church basement on Kelly Road.

"How long have you been off the juice now?" I inquired.

"It will be a year this month. Aren't you proud of me?" Valentino mentioned as he sipped his soda while stirring the limes.

"You're doing great, Johnny. Good job," I immediately complimented him. "But aren't you tempted to have a drink when you walk into a bar?"

"No, not lately. It doesn't bother me anymore. Besides, it beats sitting home and watching TV."

Valentino had been my precinct partner for the last eighteen months, and he was a great guy to have to watch your back. Johnny was an old-school veteran detective who worked very hard and wasn't afraid to play hardball. He was also very street smart, and he didn't take any shit from anyone. But for some odd reason, I always felt responsible for him, and I usually had to keep an eye out for his well-being. As we had gotten to be great friends, I always felt the need to make sure that he stayed sober. Knowing that Valentino was a recovering alcoholic who still liked to party, keeping an eye on him wasn't an easy task by any means.

"How's Marina?" I asked, referring to his once ex-wife, whom he had now reconciled. He had recently moved back to his home in Harper Woods and seemed very content with his sober, new family life.

"Marina and the boys are great," he said with a smile. "Anthony just graduated high school and will be going to Michigan State next month. He's going into Pre-Med."

"Very good," I nodded, still sipping on my Jack-on-the-Rocks.

"Dario is a junior and is still my trouble-maker. But the good news is that the Marists at Notre Dame still haven't kicked him out of school yet."

His youngest son, Dario, was a high school student at Notre Dame High School on Kelly Road. His youngest son was a carbon copy of himself and had difficulty controlling his temper like his old man. Valentino was suspended a year ago for severely beating up one of his old partners at the Third Precinct. He had made the mistake of calling him a 'dago drunk.' His son had been suspended from high school on several occasions for getting into fights with other students. Like his father, he didn't take any shit from anyone.

"How are his grades?"

"Barely passing. Says he wants to be a copper like his old man."

I smiled and shook my head, knowing that I would never want any of my children, or my friend's children, to go into law enforcement.

"And you're okay with this?"

"With his mouth and his temper, I can't see him doing anything else."

"Tell him to join the union. I hear they're looking for more young people to go into the trades. They do make a good buck."

21

"Or join the Army," Johnny quickly replied, checking out the six-o'clock news that was now blaring on all of the televisions mounted everywhere at the bar.

"How are your girls?" he asked, referring to my two teenagers while twirling the ice cubes in his glass.

"Doing well. They're both at Dominican High School."

Valentino nodded his head, then asked for a refill of his Seven-Up with limes.

"Did the Tigers win?"

"Hell, no. The Chicago White Sox kicked our asses...twelve, zip," I loudly replied, emphasizing my disappointment.

"Those pussies from the Southside of Chicago seem to always have their way with 'the boys,'" Valentino observed.

We both smiled as we nursed our drinks while glaring at the monitor mounted over the large mirror behind the bar. The bartender threw Valentino a small complimentary bag of potato chips while the homicide at the Crazy Horse Lounge was again on the six o'clock news.

"Mikie, did you hear about this? We've got a gentleman killer on our hands. This guy strangles this 'perp' in the parking lot at the Crazy Horse and leaves his derby hat at the crime scene," Johnny mentioned the matter of factly while making slurping noises with his straw and his soda.

"A derby hat?"

"Yeah, you know, those derby hats that those English gentlemen wear in London."

"You mean a bowler hat?" I corrected my partner.

"Yeah, that's it. Last time I saw one of those was in one of those James Bond movies."

"Oh, you mean 'Goldfinger'?"

"Yeah, that's it," Valentino replied as he put his empty Seven-Up glass with its half-melted ice cubes on the counter of the bar. He then made eye contact with the bartender, who knew to refill his glass immediately.

"What was the name of that movie with Pierce Brosnan?" Gina asked, immediately figuring she could participate in the conversation.

"Which one?" I asked.

"You know, there was a scene in the movie where a bunch of guys are robbing an art gallery wearing black bowler hats and dark suits, carrying a briefcase."

"You mean the 'Thomas Crown Affair'?" I interjected.

"Yeah," Gina smiled. "That's it."

We all chuckled about the movie reference while staring at the TV.

"Maybe this killer is Brit-ish?" Gina suggested, using a squeaky, mock English accent.

I nodded my head at the suggestion, thinking that it was rather strange that someone would leave their rope around the victim's neck and a black bowler hat at the crime scene.

I then confessed to my partner.

"I remember this fucking guy. This is the perp who raped and killed that high school student from Dominican during a football game at Denby last fall."

Valentino looked at me, his face drawing a blank.

"Derek Johnson. Remember? They sent that young rookie, Harrison, over to his house to pick him up on the East Side, and he found the perp's switchblade that was used in the murder."

"Oh yeah, I remember now. The crime lab dropped the ball on Johnson's evidence kit, and that young rookie confiscated and tainted the murder weapon without a warrant."

Valentino shook his head while taking a long slurp of his pretend alcoholic drink.

"That homicide still breaks my heart," I confessed.

"That perp got what he deserved, that fucking scumbag," Johnny smiled. "There truly is some justice in this world."

A silent moment while we stared at the television and pretended to be interested in the newscast.

"Who is working this homicide?" I asked my partner.

"I'm sure it's at the Fifth Precinct. But don't be surprised if it ends up on our laps. They don't have the Intel staff that we do," Valentino suggested.

"Everyone is jammed right now, so I'm not so sure we'll get it dumped on our desks," I observed.

"Don't be surprised."

By that moment, I was finished with my Jack-on-the-Rocks. Although I was tempted to have another drink, I knew I had to rush home to my girls and figure out what the dinner situation would be on that Saturday night.

"It's getting late, and I need to rush home and feed my girls," as I got up from the barstool. I then gave my partner the traditional man-hug and put a twenty-dollar bill on top of the bar counter.

"Keep it, Gina. I'll talk to you soon."

"Thanks, Mikie. Enjoy the weekend."

As I exited the Gratiot Bar & Grill, it was still light outside, even though it was almost seven o'clock. I knew I

24

had to rush home figure out the dinner situation with my daughters before they both took matters into their own hands. I lived twenty minutes away in St. Clair Shores, so I knew I could call up one of the pizzerias on Ten Mile Road and pick up dinner before going home.

As it turned out, the 'Black Bowler Hat' murder case on that summer day was never solved by the Fifth Precinct. Perhaps it was their lack of experience in solving homicide cases or their sloppiness in acquiring any solid evidence at the crime scene.

But one angle that I didn't realize at the time was that maybe the direct motive of this homicide was vengeance. Perhaps the connection in murdering this 'perp' was that someone wanted Derek Johnson dead for the murder of that teenage girl at Denby High School. Maybe this murder was retribution for his escaping justice by the Wayne County prosecutor's office.

Johnson was allowed to go free, even though the evidence from the murder weapon proved beyond a shadow of a doubt that his switchblade was used to murder that young teenage girl. It was sloppy police procedure at best, maybe even negligence on the part of the Detroit PD. This mishandled evidence allowed Johnson to go free, only to be mysteriously strangled two weeks later.

Was all of this a coincidence? Or was all of this planned and contrived by someone with authority within Detroit's legal system?

This is not how the justice system is supposed to work. This wasn't the first time a perpetrator had escaped justice because of a material flaw in the legal system in my long career. And it certainly wasn't the first time that one of the investigating detectives committed an error in gathering evidence, with the alleged convict allowed to go free. Since when was an accused murderer killed for revenge by someone within the legal system? Since when was an accused offender released by the authorities, only

25

to be mysteriously murdered two weeks later? It just didn't make any sense.

Was this a new kind of justice system?

I didn't ask myself any of those questions at the time of that 'Black Bowler Hat' murder last summer. I just figured that it was only a random homicide. It wasn't until later that I realized that this homicide would be the first of a long string of mysterious revenge murders.

This would not be the last time I would hear about someone wearing one of those black bowler hats.

# CHAPTER FOUR
A MISSING BOY – FALL, 2020

It was a late October afternoon as Tammy Stewart anxiously waited for her twelve-year-old son, Garrett, to come home from school. It was a typical fall Monday, as Tammy came home early every Monday afternoon from her job as a legal secretary to bring her son to his afternoon piano lessons. Tammy was a middle-aged single mother who doted on her only son and always ensured that he was never late for his weekly music lessons.

At just past four o'clock, it looked as though her son was unusually late. He usually came home on the bus at 3:15 from Chippewa Valley Middle School, but he must have missed the bus. She called the school looking for her son, but no one had seemed to know where Garrett was. She called his cell phone several times, but to no avail. His piano lesson at the East Side Music Conservatory on Gratiot Avenue began at 4:30 pm, and it always took forty-five minutes from their home in Clinton Township in traffic.

She continued to call everyone she knew, including several of his friends and their mothers, asking if they had seen or heard from her son.

Three hours went by, and there was no sign of her son.

At seven-thirty, she jumped in her Chevy Malibu. She drove around the school and throughout her neighborhood in Clinton Township. She drove up and down Garfield Road, south to Fraser and then to Roseville past Gratiot Avenue. Tammy then drove back north to as far as Mount Clemens. The whole time, she frantically called everyone that she knew, hoping that someone may have seen him after school.

This was so unlike Garrett. He was a good kid who loved playing baseball and football with his friends in the neighborhood. He was an ordinary boy who preferred to play outdoors with his many friends in the seventh grade rather than sit at home in front of his computer screen playing video games. When he did play, he would often be playing on his Xbox until the middle of the night, communicating with his friends online that he would be playing with until midnight during the weekends, or whenever his mother would bust him for not being in bed and asleep before ten o'clock.

It was just after nine o'clock when she finally went to the Clinton Township Police Department, nervously asking the deputy dispatcher at the front desk to assist her.

"May I help you?"

"Yes, I would like to report my son missing," Tammy said in a frantic voice, almost to the point of tears.

"What is your son's name?"

"Garrett Steward. He is twelve years old, and he's a seventh-grader at Chippewa Valley Middle School."

The dispatcher began writing down her information.

"Does he have a cell phone? Did you try calling him?"

"OFCOURSE I TRIED CALLING HIM," Tammy loudly replied, now crying and yelling at the same time.

The Clinton Township Dispatcher looked at the middle-aged woman. She was very slender, moderately pretty with dishwater blonde hair, wearing faded blue jeans and a sleeveless white shirt. She had several tattoos displayed on her right arm. At that moment, the dispatcher radioed a patrolman to come to the front desk after asking Tammy to have a seat. A tall, older patrolman, bald and wearing horn-rimmed glasses, entered the reception area within several minutes.

"I'm Officer Jerry Winer, ma'am. I understand that you have a missing little boy. When was the last time that you heard from him?"

"This morning, before I went to work. He catches the bus in front of our house on Marisa Drive."

After taking down her name and address, he asked for the young boy's cellular number. He immediately brought the information to a detective who was on duty at the time, and the two officers put a tracker on the boy's cellular phone.

The cellular phone was still active and receiving phone calls. They then dispatched a patrol car to the area where the phone was located. His Apple 10 iPhone had been discarded into the Clinton River near Clinton River Road. It was remarkably still working after being soaked and drenched in the polluted water. Several more patrol cars were dispatched to the area. It didn't take more than a few hours of searching in and around the Clinton River area to find what they were looking for.

There, located behind some thick bushes and trees near the cold dark riverbank, was a little boy's lifeless body. His body was covered with dark soot and was partially clothed as if he had been raped and badly mutilated. There were several stab wounds across his face and body, drenched in blood and black dirt. It looked as though the killer tried to partially bury the body on the riverbank after desperately trying to throw the body into the river., The murderer was probably interrupted by the nearby traffic on Clinton River Road and hastily covered the body near some thick bushes on the riverbank. The victim had been sexually assaulted before being stabbed several times.

Officer Winer observed the boy's body and removed his wallet, which was still intact in his clothes pocket. He removed his wet, soggy student identification card. After going through the contents of the young boy's wallet, there was no doubt in his mind who the young victim was.

Tammy Steward was still waiting at the Clinton Township police station when several patrolmen arrived back to inform her of the grim news that little Garrett Steward had been found. Tammy was now surrounded by several immediate family members, including her mother, sisters, and close friends. They held her up as she collapsed in their arms upon hearing the tragic news about the murder of her only son. The loud shrills of her screaming voice sent reverberating echoes throughout the police station as the rest of her family cried along with her in disbelief. A grief counselor was called immediately to assist the police department. Several other detectives from neighboring Sterling Heights and Fraser were called in to assist in the murder investigation.

The ABC Eyewitness News crew began doing a live feed in front of the Clinton Township Police Station for their late evening news. Two reporters tried to shove their microphones in front of the Steward family members as they were leaving, yelling out questions for them to answer.

"Our little boy was murdered," one of Tammy's sisters cried out loudly to the news media, as several of them assisted Tammy back to her blue, older model Chevrolet Malibu.

The Clinton Township Police Department began their investigation by acquiring the DNA evidence from the crime scene and sending it over to the FBI to match its records. Within a few days, the match came back to a potential subject.

John Michael Golan was a custodian at the Chippewa Valley Middle School. He was an older, overweight man in his late fifties, balding, and was just over six feet tall. Golan had a prior criminal record that consisted of several prior offenses, including breaking and entering, carrying an unregistered weapon, and most recently, the attempted rape of a teenage boy several years ago. Although he was a registered sex offender, he was able to stay under the radar and get hired two years ago as a nighttime custodian with the Chippewa Valley School District in Macomb County. It was unknown to the authorities at the time how a registered sex offender was able to acquire a full-time position working as a janitor at a junior high school.

Officer Jerry Winer, along with his partner, Officer Mark Bennett, picked up the perpetrator at his home on the evening of November 28, 2020. He was given his rights, handcuffed, and sent to the Macomb County Jail on Elizabeth Road in Mount Clemens. He pleaded not guilty at his arraignment and was held without bail.

By all the facts of this case, it was pretty obvious that the Clinton Township Police Department had taken custody of the right man. He had the motive and the criminal background that matched his modus operandi, or 'M.O.' that all coordinated with the profile of a sexual predator.

The Macomb County Prosecutor was so confident in the DNA evidence that he refused to offer a plea deal to the defendant's attorneys. The prosecutor believed he would have absolutely no trouble acquiring a conviction of life in prison without any chance of parole. With the age and criminal record of the accused murderer, it would be a certainty that John Michael Golan would die in prison serving his term.

But Golan's attorney, Robert Irsuto, discovered one incredible mistake made by the arresting officers that would make all the difference in the potential conviction of his client.

During the trial four months later, the prosecutors presented all of the DNA evidence, along with witnesses that attested to the perpetrator's lack of moral character and his desire to sexually rape and murder his victims.

When the defense team was asked to present their case, Officer Winer was called to the witness stand. After he was sworn in, Attorney Robert Irsuto asked the officer a straightforward question:

'Did you read the defendant his rights?"

"The Miranda Warning?"

"Yes."

Officer Winer reflected for a moment on the witness stand. He then replied:

"Yes, I did recite his rights to the defendant."

Irsuto smiled for a moment and then asked the officer the same question again:

"Officer Winer, can you please recite the Miranda Warning for us, please?"

"Certainly. You have the right to remain silent. Anything that you say can and will be held against you in a court of law. You have the right to an attorney. If you cannot afford legal counsel, one will be appointed for you before questioning. If you decide to answer questions without an attorney present, you have the right to stop answering those questions at any time."

"So, Officer Winer, you recited the defendant's rights at the time of his arrest, is this correct?"

"Yes, I did."

"Officer Winer, let me ask you again. Did you READ the defendant his rights?"

The Clinton Township patrolman sat there for a long moment, then answered the question the same way.

"I told him his rights."

Smiling, Irsuto asked him the same question.

"But Officer Winer, did you READ the defendant his rights?"

The veteran officer of nineteen years sat silently in the witness stand for several long seconds, not responding again to the defense attorney's repeated question.

"Answer my question, Officer Winer!" Irsuto loudly demanded.

"The witness shall answer the defense attorney's question, please," the judge reprimanded Winer.

After several more silent seconds, Officer Winer slowly answered the question.

"No, your honor. I recited the Miranda Warning to the defendant, as I have always done when arresting a potential suspect in the past."

"So, Officer Winer...you recited the Miranda Warning to the suspect. You did not READ the Miranda Warning as required by law. Correct?"

Another moment of silence.

"No. I did not read the Miranda Warning. I recited it to the suspect."

At that moment, Defense Attorney Robert Irsuto immediately moved to have the charges of first-degree murder dismissed by the court.

During an arrest, when the police fail to *read* a defendant his Miranda rights or fail to give them in this case correctly, any statements, including a confession, cannot be used against the defendant.

After admonishing the arresting officers for their lack of care in securing the defendants' rights, the judge regretfully dismissed the murder charges of Garrett Stewart against John Michael Golan.

There were loud cries in the courtroom as Tammy Steward, the boy's mother, began screaming out loud, attempting to approach the accused killer as he left the defendant's table with his attorney.

"How dare you? How dare you take my baby away, you rotten fucking bastard!"

The boy's mother continued to scream until two court officers apprehended her and escorted her out of the courtroom.

The next day, the Macomb Daily reported the court's decision as front-page news:

**Accused Murderer Goes Free on Court Technicality**

It was the leading story of all of the local news stations. How could the arresting officers have been so erroneous, so sloppy as to not correctly *read* the suspect's rights at the time of his arrest? It wasn't long before the arresting officers were officially dismissed and stripped of their police duties. Despite their protests and grievances filed by their local Fraternal Order of Police, they were terminated as Clinton Township police officers.

John Michael Golan was allowed to go free. He immediately made it known to his family and friends that he would be moving as far away from the Detroit area as possible.

Three weeks later, a late model Ford Escape was found parked in the parking lot of Metropolitan Beach on Sixteen Mile Road. The car had been abandoned for several days, and a powerful odor began protruding from the parked car's trunk. When the local police ran the license plates of the vehicle, they then pried open the trunk and were shocked by their discovery:

In the trunk of that car was the strangled dead body of John Michael Golan. He was bound with handcuffs, and his mouth had been duct-taped. A quarter-inch thick rope was wrapped tightly around his neck, obviously used to strangle him to death. And within the trunk of his car, next to his dead body, was another unusual item:

A black bowler hat.

# CHAPTER FIVE
### THE SANDBOX-FALL, 2020

The bright, October sun was shining brightly on the playground sand as a little girl played alone during the St. Veronica school recess on Toepfer Avenue in St. Clair Shores. She was fumbling with a blue bucket filled with sand, softly smiling, and singing to herself contently, enjoying the late autumn sunshine. Her long, curly, raven black hair was neatly combed back, not to get in the way of her white blouse, and plaid vest, and matching skirt. She couldn't have been more than eight years old but seemed undisturbed as the surrounding children played vigorously nearby. There were boys clad in their white shirts and ties, fighting for their turns on the schoolyard slide or monkey bars, while the girls in their Catholic school uniforms were playing jump rope in the middle of the school play area.

As the little schoolgirl played alone in her private sandbox, she seemed to be ignored by the other children. Boys and girls were walking and running past her as if they wished to leave her to play all alone. There was something uniquely different about her. Her neatly ironed white blouse, her almost perfect dark curly hair, and her laced socks folded neatly above her black and white saddle shoes. She seemed to stand out among the other children. It was as though she were an animated porcelain doll, playing happily and quietly alone in the schoolyard.

A dark-haired little boy, wearing a grass-stained shirt and loosened tie, began to walk over to the brunette little girl playing alone, holding a red, plastic shovel.

"Can I use your bucket?" asked the little boy, holding the red shovel up high in his hand.

"No." the girl replied.

"But you can help me fill it up with sand." She quickly added. Her soft, mellow voice contrasted the loud, laughing children playing on the adjacent swing sets.

The boy quickly sat next to her and began filling up the little girl's bucket, scooping up sand and dumping each filled bucket around them.

"What's your name?" asked the little boy in earnest.

"Sofia Maria Rigoletto," she replied, disclosing her full baptismal first, middle and last name.

"What's that?" he innocently asked.

"My name. It's Sofia Maria Rigoletto. But my Mom calls me Sofie."

"Oh." The little boy seemed undaunted by her explanation as he continued to play with the sand and a shovel and threw darker, dirt stains upon his white shirt. His feet were snuggly buried beneath the sand, not paying any attention to dirt covering his black socks and trousers.

"What's your name?" the little girl asked.

"David Andrews," he said politely, still paying more attention to his red shovel filling up her blue bucket.

"Do your friends call you Dave?" she curiously asked.

"Only the ones who want to get punched," he replied.

Little Sofie started to giggle as her new friend continued to fill up her bucket and dump the formed sand all around her.

"Let's build a castle," she exclaimed, as the two of them worked feverously at their new endeavor as the recess bell began to ring.

Within the distance of the schoolyard stood a dark-haired man, staring behind the cyclone fence, watching the two minor children play in the sandbox not very far away. He was holding a beige raincoat and had a dark brown suitcase placed neatly next to him. He watched the two children play as if he wished to walk over and play with them. He was motionless, and oddly, didn't seem to attract the attention of anyone as he studied the two children playing together. A yellow taxicab pulled up alongside the school playground. The driver motioned to the man standing along the fence that his ride to the airport was ready.

"What time is your flight, sir?" asked the cabbie.

"My flight is at 1:15, American Airlines," the gentleman replied.

"We should get on the road. The traffic is heavy."

The man continued to watch his little girl play in the sandbox with her little friend.

"Okay."

He didn't want to look suspicious, as the court order disallowing him to see his daughter had been enacted by the judge several months ago. He had not been granted visitation rights since he had been arrested several times on domestic violence charges that the girl's mother filed.

The man, with tears running down his face, slowly put on his hat and overcoat and climbed gingerly into the taxi, taking one, long last look at the little girl, playing in the sandbox, then quickly getting in line to go inside St. Veronica School with her new friend.

Little David and Sofie became fast friends in the second grade, sitting next to one another at lunchtime every day. David would unpack his peanut butter and jelly sandwich from his Batman lunchbox. At the same time, Sofie would bring along her Holly Hobby lunchbox and always split her Mortadella and Provolone Cheese sandwich with him.

They would talk and share about all of their new adventures together in the second grade. They would play together at recess, usually in the sandbox area of the schoolyard, making sandcastles, digging deep trenches, and getting themselves all dirty and full of sand before going back into class. Sofie would share her Holly Hobby books with David, bringing his Batman comic books into class to share with his friends, but mainly with Sofie.

As the fall weather became colder, David would walk from his house to Sofie's house on the corner of May and Forest Streets, pick her up, and walk together to school every morning. Along the way, there was a circular, round cul-de-sac in the middle of Forest and Oak Streets, on the way to St. Veronica School. Each morning, Sofie and David would take the time to play tag and chase each other around and around, laughing, giggling, and loudly playing together every day.

During that time, David had all but ignored his other friends, letting them walk back and forth to school by themselves. David would only play with his best friends' afterschool but always ensured that he was available for Sofie during most recesses and escorted her en route to her house and St. Veronica's School.

Early one cold, November morning, David and Sofie were playing on the cul-de-sac when, as David was chasing Sofie, she fell and badly scraped her knee. It was All Saints Day at their school, and the two of them had gone trick-or-treating the night before and had brought along some candy goodies in their lunch buckets. As David was trying to assist little Sofia with her scraped knee, a black, late model Lincoln pulled up next to them on Forest Street. Sofie recognized who was driving the car immediately.

"Daddy!" Sofia exclaimed as he opened the car door and let both of the children in. Little Sofia sat in the front seat with her seat belt on, while the little boy sat in the back. Little Sofia had not seen her father in several months.

"Where did you get this car, Daddy?" Sofie asked.

"It's a rental car, honey."

"What happened to your knee, Sofie?" as he pulled out his handkerchief and attended to her bloody, wounded knee.

"I scrapped it playing Superhero's with David."

"Are you on your way to school?" the father asked.

"Yes, Daddy," the little girl eagerly exclaimed.

"Okay, I can give you a ride to school. But I have to make a quick stop at a customer's this morning, so you're going to be a little late."

David looked at Sofie in the front seat of the car, and he immediately noticed the worried look on his little friend's face.

John Rigoletto was a traveling salesman for an automotive software company in downtown Detroit. He was usually away from home more than seventy percent of the time, spending most of his days traveling to manufacturing companies around the country that specialized in making automotive parts for the big three auto industry.

Rigoletto and his estranged wife, Nancy, had been having marital problems recently, and he moved into a small, one-bedroom apartment on Little Mack Avenue in Harper Woods.

Rigoletto was also a violent man with a vicious, brutal temper. Nancy Rigoletto had called the St. Clair Shores Police Department several times for assault and battery issues, with several domestic violence charges filed against him. His vicious temper was the direct source for his various brushes with the law, primarily on domestic violence charges. He had recently served six months at Jackson State Prison for threatening his wife with a knife and taking her and his daughter hostage in a standoff last year. He had been denied visitation rights to visit with his daughter recently and now spent a considerable amount of time stalking his little girl. At the same time, she walked to school with her little friend every morning.

On that morning, Rigoletto was at the right place at the right time. He immediately pulled his car out of Forest Avenue onto eastbound Ten Mile Road, which both children realized was the opposite direction to the location of St. Veronica's Catholic School on Toepfer Avenue.

At nine-thirty that morning, over an hour had passed since the start of the school day, and the two children did not report to class. Their teacher, Sister Monica, went down the hall to the school's front office and reported David and Sofia as unexcused absences. The school's principal and church pastor, Father Damen O'Leary, called the parents of both children, informing them of their children's truancy.

When Nancy Rigoletto received the phone call from the school principal, her heart immediately dropped down to her stomach. She had heard rumors of her estranged husband lurking around the neighborhood but didn't want to involve the authorities. She was in the process of filing for divorce, and she intended to serve him with the divorce papers. She had considerable experience with her husband's violent temper. She immediately suspected him of having something to do with their daughter's sudden disappearance.

The St. Clair Shores Police Department had been notified by noon, and a missing children's report was filed. An AMBER ALERT was issued across the metropolitan Detroit area as the authorities had feared that the father had kidnapped both children.

Both David Andrews and Sofia Rigoletto had disappeared and had been missing for more than forty days. Nightly vigils and neighborhood search parties continued in November, first starting in St. Clair Shores and then expanding through nearby suburbs and the metropolitan Detroit area. Their faces were posted on every telephone pole and almost every public building within the immediate Detroit area.

"Find Our Little Angels," the posters said, with their innocent faces posted for everyone to see. The children of St. Veronica's School prayed a daily rosary every morning for the safe return of their beloved little classmates. The nightly local newscasts on ABC Eyewitness News did a nightly story on the St. Clair Shores Police Department investigation.

The local detectives tracked down John Rigoletto at his workplace office on Jefferson Avenue in Detroit later that day after the children's disappearance. He looked distraught and said he had not seen or heard from his daughter or her little friend before they vanished. Because the Lincoln Town car he was driving on that day was a Hertz Rental Car, it had already been cleaned, shampooed, and rented to another customer. There was no DNA evidence anywhere in the vehicle. He was taken into custody and held at the St. Clair Shores Police Station for twelve hours, intensely interrogated by their detectives.

The little girl's father was then soon released.

It seemed that Rigoletto had a perfect alibi. He stated that he had arrived at Detroit Metropolitan Airport from Miami at 10:45 am on November 1st, when his daughter and her friend had disappeared. The American Airlines manifesto listed his name on that direct AA Flight 1045, leaving Miami at 7:50 that morning.

There was no sign of the two children anywhere. Forty-two days had passed without any reports, eyewitness tips, or communication regarding their whereabouts. The mothers of both children appeared on the nightly news, pleading for someone with any information to come forward and help them find their beloved children.

41

Then, on a cold December morning in downtown Detroit, a homeless man flagged down a Detroit PD patrol car in front of an old, abandoned tenement building on West Brush Street. The old, homeless vagabond had been sleeping in the abandoned building that evening when he encountered two small bodies buried underneath some broken boards, old, fractured drywall, and garbage debris located in the house's basement.

When Patrolman Anthony Crivella got out of his car and went down the basement of the abandoned tenement, he realized that the two unrecognizable bodies were the remains of two little white, mangled children. Crivella went into total shock and began shaking. He immediately radioed his Commander at the Third Precinct on Grand Avenue. He soon realized the identities of who the partially decomposed 'Little Angels' truly were.

Brutally beaten, stabbed, and sexually molested, they were the lifeless little bodies of David and Sofia.

# CHAPTER SIX

I was sitting at my desk eating a stale onion bagel from Dunkin' Donuts at my Third Precinct office in downtown Detroit. I had covered it with several globs of cream cheese, as it was a leftover victim from the weekend's donut stash. I had just raided the precinct kitchen like a hungry bear out of hibernation, looking for anything edible I could find. It was only ten-thirty in the morning, too early for lunch and too late for breakfast.

I had left a nasty note in the cafeteria to whoever had broken the toaster within the precinct. It was the only piece of equipment within the kitchen that could always resurrect a stale, weekend bagel. My hands were still greasy with cream cheese when my desk phone loudly rang.

"Detective Palazzola,"

"Mikie, it's Johnny."

My partner, Detective John Valentino, was out on the street on a stolen car investigation with another detective. It had been a busy Monday morning so far, and I was finishing some prior case paperwork from the weekend.

"What's up, Johnny? Where are you at?"

"Just got a dispatch call from Patrolman Crivella over here on Brush Street and shot over here right away."

"Why? What's up?"

There was a silent moment.

"Do you remember those two missing little kids from St. Clair Shores over a month ago? No one has been able to locate them?"

At that moment, my heart sank to my stomach as there were several long seconds of silence.

"Oh, no," I loudly said as I buried my head in my left hand. I didn't want to hear what my partner was about to tell me.

43

"They've been located here on Brush Street. They've been murdered."

A few more silent moments.

"Are you sure it's them?"

"Yeah, it's them. You better get over here. We're going to need some help before the media trucks get here."

"You got it, Johnny. I need to finish up the...."

"Can you get here quick? I don't have the stomach to do this alone, Mikie," he asserted as I was interrupted.

"Ok, Johnny. I'll be right over," I promised.

I knew that my partner always had trouble with these gruesome crime scenes, and I usually had to keep an eye on him. Valentino was a recovering alcoholic, and I had to constantly watch over him to stay sober. I was always afraid that something as gruesome as a very horrific crime scene, especially one involving children, would tip him off the wagon, and he would hit the bottle again.

I dusted the breadcrumbs from my bagel off of myself at my desk, grabbed my gun and my suit coat. I had sort of wished that this crime scene was involving anything other than a homicide concerning children. We had been seeing a lot of gangland violence lately, and discovering some dead gangbangers in a desolate Detroit alley somewhere was far better than going over to inspect a violent, horrible crime scene involving two little kids.

I jumped into my Crown Victoria police car and sped over to the Brush Park neighborhood. With the sirens on, I was at the West Brush Street address in less than five minutes. Detective Valentino was anxiously awaiting my arrival in front of the tenement building. The patrolmen had already posted the crime tape around the dilapidated broken-down house. There was a

Detroit EMT Unit and several more police cars parked in front of the crime scene.

"Hey Johnny, what do we got?" I said as we greeted each other and briefly hugged. I could immediately tell that my partner was a little shaken.

"Over there, in the basement," as he pointed to a pile of rubble that was ably covering the small children's bodies. We assisted some of the patrolmen as they removed some of the debris covering up the two children.

Underneath the pile of broken wood and rubble were the bodies of two small children. There was crusted, dried-up blood all over the bodies, and it looked as though the bodies were beginning to decay. The bodies had been stabbed several times across their torsos, and their genitals had been mutilated. Their clothing had been partially ripped off, and it was evident that the two children had been sexually molested. Their bodies were covered with black and blue marks, and their skin had turned a black and dark purple color. It was apparent that their dead bodies had been exposed to the elements for over the last month and a half, and there were missing pieces of flesh from their young bodies. The children's eyes were still open, and their eyelids gruesomely ripped off.

It looked as though some wild animals had discovered the bodies long before we did. It was a known fact that there were wild city coyotes that roamed around some of the abandoned tenements within the desolate part of the city. The wild savage animals feasted on rats, feral cats, and anything else available.

"You say Crivella stumbled on this?" I asked my partner.

"Yeah, he says a homeless man flagged him down this morning while he was on patrol with the discovery."

We both stood around, almost standing guard at the crime scene. At the same time, the Channel Eight and Channel Six news trucks had just arrived as we continued to block off the crime scene from the news reporters that were clamoring to get a story.

"Detective Palazzola," I heard someone yell out my name from a distance. At first, I had no idea who it was until I squinted over to her direction.

It was Justine Cahill, a pushy, assertive newspaper reporter from The Detroit News. She was never one of my favorite journalists, and I always had to force myself to be as kind and patient with her as possible. She was an attractive, dirty-blond-haired lady with light freckles and piercing blue eyes that distinctively revealed her distinct Irish roots.

Justine Cahill also wore her bright red, horn-rimmed glasses on the edge of her nose. She was a tough, tenacious reporter who had no problem getting in your face for any reason that suited her fancy. Her assertiveness and her determination were beyond reproach, and Cahill was someone you didn't want to fuck with. She could splash one's name all over the papers and destroy the reputation of any veteran copper with one sweeping pass of her typewriter carriage.

"Hello, Justine," I said with a forced smile as she approached me at the crime scene, giving me a very brief hug.

"How are you, Mike? Long time, no see."

"Has it been that long?"

The last time I had seen her was at Buddy's Pizza over in Corktown several months back. There she was single-handedly holding an extra-large pepperoni pizza hostage all by herself. Cahill, in the past, was a little on the chunky side, and it always surprised me that she wasn't writing a food column about all of the Italian restaurants she usually frequented. But on that morning, I could tell that she had lost a significant amount of weight.

"You've lost some weight, I see. Congrats," I said, hoping that a compliment would get me on her good side.

"Thanks, Mike. Jenny Craig has been my best friend for the last six months."

A few silent moments as she looked around the crime scene.

"Do we know the identities of these two dead children yet?"

"Not yet, Justine. We're waiting for the coroner to show up right now. We have a hunch, but we can't comment yet until we get an identification."

"It's those two missing kids from St. Clair Shores, isn't it?"

"We can't comment on that right now, Justine. Not until we can ID the bodies, which will probably take a while. If it is, we will need to contact their families first before publicly revealing their identities."

At that moment, the Wayne County Coroner had finally arrived. At the same time, we continued to stand guard and block off the crime scene from the other journalists that were now clamoring to get a story.

"I gotta run, Justine. Call me later," I politely suggested, knowing that I now had to screen my desk calls for the next few days.

I followed Detective Valentino inside the house and down the stairs to the basement. There were several other patrolmen and a couple of guys from the Detroit Fire Department. I had been on the force for over twenty years, and I have seen more than my share of dead bodies and horrific murder scenes. The gruesome crime scenes of innocent, dead children were never something that any veteran detective gets used to, and I can't say that I was getting any better at investigating them.

But after seeing their innocent faces on the six o'clock news every night, with posters splattered all over the city with their cherub faces, I suddenly broke down.

I walked over to the other side of the abandoned house and tried like hell to control my emotions. I was standing there alone for about five minutes when my partner finally approached me from behind.

"Mikie, are you okay?"

I looked at him, and my eyes were now drenched with tears.

"I wish a thousand deaths on the evil son-of-a-bitch that did this to these two little kids," I was sobbing with anger.

"I won't sleep at night, Johnny, until we find this mother-fucker!" Valentino was putting both of his arms on my shoulders. He then handed me one of his smelly handkerchiefs that probably hadn't been washed in several days, and I wiped off my tears as quickly as I could.

I continued to study the victims, trying to process the whole murder scene. I kept staring at the bodies, then walked around the basement, looking for any obvious clues.

Valentino was looking around with me as he asked,

"Are there any signs of a struggle?"

"No, these bodies are too far gone. They have been buried in all of this rubble and exposed to the elements. There isn't much evidence left on these bodies. We need to have the coroner take them right away and see what an autopsy turns up."

At that moment, the coroner had thrown a white sheet over both of the young, mutilated bodies and began to load them up on gurneys while the other patrolmen were guarding the crime scene. They were doing their best to keep the reporters and the crowds of people away that were starting to gather on Brush Street. The media trucks with the cameras and crews were now doing their live news feeds from the front of the tenement building, as other patrolmen were trying to push them as far away from the crime scene as possible.

After several hours of supervising the crime scene investigation, I went back to my office at the Third Precinct and started writing up my investigation report. I had a feeling that, unless CSI could come up with any DNA evidence at the crime scene, find any witnesses, or come up with any clues or suspects, this murder investigation was going to remain open for a very long time. Whoever this murderer is, is no amateur.

Getting a 'collar' on this murder was going to be difficult. I had read in previous reports that the father of the little girl, John Rigoletto, had been initially picked up by the St. Clair Shore investigation unit hours after the children's disappearance, but he had alibied out. According to their reports, he arrived at Detroit Metropolitan Airport when the children were abducted from a direct flight from Miami. His name was listed on the flight manifesto.

Rigoletto had a criminal record and had served six months in Jackson State Prison last year for a domestic violence incident. His estranged wife is in the process of divorcing him. She is on record saying that he displayed a very dangerous temper and abusive behavior towards his wife and little girl. That would motivate him, especially if he psychologically took out his anger towards his innocent daughter and friend.

But what about the American Airlines Flight manifesto and the fact that he was en route to Detroit on November 1st? I then remembered a criminal case I was investigating years ago where we found that the flight manifesto was erroneous. Several of the last-minute passengers who had traveled stand-by were not listed on that particular flight.

Could there have been an earlier flight where John Rigoletto had traveled as a stand-by passenger?

I called American Airlines and was on the telephone with them for almost an hour until they finally confirmed my hunch: There was a previous flight that was half empty that arrived at Metro Airport earlier that morning, at 6:47 am. Could Rigoletto have been on that earlier flight?

Without looking for further evidence, I jumped from my desk and walked over to Valentino's cubicle.

"Johnny, grab your jacket, your gun, and your temper. We're going to need all three."

My partner looked at me suspiciously.

"Where are we going?" he asked.

"We're going to pay a nice little visit to this little girl's father."

The drab, gray walls of the ten by twelve-foot prison cell were dreary and dilapidated on that cold December day. John Rigoletto sat on a single worn-out mattress, situated within the middle of the room, waiting for his attorney. He had been at the Third Precinct at 2875 West Grand Avenue for over forty-eight hours now and knew very little about why he was being held in jail. He only knew that he was being accused of the murder of his young daughter Sofia and her little friend David Anderson but knew nothing else.

Detectives Mike Palazzola and John Valentino picked up the software salesman at his place of work within several minutes after he had learned on social media that the bodies of those two children were that of his little girl and her friend. Their partially decomposed bodies had been discovered in some old, dilapidated tenement on Brush Street. As the news broke over the newscasts, two police detectives from the Third Precinct were immediately at his office to arrest him.

Other than mentioning that he was getting picked up on suspicion of murder, they said very little else to the alleged suspect. Rigoletto was quickly handcuffed in front of his fellow employees and hauled off downtown to jail. Knowing that he was about to be interrogated by the police again, he had this time requested that he 'lawyer up' and asked for his attorney to be present. Rigoletto was not about to make the same mistake that he had made before. He was not going to let himself be questioned unless he had an attorney present.

When he originally intended to hire a defense attorney, he had no idea who to call. He only knew that, with the privilege of only one phone call to make if he ever got arrested again, that there was only one person in the whole world that he should immediately contact.

After being picked up by the St. Clair Shores police after the disappearance of little Sofia, he had contacted and retained a popular criminal attorney to defend him if or when the bodies of the two minor children were discovered.

Rigoletto contacted a veteran criminal attorney by the name of Daniel J. Breazie, an experienced sixty-something lawyer who has had more than his share of prevalent run-ins with both the Detroit police and the local media.

Breazie was a top-rated legal counselor in the Detroit area. He frequently advertised his legal services on television, usually after the late evening talk shows. His 1-800-NO-JAIL4U was a famous jingle after hours. He had defended murderers, rapists, gangbangers, crooked politicians, embezzlers, swindlers, and corporate thieves in the past with sometimes less than favorable results. He acquired a very sleazy legal representation within the local federal courts. It wasn't often that he didn't acquire a favorable legal ruling on his almost always guilty clients. The Wayne County Prosecutor's office had effectively referred to him as 'Sleazy Peezy Danny Breazie.'

Breazie's success came with his broadcast television persona. He recklessly advertised his expert legal abilities as 'almost always' acquiring a successful verdict for all of his felonious clients, calling himself 'Perry Motor City Mason.' With a large cash retainer requirement and a billing rate of $550 an hour, 'Sleazy Peezy Danny Breazie' had done quite well for himself in his legal practice. He had been threatened with disbarment several times by other county prosecutors and federal judges who were more than familiar with his questionable, slimy legal methods.

But what evidence could the Detroit detectives possibly have against Rigoletto? He had an ironclad alibi, as he was on the return flight from Miami to Detroit on that same morning that his daughter and her friend disappeared. He had proven to the St. Clair Shore coppers that he was on that flight, as he was listed on their flight manifesto.

After twenty-four hours, Rigoletto was escorted in handcuffs and ankle chains out of his jail cell and into a conference room with only three filthy, high ceiling windows. The walls bore a drab, green paint color that was so old and dirty; it was starting to turn yellow. As he sat down on that cold, steel chair, he overheard his new lawyer's voice that he hoped would make this incredible nightmare go away, coming down the hallway towards the conference room.

'Perry-Motor-City-Mason' was loud and gregarious as he entered the prison conference room. Breazie was not an attractive man. He was of average height and build, balding, and prided himself with the $1,500 custom-made suits that he usually wore daily. He flashed around his $25,000 Rolex gold watch on his left hand while sporting a two-carat diamond pinky ring on his right. Breazie was twice divorced and lived alone in an exclusive townhouse in Grosse Pointe Woods.

On that day, the criminal attorney was holding a large briefcase with one hand and his beige, London Fog overcoat with the other. The attorney placed his belongings on top of the conference table as the reflection from the room's fluorescent lights sparkled brightly upon his eighteen-karat gold Rolex watch. He briefly glanced at the time on his left hand, which bore a large gold diamond pinky ring that mirrored the dreary conference room lights above.

"Dan Breazie," he loudly announced himself as he extended his right hand to the prisoner.

Still wearing his handcuffs, Rigoletto reached out with both of his hands to his newly acquired lawyer, clasping Breazie's hand with shackles tightly attached to both of his wrists.

"How are they treating you here," he immediately asked as he placed a stick of Big Red chewing gum into his mouth.

Breazie was a gum chewer, which resulted from his constantly trying to quit his life-long habit of cigarette smoking. His futile attempts at quitting never lasted more than a few days at a time. Breazie was a three-packer and would often go through the phase of throwing out all of his cigarettes and hiding his cigarette cartons in his office for four or five days. His nicotine withdrawals would regularly follow afterward, and Breazie would become exceptionally desperate for a smoke. After becoming extremely irritable and moody for several days, the criminal attorney would immediately run back out to the nearest 'party store' (a synonym for convenience stores in Detroit) and re-stock his inventory of Marlboro Lights.

"I'm okay," Rigoletto answered, realizing that his lawyer was too busy fumbling through his briefcase to care about his response.

"I'm getting three squares a day, and nobody bothers me," the accused child killer cheerfully said, still trying to get his attorney's attention.

Breazie briefly looked up and smiled, continuing to shuffle more papers out of his dark, leather briefcase and began spreading them across the table. There were several moments of silence as the criminal attorney began reviewing his notes while rearranging more papers on the table.

"Says here you were on a flight from Miami to Metro Airport on the morning of the murders. What time did your flight come in?"

"10:45."

The sordid attorney smiled at his client's answer.

"Really? Look, Rigoletto...if you want me to defend you, you have to tell me the truth. There seems to be some evidence here that points to the fact that you probably arrived at Metro Airport on an earlier flight. You were able to arrive at the airport, pick up a rental car and you would have had more than enough time to commit these murders," he admonished his client.

"As if all of this isn't bad enough, please don't make the mistake of lying to your lawyer as well."

The accused child killer began turning red in the face, knowing that he had been caught in a blatant lie.

"I don't like surprises," the criminal attorney emphasized loudly.

"Don't lie to me."

There were several moments of silence as Rigoletto tried to gain his composure. He then swallowed hard and recited the whole story to his lawyer.

Rigoletto's narrative began with arriving on an early flight from Miami to Detroit Metropolitan Airport, traveling standby. He landed at the airport before seven o'clock in the morning, where a rental car was already waiting for him. He hadn't seen his daughter in a few months, and he knew that his estranged wife would never consent to his seeing her at their home. Rigoletto then decided to meet her on her way to school and found her walking with her friend a few blocks away.

His original intention was to take them somewhere for breakfast. But her little friend began to protest that he had to be at school for class immediately. When they both started crying incessantly, Rigoletto lost his temper. He pulled the car over to an abandoned lot off of Gratiot Avenue. He beat them relentlessly until they were unconscious. At that immediate moment, Rigoletto went into a psychological rage and couldn't control his sexual urges. With the both of them knocked

55

out and in an unconscious state, he began to have his way with them until he had hurt them severely. Rigoletto felt that he had no choice but to beat them until they were no longer breathing. He then drove around downtown Detroit for a couple of hours until he found a dilapidated tenement. He buried both bodies under the extensive debris down the basement. Rigoletto then returned the rental car to the airport and took an Uber back to his place of work.

Breazie took extensive notes while Rigoletto recited his story. Because of the evidence that Detectives Palazzola and Valentino had recovered, and because they could prove that his client had the motive and arrived early from his trip to Miami, the criminal attorney felt he had only one choice for his defense.

The lawyer sat with his client in the conference room of the Third Precinct for several more hours, summarizing his past, his prior relationships in his childhood, and assessing the mental and emotional damage that had been inflicted on his client while he was growing up. He immediately knew that Rigoletto was a very sick man, both psychologically and emotionally. He needed extensive psychological help and needed to bring in a forensic psychiatrist to complete his assessment of his client. He now knew what he had to do.

Rigoletto would plead not guilty by reason of insanity.

# CHAPTER EIGHT

The morning newspaper was sitting on my car's front seat as I headed to the Theodore Levin Federal Courthouse at 231 W Lafayette Blvd early that morning. I had an early appointment with the federal prosecutor, Kevin Scanlon. We were about to go over my testimony and how the two bodies of those St Clair Shores children had been found. I had only had a brief chance to read the article, which was on page one of the Detroit News:

### Accused Child Murderer Goes On Trial

My Dunkin' Donuts coffee was sitting in the cup holder of my car, with droplets of caffeine spilling onto the newspaper that was lying on the passenger seat of my patrol car. Whenever the opportunity of a traffic light turned red, I pursued the news article, which coincidently, was written by my reporter friend, Justine Cahill.

Each time I read the details of that article; my stomach got more nauseated. The news article discussed how the bodies of those two small children had been discovered and found in that Detroit tenement building on Brush Street last December. It discussed how the accused killer possibly arrived early from a business flight from Miami to murder those two children. How could someone, who had put on such a professional act in front of everyone, so callously molest and murder his daughter, then leave her and her little friend abandoned in some tenement building downtown? Each time I read that newspaper article, I became more enraged with every sentence, every paragraph, every word. John Rigoletto, I had already surmised, was a fucking monster. There wasn't another cold-hearted human being in this world who deserved to rot in hell for his murderous actions more than Rigoletto, I thought to myself. I had already convicted him in my mind, and justice certainly needed to be served in that courthouse that day. I was going to do everything in my power to make sure that Rigoletto got nothing less than two life sentences and a thousand deaths that went with them.

My cellphone went off as I pulled my squad car into the parking garage adjacent to the courthouse. I looked at my phone and immediately noticed who it was.

"Hello?"

It was Johnny Valentino, my partner.

"Hey Mikie, do you need me to come there and assist you during the trial? There may be some details you might forget in your testimony," he suggested in a joking tone of voice.

"Are you kidding? I've been dreaming for three months about this trial and how much pleasure I was going to get when the judge throws the book at this son-of-a-bitch."

"Really? I don't know pallie, you might need some assistance on this one," he said as if to throw in a curse of bad luck into this trial.

"You might need me there to give you a hand on this case. Tell Scanlon to put me down on the witness list."

"Why?"

"Come on, Mikie. You know this asshole's lawyers are going to plead the temporary insanity defense. They will come into that courtroom with some bullshit about the terrible childhood this monster had and how it affected his adult life. You know that's coming."

"I doubt it, Johnny. There is no way the jury is going to buy an insanity plea on this one. Especially regarding the murder of his daughter and her classroom friend."

"Let me come down there, Mike...at least for moral support. You know how sideways these murder trials can go."

"It will be fine, Johnny. I'm sure Scanlon won't have any problem getting a conviction on this perp. I'll call you at noon and let you know what's going on."

As I quickly hit the 'end' button on my cell phone and fumbled with my briefcase, my coffee, and my keys, I started to wonder.

An insanity plea for the murder of these two little children? There is no way the judge and jury are going to buy that.

I walked into the courthouse, passed through security after showing them my police badge, and walked over to Room 107-A, which was the lawyer's conference room that was down the hall from the courtroom where the trial was going to take place. They had already had the jury selection the day before, which went most of the day until five-thirty. Breazie and the prosecutor had finally come to a compromise on the jury selection. Of the twelve jurors of seven men, four were African American, three of them white, and five were women. All of the women were housewives who, incidentally, didn't have educations beyond high school.

Kevin Scanlon and I briefly shook hands, and I was still fumbling with my coffee, my keys, and my briefcase, which had all of the police report and crime photos of the two deceased children.

And then, as my partner had correctly predicted, Scanlon immediately sprung it on me.

"Breazie is going to enter an insanity plea, Mike."

I looked at him in total shock, not believing that such a plea, in this case, was even possible.

"You fucking kidding me? How is he going to make that fly?"

"Breazie got a hold of some psychological reports from over twenty years ago, documenting

59

Rigoletto's mental issues from when he was a teenager in high school."

"What?" I was in total shock.

"What possible report could justify such a plea after these brutal murders?"

"The defense is going to play out his temporary insanity based on his being consistently molested and raped by his father when he was a child. Breazie sounds pretty confident that he will be able to sell it to the jury and the judge."

I only stood there, still holding my half-filled Dunkin' Donuts coffee. My right hand was now shaking.

"Danny Breazie is a fucking slim-ball," I immediately reacted.

I was all too familiar with criminal defense attorney Daniel Breazie and his slimy, unorthodox reputation. I was always convinced that the saying of 'lawyers being lower than pond scum' analogy was purposely contrived for criminal attorney Dan Breazie. The words 'slim-ball' and 'scum-bag' were far too gracious in describing the legal methods of this legal counselor. It was a minor miracle that he was even still allowed to continue to practice law in any Michigan courtroom.

I usually did my best at not getting too emotional when having to testify at a criminal trial, especially a homicide trial. But this one was different. Because I had two daughters at home and knew what it was like to be a father to two small children, this one was now personal. I knew that Rigoletto's defense attorney was capable of anything, and I had heard about some of his pretty farfetched defenses when it came to some of his monstrous clients. But pulling out an insanity plea on the blatant murder of two young children was not only reckless and absurd but was irresponsible to be allowed by the judge in this case.

The presiding jurist was an African American judge named Paul Michael Nelson, who had been on the bench for several years. This judge was elected to the court as a Democrat and was quite liberal in his rulings. From what I had heard from some of the other coppers in my precinct, Nelson was not your typical 'hard-nosed, hang 'em high' kind of judge. Quite the opposite. If an absurd insanity plea could be entered and successfully litigated in any murder trial into anyone's federal courtroom, it was Nelson's. This guy probably wore a 'Black Lives Matter' tee-shirt under his judicial robes and was as liberal as the day was long. I now realized deep down in my gut it was going to be a difficult task getting Rigoletto convicted on two homicide charges.

As the trial began that day, it became quite evident early on what was going to happen. I was put on the witness stand immediately, and I described the murder scene of those two young children found on Brush Street last December. I read through the police reports with the prosecutor and reintroduced some of the defendant's prior convictions regarding domestic violence. During the cross-examination, Breazie emphasized how emotionally involved I had become with these homicides and how partial I had become towards the alleged murderer. He had brought up some of the statements I had made to Rigoletto during his arrest: 'I hope you rot in hell' and 'you should die a thousand deaths' remarks that I had allegedly said to the perpetrator. Of course, I denied making those statements. Scanlon objected several times, but Judge Nelson allowed the comments.

The picture that criminal defense attorney Daniel Breazie was painting during that murder trial became quite clear early on. He portrayed John Rigoletto as some kind of psychological victim, a lifelong casualty of physical and mental abuse suffered early on in his lifetime by his parents, family, teachers, and peers. Several other witnesses were brought onto the witness stand, supporting Breazie's insanity defense. One grade-school teacher from Rigoletto's past had even stated under oath that she had witnessed Rigoletto being beaten by his father after school for cheating on a math test in the fourth grade.

A forensic psychiatrist, Dr. Jeanne O'Brien, testified that it was quite possible that a lifelong abuse victim such as John Rigoletto could quite possibly take out his physical frustrations on the likes of his small daughter and her friend. The reason, she explained, was not wanting them to grow up and suffer through adulthood the way he had. Dr. O'Brien explained that Rigoletto was the lifelong survivor of intense childhood physical and emotional abuse. He had erroneously and inappropriately inverted his mental intentions onto his young daughter, not wishing her to grow up mentally twisted the way he had. John Rigoletto was a victim of *chronic maltreatment*, defined as 'recurrent incidents of maltreatment over a prolonged period during childhood.'

The murder trial went on for two full days, and to say that Breazie had his way in court was an understatement. Each time prosecutor Kevin Scanlon objected against Breazie's absurd introductions, Judge Nelson ruled against him. By the end of the trial, it was quite clear that Breazie had successfully gotten the judge and the jury to feel sorry for Rigoletto and his mental state of mind. Daniel Breazie had made a trial summation to the jury that entirely painted Rigoletto as a victim of not only his abusive father and family but a tragic victim of society. Scanlon's retort to Breazie's trial summation was weak at best. By the time Judge Nelson was giving deliberation instructions to the jury, I was utterly sick to my stomach. The jury deliberated on the morning of the third day, and by that afternoon, had delivered their results.

John Rigoletto had been deemed not guilty by reason of temporary insanity.

I had grabbed my stomach when that verdict was read out loud. It took all of my strength to keep from throwing up in the middle of that courtroom.

Not guilty by reason of temporary insanity.

A perpetrator who is deemed not guilty because of a provisional mental, psychological disorder or temporary psychological insanity must undergo psychiatric treatment in a state mental institution. Judge Nelson mandated a long-term mental hospital court order against Rigoletto. It was a restrictive sentence where the release from the mental institution would require the permission of the criminal courts and a "supervision and treatment" order in favor of the defendant. This ruling would eventually amount to an absolute discharge of the murders of those two small children.

Unlike defendants who are found guilty of a crime, they are not institutionalized for a fixed period but rather held in the institution until they are determined not to be a threat to society. The criminal courts in making this decision are supposed to be cautious, making sure that the alleged perpetrators are institutionalized for a more extended period than what they would have usually been incarcerated in prison. But in this case, I knew Rigoletto would be back out on the streets in less than eighteen months if he played his cards right.

Federal Prosecutor Kevin Scanlon approached me after the trial as I sat there in the courtroom in complete and total shock. He looked at me as if to try to console me with the irresponsible verdict that had been given to this alleged child murderer.

Scanlon looked at me with a gleam in his eyes.

"Don't worry, Mike. This monster will get what he has coming," he only said.

It was as if he was referring to some kind of inapplicable act of 'karma' that was going to be asserted against this juvenile killer miraculously.

"Are you fucking nuts, Kevin? This judge and this jury just gave this bastard a 'Get Out Of Jail Free' card. Where the hell do you see the 'karma train coming' here?" I angrily asked.

Scanlon only smiled. He then promptly turned and grabbed his briefcase on the courtroom table and quickly walked away.

As I sat there alone in silence, I only kept shaking my head. This was not the first-time justice had not been served during my long career as a Detroit police detective and criminal investigator. But this verdict hurt the most. I continued to shake my head as the courtroom cleared until I was practically the only one left sitting in that courtroom.

There were tears in my eyes. I was tired. I was angry. I was hurt. Justice had not prevailed for those two small, innocent children. It was as if I had been given the responsibility of making sure that the rightful killer had appropriately been locked away in federal prison for the rest of his life. I had let those two innocent little angels down.

Later on, I came to find out that there was indeed a 'karma train' coming down the tracks.

And Kevin Scanlon would be one of several people driving that train.

# CHAPTER NINE
## STATE'S ATTORNEY KEVIN SCANLON- FOUR YEARS AGO

On that spring afternoon in April 2017, the city was bustling with traffic, especially in front of 1441 St. Antoine Street. Wayne County State's Attorney Kevin Scanlon sat in front of his fifth-floor picture window, silently contemplating, his feet on top of his desk. It had been a busy spring for the State's Attorney's office. With all of the drive-by shootings, looting, and rioting that had been going on, his office had been busy.

Kevin Scanlon, age 45, was a good-looking, blond-haired family man with a wife and three children, living in the posh, western suburb of Rochester Hills. He had been the head of the Wayne County Attorney's Office for the last five years. With more than 300 attorneys and more than 500 employees, the Wayne County State's Attorney's Office is the seventh-largest prosecutor's office in the nation. The office is responsible for prosecuting all misdemeanor and felony crimes committed in Wayne County, one of the United States' largest counties. In addition to direct criminal prosecution, Assistant State's Attorneys file legal actions to enforce child support orders, litigate to protect consumers and the elderly from exploitation and assist thousands of victims of sexual assault and domestic violence each year. The State's Attorney also serves as legal counsel for the government of Wayne County. Overseeing all of these activities was an all-consuming job indeed for any State's Attorney.

On that day, Kevin Scanlon was exhausted. His twelve-hour days included an intense judicial meeting schedule, court appearances, press releases, and staff conferences five days a week. Since his recent re-election into the office last November, Scanlon had been busy scurrying against the current soft line policies of the federal judicial system.

But also on that day, Scanlon finished a murder trial in which the accused murderer of a ten-year-old little girl had been acquitted in a jury trial that afternoon.

Scanlon was discouraged and extremely disheartened on that late April day.

Besides overseeing the prosecution of federal cases involving homicide convictions, Scanlon was highly engaged in the intense politics of his office. Until the recent mayoral election of white conservative Mayor Donald Stafford in 2016, the staunch Republican prosecutor had always been armed with the prior mayor's policies on seasoned, career criminals. He was trying to find a compromise between previous Mayor Lorenzo Adam's flexible, sympathetic platforms and the Detroit Chief of Police Byron Davies' hard-core, right-wing procedures in arresting all recent violent perpetrators.

When four juvenile African Americans raped and killed a young twelve-year-old white girl in the Indian Village neighborhood two years ago, Scanlon got a rude awakening of the current, deplorable state of the federal justice system. Because all of the perpetrators of that heinous crime were only fifteen years old, he was forced to prosecute those four individuals for standing trial as juveniles. Knowing that if his office had taken a hard line against those criminals and charged them as adults, the public unrest that this would have caused would have pushed the black community to the point of no return. Had those four young men been white Caucasians, raping and killing a young black girl, the black community would have demanded a death sentence for those four young men.

There was now a double standard that had drawn a hard line in the city. He was constantly fighting the intense prejudices of the black and white communities. It was the political platforms of many of Detroit's politicians that, until the racial lines of Eight Mile Road are permanently abolished, it will always be the city blacks versus the suburban whites. There were very few who wished to cross that imaginary line and integrate and improve those city neighborhoods.

Two summers ago, an African American ex-convict killed a white, eighteen-year-old girl in Greektown who was out with her friends. She was a straight-A student, about to graduate from Warren Woods High School. It would have been an open and shut case of murder in the first degree until the perpetrator's lawyer had presented some evidence that the young girl was downtown to buy drugs from the accused killer. When a scuffle ensued, he claimed that the high school student attacked him and killed her in self-defense.

Because he was painted to the racially mixed jury as a poor, indigenous victim of his drug-infested community. He was convicted on a single manslaughter charge. He was now up for parole after only serving eighteen months in prison.

The racial double standard, Scanlon now believed.

The African Americans were getting away with murdering their own and those of a different race. At the same time, the black community blamed the whites for years of slavery, racial mistreatment, and decades of prejudice. All of this was the aftermath of poor African Americans who were now excused from the basic standards of society. The federal judicial system was now expected to make exceptions to those who have been victims of the poor, inner-city conflicts that were now rampant in Detroit.

Was the 'Thou Shall Not Kill' commandment not applicable to the racial minorities? Was it not usurping to those who take another's life without a conscience? Was the 'Eye For An Eye' scripture too harsh to those who ruthlessly kill?

It was almost four-thirty in the afternoon, and the prosecutor had a dinner date with his close friend. Judge William Ellis was a retired federal judge for the Eastern District of Michigan and was a very close friend of the prosecutor for many years.

Scanlon went into his private bathroom in his office, freshened up, and changed his white shirt and tie. He had requested to have dinner with the respected judge because he had something significant on his mind that he needed to discuss:

Wayne County State's Attorney Kevin Scanlon was now considering his resignation.

---

Sogni Per Tutti is an upscale Italian restaurant located on Michigan Avenue in Corktown. The beige chairs and modern décor of the upscale restaurant blended nicely with the ambiance and the casual atmosphere of downtown Detroit's Old Town neighborhood. The popular restaurant and bistro was a trendy, contemporary nightspot for those wishing to enjoy its top-shelf martinis and food menu, along with its classy, elegant dining room design.

A beautiful young hostess brought Kevin Scanlon over to the distinguished gentleman. He had a table next to the picture window, where they could observe all the foot traffic on Michigan Avenue. He had been patiently waiting for the State Prosecutor to arrive.

"Sorry I'm late, Judge," as they greeted one another with a firm handshake and a brief hug.

Scanlon had made the mistake of ordering an Uber to the restaurant. The driver was several minutes late in picking him up from his office on St. Antoine Street.

"How are you Kevin," the judge curiously asked as they sat down to order drinks and peruse the menu.

"It's been a brutal few weeks, Bill. I've got a lot on my mind that I wanted to bounce off you."

"I heard about that case that you lost regarding the homicide of that little girl," the judge sympathetically mentioned.

At that moment, his Chivas Regal on the rocks had just arrived, while the judge was on his second Crown Royal. Scanlon began lamenting while taking long swallows of his cocktail.

He and his staff of prosecutors had been trying to get a conviction of a 38-year-old white offender, John Purcell, a criminal with a very violent past, against a ten-year-old Livonia girl who had been brutally raped and stabbed to death less than a year ago. The little girl was kidnapped while going into the bathroom of a small pizzeria in Greektown. Despite the eyewitnesses that had seen Purcell leaving the restaurant out of the back door with the little girl, the DNA evidence didn't match up with the murder weapon found next to her body when she was discovered in an abandoned tenement building near McNichols Road.

Despite the eyewitness putting Purcell at the kidnapping scene, the accused offender had a solid alibi and was found not guilty by a racially mixed jury of five men and seven women.

Judge Ellis listened to the young prosecutor intently as he began to lament his disappointment with the jury's verdict that day. The two had known each other since working together at a prestigious law firm in downtown Detroit twenty years ago, and the two had become very good friends.

As their entrées of veal scallopini and gnocchi with vodka sauce arrived, the exhausted prosecutor made his announcement:

"Bill, I'm going to announce my resignation next week."

The judge's face became contorted, as he was now in disbelief.

"Why? You and your office have been doing such an outstanding job in your handling of so many of these convictions and trials."

"Are you kidding me? We have been working so hard to get so many of these murderers convicted and locked up, only to watch so many of these perpetrators get off on a technicality and walk back out on the streets scot-free. I can't mentally take it anymore."

The judge listened intently.

"Kevin, you've made quite a name for yourself in the county prosecutor's office. Your hard work and tenacity have not been going unnoticed by everyone in town. Any criminal defense attorney in this city now knows they will always have their hands full when they go up against you or any of your prosecutors in your office."

Then the prosecutor began to raise his voice.

"But that's not enough, Bill. These bastards are all walking out of jail free as a bird, and the incompetence of some of these police detectives have made our jobs even more difficult."

The two of them began eating their meals while Kevin Scanlon continued to voice his discouragement and disgust.

"It's been a long five years, Bill. I'm ready to move on."

While they finished eating, they both ordered drink refills and continued their intense conversation. As the crowded dinner hour of the restaurant began to recede, Judge William Ellis pulled out his ball-point pen. He scribbled something on a paper napkin next to his drink. He then handed it to Scanlon.

Looking at it briefly, Kevin Scanlon had only a confused look on his face.

"What is this?"

The judge looked at him and smiled.

"What does it say?"

The prosecutor read the judges' scribble on the napkin.

"It says "Deliverance, Roma Café, June 13th, 2017."

Judge William Ellis smiled, taking another sip from his drink.

"What the hell is this?" Scanlon asked again.

"It's an invitation to our closed society of archangels. When we invite someone to join our group, we call it 'deliverance.'"

Scanlon, who was a Protestant and was not very religious, immediately protested.

"Look, Bill, I'm not into any of these 'Praise The Lord' and 'Born Again' religious groups. I don't need to be finding the church and...."

Ellis interrupted him.

"No, Kevin. This is not a 'Born Again' Christian group. We are anything but," the judge smiled.

The two of them sat there in a long silence as the judge had now finished his third Crown Royal.

"We are called the Malizia Society of Detroit, and we've been around since 1927. We call ourselves 'The Archangels.' We are a discrete, secret society of thirteen members from the community, who meet in the back room of the Roma Café every three months. Different criminal cases that concern the miscarriage of justice are presented to us as a board, and we discuss and vote on their mortal redemption."

Scanlon looked at him with a confused look on his face.

"Mortal redemption?"

"Yes. We are a very discrete group of men who carry out justice against those whom the courts have failed to convict."

At that moment, the waiter came to their table, and they both ordered another round of drinks. There were several more moments of silence as Ellis could see the wheels in Scanlon's head beginning to turn. When their refills arrived, the judge continued the conversation.

"We then carry out justice," he softly said.

Scanlon looked at Judge Ellis intently.

"And how do you do that?"

William Ellis took another long sip of his Crown Royal.

"Over the years, a judge in our society grants a pardon and freedom, based on a legal technicality or a judicial mistake of some kind, to a prisoner who has been convicted of first-degree murder. He is then hired and 'retained' within our group to carry out whatever formal sentencing that we as a formal society decide upon and see fit."

Scanlon looked at the judge, now in disbelief.

"Bill, you're kidding, right?"

"No, Kevin, I am not kidding."

The prosecutor looked at the judge intently and then began to smile slowly.

"And how long have you guys been doing this?"

"Our founder, Judge Anthony Siracusa, founded 'The Archangels' in 1927, and we have been meeting and carrying out our brand of retribution ever since. We do it quietly and discretely. Many years ago, we used guns and knives as our murder weapons but found them too messy and easy to generate DNA evidence. We now prefer strangulation."

Scanlon looked at the judge intently. He then smiled at the retired judge. Was this old man on the level? Was he really serious? The county prosecutor smiled to himself, not believing at first what the former judge was referring.

"I've been a federal prosecutor for over twenty years. How come I've never heard of you guys?"

Ellis smiled. "Then we've done a good job, then. Wouldn't you agree?" referring to the clandestine society's secrecy.

Scanlon took another long sip of his drink while Ellis continued.

"We've had a vacancy in our group recently. One of our beloved Archangel brothers has passed away with glioblastoma, and your name was brought up as a special candidate for deliverance."

Kevin Scanlon was now silent. As he was drinking his Chivas Regal on the rocks, he was without words.

The waiter then came back to their table, and Judge Ellis picked up the dinner bill. They then rose from their table in silence, walking out of the restaurant onto Michigan Avenue. It was as though Scanlon was in shock and could no longer speak. As they were both standing outside on the sidewalk on that pleasant April evening, the judge made a final pitch to his longtime friend.

"Look, Kevin, I know this is all very unbelievable to you right now. I volunteered your name to our society because I know that I could trust you with this information. I know that my

Archangel brothers can trust you as well," the judge exclaimed, talking over the bustling nighttime traffic of Michigan Avenue.

"Promise me that you won't decide on this resignation until you come to our meeting in June. There, you will learn more about us and being an Archangel to our community."

Still speechless, Scanlon shook the judge's hand, and they both hugged each other intently.

"Remember, Kevin...deliverance."

Scanlon looked at the judge and smiled.

"Okay, Bill. I will be there," he replied.

As he was about to walk away and hail a taxicab, Judge William Ellis gave the prosecutor one last directive:

"By the way, Kevin. When you come to your first meeting, wear a black bowler hat."

Scanlon looked surprised. "But I don't wear hats. What if I don't have one?"

The judge then gazed sternly at the prosecutor.

"Get one."

# CHAPTER TEN
## ROMA CAFÉ- SPRING 2021

The wet pavement of Riopelle Street was turning into black ice on that cold spring evening as I maneuvered to parallel park my Crown Victoria squad car. The calendar said the middle of March, but 'old man winter' still held the Motor City hostage. After several days of warmer weather, it was a fair assessment to say that everyone in Detroit was suffering from spring fever. Everyone couldn't wait for the warm weather to come back as soon as possible.

I was meeting Justine Cahill for dinner at the Roma Café that Saturday evening, and to say that I was excited to meet up with her was a bit of a stretch. She had called me the day before asking me questions regarding the Rigoletto murder trial and the jury's verdict in that case. She asked many pointless questions, letting me know that she was more than snooping around for more information in her investigation.

But it was very obvious what she was really after, and I was somewhat reluctant to play along. Justine has always been extremely friendly to me, even flirting, and she has more than told me in so many words that she would enjoy our getting together socially on a personal level. She had asked me a few personal questions over the last few months, and she knew that I was available.

Being a widower for the last six years, I was still recovering from the loss of my wife Laura to breast cancer. We had been married for eighteen blissful years. I have two teenage daughters, Adrianna and Sara, ages fourteen and sixteen, that more than keep me on my toes. As a freshman and junior at Dominican High School, keeping them focused on their studies while trying to fight off all of the boys was a challenge. As a single father, I realized how difficult it was working full-time as a police detective while taking care of my two children.

I missed my wife, Laura. Since her tragic passing, not a single hour of my life has ever gone by that I didn't think about her. For me, the grieving process has never ended, and I have struggled to keep my life in order while psychologically, physically, and emotionally holding it all together. If it hadn't been for my responsibility to my two young daughters, I probably would have gone the same direction as my partner, John Valentino, and become an alcoholic. And my going out to social events and gatherings, or even on 'dates,' still makes me feel guilty and uncomfortable. Venturing out and being social without my wife is still a challenging task for me.

I have not looked forward to dealing with the dating scene, and I'm not sure if I ever will be. Throwing my picture and profile onto an online dating service was still completely out of the question. Since losing Laura, I just didn't know if I would ever be ready to bring another person into my life again.

The only reason I had agreed to meet Justine for dinner that evening was that I was afraid of what rejecting and crossing her could do. That last thing that I needed was a scorned newspaper reporter on my hands, especially an influential, shrewd, take-no-prisoners reporter like Justine Cahill.

So I decided to accept her dinner invitation, knowing that meeting her as friends for dinner couldn't possibly cause any harm.

Or so I hoped.

The Roma Café was one of those cliché type restaurants typical in their popular Italian cuisine and décor. It has been said that this Detroit eatery is the city's oldest Italian restaurant, has been a part of the Eastern Market since the late 1880s. It has been a family-run establishment for over one

76

hundred and twenty years, serving Italian dishes and old-world classics that still keep the crowds coming back for more.

The tables are all covered in red and white checker cloths, with straw-covered wine bottles hanging from the various areas of the bar and ceiling in the restaurant. There was old walnut wooden trim around the whole ceiling, and the shiny, wooden mahogany bar with all of its classic woodwork made me feel as though I was traveling in time. It had been several years since I ate there, and I remembered the food being pretty good.

As I looked around the antiquated, old-style restaurant, I smiled to myself. I wondered out loud what those wooden paneled walls erected over one hundred years ago would actually have to say if they could talk. Rumor has it that the Roma Café has seen more than its share of colorful characters and certified wise guys.

The restaurant was well packed with seated patrons for a weeknight, and I was afraid we would have trouble getting a table.

"Hey Mike," Justine immediately exclaimed as she entered the front entrance of the restaurant behind me. She put her arms around my waist and gave me a wet kiss on the lips, which took me by surprise.

Justine was dressed in a black, low-cut Armani dress, which stylishly showed off her shapely, well-endowed figure very nicely. She was extraordinarily stylish and looked very desirable in a different light. Justine had on make-up that accentuated her deep blue eyes and her soft cheekbones. I had never looked at her as anything other than a cut-throat reporter, and I had to admit that she looked beautiful that evening. Her well-dressed, alluring appearance accentuated her weight loss, and she looked several years younger as a result.

I had already given the hostess my name, and she promised us a table within the next ten minutes. Since the old mahogany bar was only steps away from the entrance, I escorted Justine to the bar, and we ordered drinks while we waited for our table.

"Your table is ready now, Mr. Palazzola," the hostess promptly said as I said a quiet prayer of thanks to the patron saint of dinner reservations.

Ordering a bottle of Pinot Noir, we made ourselves comfortable at our table while talking about our jobs, our families, and our investigation recently into those brutal child murders.

"Did you make the reservations tonight?" Justine asked.

"No, I didn't. It escaped my mind as I was so busy today."

"I didn't either. So glad we're able to get a table tonight. This place is always jam-packed," she observed.

We walked through the aisle of neatly arranged tables filled with well-dressed couples warming themselves with appetizers and huge glasses of wine. As we followed the hostess to our table, I heard my name being called out in the background.

"Mikie! Mikie!"

I looked to my left and noticed a familiar face I hadn't seen in over a year. He was sitting with a beautiful brunette whom I had never seen before. We both gave each other a man-hug while shaking hands.

"How are you, Anthony?"

"I'm great! This is my wife, Cassandra," he introduced her as we shook hands.

"How have you been, Mike?" he asked. "Still chasing around bad guys?"

"Doing my best, Anthony. It's never an easy task working with your brother."

Anthony Valentine Carleton was my partner's half-brother, who worked for the Treasury Department in the Internal Revenue Service. They discovered each other only recently, within the last year, and it's been a godsend to Johnny that he now has a little brother to look after.

Watching and hearing about them getting closer in their fraternal relationship was the very thing that was probably missing in Valentino's life. Since they met up, my partner Johnny has been more at peace with his life and no longer drinking. He had moved back home with his ex-wife and family in Harper Woods and stopped drinking, which was a massive step in the right direction for him.

Since the 'Water Pistol Murders' were solved last year with the death of our commander Joe Riley and the sudden death of Detective Frank Partridge, Johnny finding his brother was probably the only good thing that came out of that killing spree. It appears that the 'Water Pistol Murders' of his father's killers forty years ago has been solved, although Frank Partridge's sudden homicide still hasn't been cracked.

With Valentino discovering a half-brother in that investigation, their constructive relationship positively influenced his life. I had gotten together with John and Anthony to play cards a few times and have gotten to know him as a great guy. And his position in the Treasury Department also makes him a great asset in any of our investigations.

By that moment, the hostess motioned us to continue to follow her before we lost our table. We sat down at a quaint little spot next to a large picture window opposite Riopelle Street, facing all the hustle and bustle of that typical cold spring evening in the Eastern Market section of Detroit.

We were given the wine list, and I immediately recommended the Belle Glos 2019 Pinot Noir

Telephone & Clark vintage, which she was more than happy to try. I hoped that by being daring enough to order an expensive bottle of red wine immediately, our glasses would be well filled, and our conversation would stay light and breezy.

As we started to make ourselves comfortable, we made a toast to our good health, and Justine then gazed at me, taking a long sip from her wine glass.

"So Mikie, why has it taken so long to get you to have dinner with me?" she brazenly asked.

Justine was unusually forward, which didn't surprise me.

"No real reason," I replied. "I haven't been out much these last several years since I lost my wife. My girls keep me pretty busy when I'm not playing cops and robbers at the Third Precinct."

Justine looked at me with those piercing blue eyes of hers. She then took another long sip of Pinot Noir wine which I could tell she was thoroughly enjoying.

"I've always wanted to tell you in person how much I admire and respect you. You're very old school, Mike. There are not a lot of guys like you around anymore."

I found it suddenly refreshing that she was paying me such a nice compliment.

"Thank you, Justine. Coming from you, that is a compliment."

"Does that surprise you?"

"Well, kind of, sort of, I guess...." I stumbled for words, looking for my wine glass to rescue me.

There were several long moments of silence as she continued to glare at me with those hypnotic blue eyes of hers.

"You're afraid of me, aren't you?"

Now I was going into mild shock. I was without words as I tried to stick my face as far as I could into my wine glass to cover up my fears. I certainly wasn't ready to admit the fact that she scared the living shit out of me.

"You're a class act, Michael. I would never do anything that would hurt you or your reputation. You're a great cop and a wonderful father. That is a very unusual combination for any Detroit detective."

I only smiled, initially believing her sincere statement and personal observation for about three seconds.

"You're a tough lady, Justine. Your typewriter and your magic pen have proven to be far mightier than any sword on this town."

She smiled and took another sip of her wine.

"I have to be, Michael. Detroit is a gritty, tough newspaper town, where only the strongest survive," she smiled.

"I'm not that tough, Mikie," Justine made it a point to say.

"I like to get all dolled up, wined, and dined like any other girl," she mentioned.

I smiled, trying to control myself from saying what I was thinking. By that point, I wasn't sure if I should have been ducking for cover underneath the table or grabbing my testicles for personal protection.

We were now staring at each other and our empty wine glasses, so I decided to live up to my old school reputation and keep her wine glass well-filled. We made another toast as the waitress came over to recite the daily specials.

While glaring at the menus, I notice two well-dressed men in dark suits, black ties, and winter overcoats entering the restaurant. They had a quick conversation with the hostess, and then they were led to the back of the restaurant in an adjacent room, which was a closed meeting.

The only reason the two men had caught my eye was that they were wearing black bowler hats.

I glared at the two gentlemen as they walked past our table, led by the hostess.

I then made it a point to mention something to Justine.

"That's unusual," I said out loud to Justine, still grasping my wine glass for comfort. "You don't see anyone wearing black bowler hats like that anymore."

She watched the two men walk past our table but then immediately dismissed it.

"I hear that men's hats are making a comeback."

"Really? That's interesting. Nobody wears hats like that around in public that I've seen."

The waitress came back to our table and took our entrée orders. That evening, I decided to keep it light and ordered Chilean seabass. In contrast, Justine ordered a ravioli dish with ricotta cheese.

She then made it a point to fill my wine glass.

"I'm so sorry about that Rigoletto murder case. After talking to you yesterday, I can tell you're taking this verdict pretty hard."

A silent moment.

"I feel so bad for you and Valentino. You guys worked so hard to get that scumbag convicted. That perp should be rotting in hell for what he did to those two little children."

"I know," I said out loud, then took a loud sip of wine from my wine glass. For some odd reason, I wasn't in the mood to talk about that court case.

"I guess that's what you get when you go up against a late-night TV ambulance chaser like Sleazy-Peezy Danny Breazie."

If any attorney needed to die a slow death for keeping these violent perpetrators on the street, it was Breazie. Just saying his name brought back raw emotions of hurt, pain, and relentless anger deep down inside of my stomach.

"I can't sleep anymore. I keep thinking about those two little kids, believing that they were going for a ride with her father and that he was going to take them out for breakfast."

"I'm so sorry you're going through this, Michael. In your line of work, it's gotta be tough to watch some of these sleaze-balls walk out of the courtroom and back on the streets."

We both took a long sip of our Pinot Noir, and there was a moment of silence.

"Sleazy Breazie has quite a reputation of pulling these rabbits out of his hat and selling it to any judge or jury."

"No shit," I agreed. "Who the hell can get their clients an insanity plea and successfully sell it to a jury, especially for the murder of two little children?"

Justine continued to shake her head in agreement.

"When I first heard about Rigoletto's insanity plea, I thought for sure that the jury would never fucking buy it. When they came back with that 'guilty because of insanity' ruling, I was sick to my goddamn stomach," I mentioned.

My throat was starting to get dry, especially after thinking about that murder trial. I took another long sip from my wine glass.

"Kevin Scanlon had enough to convict this fucking perp. He had a motive and a history of family violence. He even spent several months in Jackson last year for a domestic violence charge," I emphasized.

"That's Danny Breazie. They don't call him Sleazy for nothing," Justine commented.

Another silent moment as I stared out of our picture window facing Riopelle Street.

"I just wonder how that fucking guy can sleep at night, knowing that he put a child-killer in the psycho ward. Everybody knows he'll be out and back on the streets in less than two years. The Detroit mental hospitals are crowded with crazies, and they're looking for any excuse to clear out their psych wards."

A few more silent moments as we were finishing our bottle of wine. At that moment, four more men were standing at the entranceway of the restaurant, waiting to be seated. All of them were well dressed in suits and ties, wearing long winter overcoats.

And black bowler hats.

I glared at the four of them walking past our table and then again led to the private room adjacent to the restaurant's back.

Now I was getting curious. When the waitress brought us our entrees, I decided to be nosey.

"Excuse me, ma'am? Is there a formal party going on tonight?"

"Why do you ask?"

"I see a few dapper men entering the restaurant, all wearing black bowler hats."

The attractive, middle-aged waitress looked at me for a few seconds. She must have figured out that I was a cop because her response sounded particularly guarded.

She smiled and responded coyly, "Well, officer, it is cold outside."

She then quickly changed the subject, "Will you both be needing anything else?"

"No, thank you," Justine quickly responded.

I watched the waitress walk away before digging into my food, which looked incredibly delicious.

"How did she know you were a cop?"

"Good question. I must have that Detective Stabler from 'Law & Order' look on my face," I smiled.

I suddenly remembered that murder case last summer on Eight Mile Road, where the victim was strangled in the parking lot of a strip club. For some strange reason, the detectives found a black bowler hat in the back seat of the victim's car.

I decided to temporarily dismiss the 'Men In Black' before enjoying my Chilean seabass entrée. The waitress came back to check on us, and I ordered another bottle of that Pinot Noir wine. I could tell Justine was thoroughly enjoying it, and I was finally starting to feel relaxed around her. The wine was going down incredibly smooth, as her deep blue eyes were glaring back at me all evening. I never anticipated her being so easy-going and so comfortable to talk to. Perhaps, with her hard newspaper reputation, I had misjudged her. I was getting a completely different impression of Justine Cahill.

I admit that perhaps I was starting to let my guard down, thanks to that third glass of Pinot Noir and her strategically exposed cleavage from her black Armani dress.

"Here's to tough reporters," I kiddingly saluted as I laughed and raised my glass.

"Here's to good detectives and great fathers," she responded.

After a few long moments, she hypnotically stared into my eyes.

"Did anyone ever tell you that you look like that actor from 'The Fast & Furious,' Jason Statham?"

I didn't know if she was sincere or if the wine was taking an early effect on her 20-20 vision. I smiled, trying not to blush.

"You mean that bald tough guy in the movies? Now and again," I only said.

"He's very handsome, you know," she only said—what a difference from that cold, mean, ballsy reporter who pushed her way around Detroit's police precincts.

"You're not trying to take me to bed on the first date now, are you?" I brazenly asked.

I figured by that point, since we were doing a great job polishing off our second bottle of wine, that I had nothing to lose.

She smiled and winked her eye, giving me the distinct impression that nothing was off the table. I wisely decided to control my animalistic urges and discuss more trivial subjects like sports, weather, and current political events.

After several minutes of engaging in a more mundane conversation, I looked over at the front entrance. Five or six more men were now gathered at the front door, waiting to be seated. All in black, upscale suits. All in black bowler hats. This time, the hostess brought them to the adjacent back room from the other side of the restaurant so they would not be noticed by any more customers.

At that moment, I decided to excuse myself and go to the restroom. Knowing that the men's room was in the back of the restaurant, I decided that this would be an excellent time to get up and formulate any excuse to see what was going on. Before entering the men's room, I noticed that the back room of the Roma Café was filled with several well-dressed men, making themselves comfortable and seated at a long table, with two or three waiters attending to their needs. They had all hung up their coats in the adjacent coat room but were oddly still wearing their black hats.

Very strange.

I washed my hands and then went back to the table, where Justine was anxiously waiting.

"What do you think is going on back there? There are a lot of dapper guys eating dinner with their hats on," Justine smiled with amusement. "Always a detective, I see."

"I wonder who they are?"

"Maybe they're Jehovah's Witnesses," she suggested.

I just sat there shaking my head. I thought about her answer, and then I just figured there had to be some other logical explanation that was none of my business. So I again put it out of my mind, and we both amicably finished out entrée's.

We then ordered espressos with a large portion of tiramisu cake, and we made more small talk about our background and our families.

Justine had just celebrated her fifty-first birthday a few weeks ago and had worked for the Detroit News throughout her whole career. She originally got her job with the newspaper as a copy girl in the summer of her junior year at Wayne State University. She had never looked for another job since.

Justine was a divorced mother of two grown-up girls, both with productive careers in something other than journalism. Her oldest, Brittney, was a legal receptionist for a law firm downtown and was living with her boyfriend in an apartment in Corktown. Her youngest daughter Bridget had just finished a sales and marketing degree at Michigan State. She had started a job with Oracle's sales office in the suburbs. Justine had a comfortable home in suburban Birmingham. She enjoyed having her youngest daughter around and still home living with her, even though she seldom saw her daughter between her working and partying with her friends.

Justine also mentioned that she had been married for almost twenty-four years before separating from her ex-husband, William Cahill, a very successful tax attorney. He decided one day to trade her in for a younger, thinner, more attractive model with less mileage. That was a brutal divorce that took her years to recover emotionally. She has had an acrimonious relationship with her ex-husband ever since.

When the bill finally came, Justine wanted to make good on her offer to buy me dinner, but I pulled out my American Express card and beat her to it. I helped her with her coat, and we both began to leave the restaurant. As we were exiting, we walked past the bar, and I made eye contact with the bartender, nodding his head and thanking us for our patronage. At that moment, I walked up to the bartender and asked him:

"Any idea who all the 'Men In Black' guys with the hats are?"

He looked at me, then thought for a moment.

"Archangels," he said. "They're a bunch of well-dressed guys that get together here every three months. They have their dinner meetings here in the small banquet room. They've been coming here for as long as I remember. They're great tippers."

"And how long has that been?"

The bartender thought for a moment.

"My boss, who is the owner here, says that they've always been coming here for the last ninety years or more. His grandfather, who used to own the restaurant, remembers them coming here every three months. They usually have a ten-course meal with unlimited liquor and wine, and then they lock the doors in meetings for several hours. We usually have to stay late, well after closing until they all leave, sometimes not until after two o'clock in the morning."

"Archangels, huh?" I repeated.

"Yeah, that's what they call themselves."

There was a long pause in the conversation.

"And nobody knows anything about these guys?"

The bartender smiled, now figuring that I was a copper.

"I just serve drinks here, sir. I don't ask any questions."

Justine was standing next to me while asking the bartender questions, so she overheard the whole conversation.

"Michael, I will do some digging when I get back to the newsroom tomorrow," she said as I walked her to her dark blue, late model BMW parked around the corner. She grasped my hand at first as I opened the passenger door, trying to be cordial. Then, as if to not want to let it go, she kissed me on the lips for several long seconds. It was a very wet, passionate kiss.

"I had a great time, Michael. Thank you for dinner." Justine then gave me another wet, passionate, three-second kiss.

"Don't be afraid of me. I don't bite."

I looked at her in silence for several long seconds. I then looked down and made sure that my testicles were still intact.

"Call me tomorrow," she smiled as she got into her car. She then closed her door, winked her eye, and waved as she drove off down Riopelle Street. The wet mud and the water from the street puddles splashed my shoes as I stood there, momentarily speechless. As I began to walk towards by squad car parked nearby, only one question kept going through my mind:

Who were these guys wearing black hats?

# CHAPTER ELEVEN
### THE DONUT SHOP – SPRING 2021

Warm temperatures and the spring season were definitely in the air on that sunny afternoon as a Wayne County Sheriff patrol car pulled up in front of the Wayne County Jail at 570 Clinton Street. Two county sheriff patrolmen were inside that unmarked police vehicle as they sat there in front of the county jail to wait for their prisoner to be escorted out that old, red brick building.

They had been instructed to pick up a prisoner and bring him to his final destination, the Wayne County Health Psychiatric Center on Newburgh Road in Livonia. Their prisoner had just been sentenced to intense psychiatric care by Judge Paul Michael Nelson two weeks prior, and the Wayne County Sheriff's office was in charge of transporting the prisoner that afternoon.

But the unusual part of this transport was the fact that the head of the Wayne County Sheriff's office was one of the two patrolmen transporting this prisoner. Sheriff Raymond Monroe was elected as the Wayne County Sheriff's office head at 1441 St. Antoine Street for the last six years. Monroe was a conservative, African American county deputy who had been recently re-elected based on his conservative, Republican views. He was not your typical, black, liberal elected official. Monroe was a dedicated patrolman with a hardline approach to the Wayne County justice system. And Sheriff Monroe was quite vocal in expressing his political views.

He still had a 'Trump 2020' flag hanging proudly in his office and had no use for the 'Black Lives Matter' movements that were the current theme of the recent Detroit inner-city protests.

His department suggested that Sheriff Monroe take personal charge of the transport of this prisoner, as several violent threats had been made against the personal safety of this exonerated child murderer. Both Sheriff Monroe and another patrolman were waiting patiently outside in their patrol car for over thirty minutes.

It was just past two-thirty that afternoon when the prisoner was finally escorted out of the Wayne County Jail for his ride to the mental hospital in Livonia. John Rigoletto was wearing a bright orange prisoner jumpsuit when escorted out of the Wayne County Corrections facility. His hands were handcuffed behind his back as Sheriff Monroe assisted him in putting him in the back of the car.

"Remove the prisoner's handcuffs," the sheriff ordered the other patrolman as he climbed into the back seat of the patrol car.

"It's a long, uncomfortable ride to Livonia in traffic," the Sheriff stated as he climbed into the passenger side of the Wayne County Sheriff's patrol car.

Rigoletto was smiling to himself as he sat comfortably in the back seat of that vehicle, rubbing his wrists from the painful feeling of those tight handcuffs.

The temperature was warm on that spring day in March, as the afternoon temperatures soared to the middle sixties on that day. Monroe decided to put on the air conditioner, blowing comfortable cold air into the vehicle's back seat as Rigoletto was making himself comfortable.

The patrol vehicle immediately merged onto the John Lodge Expressway and quickly encountered the usual afternoon traffic that went with traveling on that busy expressway. The ride to the mental health facility usually took no more than forty minutes from the Wayne County Corrections building, but the added traffic would make the drive exceed ninety minutes.

As the patrol car exited the Jeffries Freeway and onto Telegraph Road, Sheriff Monroe decided to make an unusual stop. The patrol car was approaching a Dunkin' Donuts shop on the east side of Telegraph Road, and the Sheriff wanted his usual afternoon iced coffee. The other patrolman had mentioned earlier that he needed a bathroom break. As they pulled up to the donut shop, Sheriff Monroe and the patrolman driving the vehicle undid their seatbelts.

"Would you like anything?" Monroe politely asked the prisoner.

"Sure. Get me a large coffee, extra cream, and sugar," Rigoletto requested as he sat comfortably in the back seat.

Being very familiar with police prisoner transport procedures, Sheriff Monroe handcuffed the prisoner's hands behind his back. He did not want to leave the prisoner unattended without being handcuffed.

The patrolmen then exited the vehicle. Both proceeded towards the entrance door of the donut shop, where there was a line forming on the inside.

Rigoletto sat in the back seat of the car, alone and unattended.

For some odd reason, the patrol car was left unlocked, with the exit door handles still attached to the passenger doors of the vehicle. This was unusual, as most patrol cars do not have any exit handles for the passenger to leave. There was a vacant city lot next to the donut shop, with high brushes and wildly grown trees scattered around the vacant property. These bushes and wild-grown trees would be enough to camouflage anyone who wished to hide their appearance.

Fifteen long minutes passed.

As the patrolman exited the donut shop, they noticed that the rear passenger door was wide open. At first glance, Sheriff Monroe thought that the convict had escaped the patrol car. When he approached the unmarked vehicle, he found a gruesome discovery:

John Rigoletto's body was lying face down on the floor of the patrol car, his hands still handcuffed behind his back. Rigoletto's neck was wrapped tightly with a thick, quarter-inch rope, and blood, saliva, and other bodily fluids had protruded out of his mouth. He was lying face down in his own blood and vomit, and he wasn't breathing.

He also noticed something unusual: A black bowler hat laying in the back seat next to the body.

Sheriff Monroe checked his neck for a pulse and then immediately called for an ambulance on his radio. Several patrol cars soon ascended the parking lot of the donut shop as an EMS truck quickly arrived. Rigoletto's body was taken out of the patrol car's back seat, and several paramedics tried in vain to revive him. He was then taken to Beaumont Hospital, where he was pronounced dead on arrival.

By five o'clock, several news crews had arrived with cameras and news vans, doing live news feeds and reporting the circumstances of the prisoner's apparent murder while in police custody.

Although the media did not directly question Sheriff Monroe, several other police detectives at the crime scene questioned why the prisoner had been left alone in an unlocked patrol car, with the two escorting policemen standing in line at a donut shop. Sheriff Monroe was interviewed by several of the investigating detectives from the Detroit Police Department. He was later criticized for leaving the prisoner alone in an unlocked patrol car.

---

Wayne County Prosecutor Kevin Scanlon was still at his desk at six-thirty that evening when his desk phone began to ring loudly.

"Hello, Kevin Scanlon speaking," he answered.

"Kevin, turn on Channel Six News," a familiar voice said on the other end before quickly hanging up the phone.

Scanlon walked over to his television and turned it on with the remote control as the news reporter was doing a live news feed from Telegraph Road.

"*This is Denise DeVito, Channel Six Eyewitness News. There has been a murder at the Dunkin' Donuts store here on Telegraph Road here in Livonia. The escorted prisoner, John Rigoletto, was handcuffed and left alone in the patrol car he was being held while the two patrolmen from the Wayne County Sheriff's office were inside. Someone broke into the patrol car and strangled the handcuffed prisoner while the two patrolmen were inside the donut shop. There were no witnesses. A quarter-inch rope was used by the killer, and a black bowler hat was left behind at the crime scene.*

*One of those patrolmen was the Wayne County Sheriff, Raymond Monroe. He was assisting the department in transferring the prisoner to a mental health facility here in Livonia when this tragic episode occurred. The circumstance of this murder is still under investigation by the Wayne County Sheriff's Office and is ongoing.*"

Prosecutor Kevin Scanlon smiled as he watched the Channel Six newscast, the volume blaring out loudly in his office.

The Karma Train had arrived indeed.

Charlie's Pancake House, an established morning restaurant on the corner of Mack Avenue and East Outer Drive, was busy with its customers going in and out on that early Wednesday morning. Criminal Attorney Daniel J. Breazie pulled his black, late model Porche Cayenne SUV into the parking space on the east side of the store. Arriving at the same greasy spoon for breakfast every weekday at six in the morning was a daily routine that he had done for years, as he locked his car and immediately walked toward the entrance.

As he grabbed the entrance door, he instantly remembered that his new pack of Marlboro Lights was still in his central dashboard, so he returned to his car to retrieve them. Although he knew that he couldn't smoke inside the coffee shop, feeling his pack of cigarettes in his front shirt pocket first thing in the morning was a security blanket of sorts. He would have plenty of time to enjoy a smoke on his way to the federal building, he said to himself. As he retrieved his morning smokes, he had forgotten to re-lock his car doors for some strange reason.

"Good morning, Danny," Charlie immediately greeted his good customer as Breazie sat at the counter. At the same time, he filled his ceramic cup with freshly brewed, black coffee. The lawyer placed his London Fog raincoat and laid it on the stool next to his.

"Morning, Charlie. How's the rat race treating you?" he casually asked, noticing that he was getting more than his share of take-out orders that morning.

"A lot of take-outs this morning. Nobody wants to come in and enjoy breakfast anymore," Charlie observed. He knew that Breazie enjoyed reading the paper in the morning, so he walked over to the far corner of the counter to retrieve the Detroit News for him.

The attorney then ordered his usual breakfast that morning, which consisted of three-scrambled eggs, two sausage links, and hash browns with wheat toast, slightly buttered. There were two overhead television sets mounted above the counter, so several customers were watching 'Good Morning America' while enjoying their early morning breakfast. Breazie made small talk with several of the other patrons while enjoying his breakfast. At the same time, Charlie continued to keep his coffee cup well-filled.

By seven o'clock, Breazie had finished his morning breakfast and threw down a twenty-dollar bill on the counter to cover his $10.76 breakfast tab.

"Have a great day, Charlie," the attorney loudly said to the coffee shop proprietor as he grabbed his London Fog raincoat and headed towards his parked car. He was mildly surprised that he had forgotten to lock the doors of his Porche SUV but didn't think anything of it as he started his vehicle and began driving towards the Ford Freeway. He opened his window slightly, then lit up a cigarette while he approached the usual morning traffic.

While Breazie was driving, with his Sirius radio station blasting oldies music and as he was smoking a cigarette, he neglected to notice one small problem:

He wasn't alone.

Behind the backseat of his sport utility vehicle, a well-dressed man, wearing a dark suit, white shirt, and tie, was lying across the floor of his car. He was silently waiting for the right opportunity to carry out the duties he was hired to perform.

The silent stranger was 'Raphael,' one of the 'Black Bowler Hat Killers.' He was one of three assassins that they referred to as 'Black Angels.' He had been hired by the Archangels, or the Malizia Society of Detroit, to perform murders and assassinations against all those perpetrators who had legally escaped the justice system. As one of the hired assassins, Raphael had committed several murders against those acquitted convicts who were now back on the streets over the last several years.

The stranger was always well dressed. His usual dapper attire included a dark suit, white shirt, and a black-tie, allowing him to blend in with the crowd in public. And as always, in keeping with the Archangels tradition, he always either carried or wore a black bowler hat while on assignment. He had been stalking the criminal attorney for over two weeks and was now familiar with his usual routine. The stalker knew he would be parking his car at the parking garage on East Lafayette Street like he did every morning, and he would have the perfect opportunity to complete his task.

The Bowler Hat Killer, as one of three hired assassins, was very well compensated for his services. His particular code name was 'Raphael' and was always referenced as such by society. He was blatantly kept unaware of his two other associate assassins, or 'Black Angels' who the organization referred to as 'Gabriel' and 'Michael.' His contract with the Archangels included payment of twenty-five thousand dollars in cash for every contract hit, plus expenses. His mortgage and utilities on his luxury condominium in Harper Woods were paid in full by the Archangels every month.

As one of the Bowler Hat Killers, Raphael paid most of his monthly living expenses in cash. He was very successful at staying anonymously under the radar. He also had a day job and blended in well with the crowd. Unless he were openly wearing his black bowler hat in public, one would never suspect who he was affiliated with or his true identity.

On that morning, he knew that the only way he would be able to get to Breazie was if the killer snuck into his car while he was having breakfast at Charlie's Pancake House. He went to great lengths to acquire a duplicate key fob for his Porche Cayenne SUV. The assassin had it duplicated so that he could easily break into his car and wait for his victim. But the Black Bowler Hat Killer caught a break that morning when Breazie inadvertently left his vehicle unlocked.

Unlike the other assassin's victims, this lawyer was not a hardened criminal. 'Sleazy-Peezy Danny Breazie' was a very successful criminal attorney. He had effectively acquired freedom and acquittals for many of his felonious clients. With his famous reputation, he has been able to enjoy a very lucrative law practice, always arrogantly touting his past successes in beating the justice system.

But after many years of assisting his clients in defeating the criminal justice system, Sleazy-Peezy-Danny Breazie had beaten one murder charge too many. He had come into great disfavor with many of the federal judges and prosecutors within the Third Circuit Court of Wayne County. The legal community within the Motor City was more than aware of his questionable legal maneuvers, and the State Bar of Michigan had repeatedly been unsuccessful in getting Breazie disbarred in the past.

Daniel Breazie had a significant number of enemies. And some of those enemies were now members of the Malizia Society.

After the last meeting of Archangels at the Roma Café last March, it was decided that Daniel J. Breazie needed to be eliminated, once and for all. The jurists and the prosecutors in Detroit had realized long ago that Danny Breazie was 'too sleazy' for his own good, and he definitely had to go.

And the Malizia Society was all too happy to assist in delivering his just reward.

The attorney flicked his cigarette out of the window as he pulled into the Lafayette Street parking garage. As he parked his SUV on the first floor, he suddenly heard a strange voice from the back seat of his car.

"Sleazy-Peezy Fucking Breazie," 'Raphael The Black Angel' said from the back seat of his SUV. As the victim quickly glanced at his rear-view mirror, he saw his assassin. Wearing a black bowler hat, the killer quickly wrapped the quarter-inch rope around the lawyer's neck. As he immediately began choking his victim, the assassin whispered a message into the lawyer's ear, making sure that he would remember his last words as he was about to be ascended into the hot, fiery depths of hell.

"I have a message from the Archangels," he whispered softly, as his victim was struggling to pull off the rope around his neck. His face was now turning a deep color red, and his loud gurgling noises could not be heard by anyone else in the parking garage. His feet were now violently kicking the Porche dashboard as he began to urinate all over himself.

"For every murderer, you helped escape justice; you will burn in hell and die a thousand deaths, you rotten bastard."

Within minutes, the criminal attorney, with his eyes still open and a rope tied tightly around his neck, was now dead. His eyes were blackened, and blood and saliva protruded from his nose and mouth. His face was now beginning to turn a light shade of blue.

Raphael, noting that no one else was in the parking garage, quickly exited the black SUV, leaving his black bowler hat in the back seat of the car.

Following the contract orders of the Malizia Society of Detroit, the mortal redemption of Daniel Joseph Breazie had now been successfully completed.

# CHAPTER THIRTEEN

The Highlands Restaurant on the seventy-first floor of the General Motors Renaissance Center was exceptionally busy for lunch that day. With everyone's impending spring fever on that sunny afternoon, the popular restaurant didn't have any shortage of patrons for lunch that day.

An elderly tall gentleman in his early sixties entered the restaurant, wearing his usual Brook Brother dark suit, crisp monogrammed white shirt, and striped tie.

"A table for two, please."

"Do you have a reservation?"

"Yes, Thomas Blakely from Comerica Bank."

The young, blonde hostess checked her computerized reservation list, and indeed, confirmed the banker's lunch booking.

"Come right this way, please."

The handsome, dapper businessman looked like an upscale version of Kevin Costner, with his light brown hair sprinkled with gray and combed to the side.

"Thank you," he said to the hostess as he sat down near the window of the restaurant. His lunchtime seat had the perfect view of the Detroit River overlooking Windsor, Canada, and the Ambassador Bridge lurking in the background. It was a fabulous spring day, he thought to himself.

He had been asked to lunch by a good friend and fellow Archangel, Judge William Ellis. He didn't elaborate over the telephone about the subject of this lunch meeting entailed. Still, Blakely had a suspicion, and he was rightly concerned.

His twenty-three-year-old grandson, Trevor Blakely, had been a heroin and cocaine user since he was a young teenager in Birmingham, Michigan. Despite all of the help and assistance,

**101**

his family tried to impose on his young grandson, Trevor Blakely decided to walk on the wrong side of the law. He was suspended from Brother Rice High School and later public school at the age of sixteen. Despite all of their efforts, Trevor hung around with the wrong kind of friends, who introduced him to all of the intense drugs and alcohol that were now ruining his life.

At a party two years ago, 21-year-old Trevor Blakely murdered Sara Anne Crandell, a sixteen-year-old girl from West Bloomfield High School. He claimed to the police that the high school teenager had owed him a significant amount of money for drug sales that she never paid him for and was receiving payment from her in the form of sex.

At first, the sex with the high school teenager was consensual. But one summer evening at a party in West Bloomfield, Trevor met the girl outside in the backyard and attempted to have sex with her. When the young girl refused and rejected him, Trevor, who always carried a switchblade, stabbed her and left her for dead behind the bushes. He claimed that the girl attacked him for refusing to supply her with more cocaine and heroin.

Trevor Blakely was immediately picked up and booked on first-degree murder by the West Bloomfield police. He was held without bond in the Oakland County Jail for several months while his family, particularly his grandfather, planned for his legal defense.

Still believing that his grandson could be rehabilitated, Thomas Blakely hired a prominent Detroit criminal attorney, Sydney Rothstein, to defend his grandson. The criminal lawyer was retained by Blakely, paying him more than $100,000 in legal fees.

At his criminal trial in Oakland County, Rothstein recruited several witnesses at the party who claimed that they saw sixteen-year-old Sara

Crandell hitting and beating Trevor in the backyard during the party. Even though Trevor was over six feet tall and towered over Crandell's small, petite frame, Blakely felt he needed to defend himself against the young high school girl. Other witnesses at the trial collaborated with the defense, and the jury ruled that Trevor had successfully defended himself in stabbing young Sara Crandell. Due to her past violent temper, Rothstein was able to prove that Trevor's life was in danger and that he stabbed her in self-defense.

Trevor was acquitted and eventually set free. Without a job and now homeless, Thomas Blakely's grandson was back on the streets, dealing drugs and stealing whatever he could to finance his intense drug habit. His family could not get him the psychological and mental health that he so desperately needed.

Thomas Blakely, needless to say, was very frustrated with his grandson. He wondered if young Trevor would have been better off rotting in a jail cell for murder rather than financing his defense and allowing him to go free.

The media had chastised Sydney Rothstein's legal defense, saying that many of his witnesses at that party had willfully lied in court, some of them compensated for their false testimony.

As the publicity for this wrongful exoneration began to spread across social media, word had reached the Archangels. Several members of the society had discussed privately with Judge William Ellis about rendering some sort of mortal redemption against this drug addict and murderer, even though he was the grandson of one of their own.

"Good afternoon, Judge," Blakely said as the older, retired circuit judge entered the restaurant and sat at the table. They shook hands, and the Comerica banker tried not to look annoyed, as the judge was almost twenty minutes late for their lunch date.

"I'm sorry I'm late, Tom. I had some business to attend to at home."

"I understand, Bill. Things do happen these days. I'm glad you could make it," Blakely said, trying his best to be pleasant. He knew that Judge Ellis had a sickly wife with Alzheimer's Disease that he needed to attend to at home.

They made some small talk regarding sports and current affairs as they ordered cocktails and their lunch entrees. When the conversation started to lag, Blakely could no longer control his curiosity and suspicions.

"So, why did you ask me for lunch, Bill."

The judge took a long sip of his Vodka Gimlet cocktail and then proceeded to explain.

"There have been some rumblings within the Society, Tom...rumblings about your grandson."

Tom Blakely looked at the elderly judge; his eyes began to widen.

"My grandson was legally exonerated from that murder charge, Bill. My family affairs, and especially my grandson's, shouldn't be anyone's business."

Judge Ellis looked intently at the banker.

"I truly wish I could agree with you, Tom. Unfortunately, one of our members is close friends with the Crandell family, the young girl who was stabbed to death. They're members of the same country club, and they're completely troubled about the way the jury ruled on this homicide case."

Blakely looked at Judge Ellis.

"Trevor is my grandson, Bill. What was I supposed to do? Feed him to the wolves? He needed our family's help, and we found him the best lawyer that we could to defend him in this case. I don't believe for one minute that my grandson would willfully kill another person if it weren't for self-defense."

"Your grandson is a coke-head, Tom. I understand that he is practically homeless and roaming the streets of Oakland County right now. He's still dealing drugs, more than likely to more high school kids."

"And how do you know this, Bill?"

"We have our connections, Tom. You know this. We have an obligation to the community, and you know we can't allow a murderer and drug dealer like your grandson to continue to roam the streets."

The waitress then brought over their lunch entrées. Thomas Blakely had ordered a Bacon, Lettuce, and Tomato sandwich, while Judge Ellis had ordered a Caesar Salad. As their lunch orders had arrived, the Comerica banker had suddenly lost his appetite.

"So what are you saying, Bill."

The judge looked at the banker with a cold expression on his face.

"Your grandson's name will be submitted for redemption at the next meeting."

Thomas Blakely then slammed his open hand on the table, tipping over his almost empty glass of water onto the floor. The loud noise caught the attention of several other patrons who were trying to enjoy their lunch at the upscale restaurant.

"Fuck you, Bill. You can't do this. This is my grandson that we're talking about here."

"You and your family have had enough time to get your grandson the help that he needs."

"We've fucking tried!" Blakely said loudly.

"Well, it hasn't worked now, has it? Now, this kid is walking the streets dealing drugs, and God knows what else!"

Blakely glared at the judge, completely speechless, for several long minutes.

"You should have left him in prison, Tom. He would have recovered from his drug habit, and he would at least be safe in the Oakland County Jail.

**105**

You're financing his defense with some hot-shot criminal attorney was the worst thing you and your family could have done. You're partly responsible for this, Tom."

Blakely continued to glare at Judge Ellis as he was casually enjoying his Caesar salad.

"Fuck you, Bill. I am not going to ideally sit while 'the society' puts out a contract on my grandson!" he thundered, putting his suit jacket back on and leaving his BLT sandwich untouched.

"I'll destroy you, Bill," he loudly threatened. "I will fucking destroy all of the fucking Archangels," he roared.

Several onlookers were taking notice of Blakely's loud threats as the skyscraper restaurant became suddenly silent.

Judge Ellis looked at the Comerica banker and smiled, still enjoying his lunch.

"You wouldn't dare," the judge said softly, shaking his head with a smile on his face.

The banker stormed out of the Highlands Restaurant, taking the elevator and exiting the Renaissance Center onto Jefferson Boulevard.

Judge William Ellis casually finished his lunch, informing the waitress to wrap up Blakely's untouched BLT sandwich to go.

Thomas Blakely was furious. He was not going to allow the Malizia Society of Detroit to put out a 'mortal redemption' contract on his derelict grandson, no matter how responsible he was for the murder of that young teenager. He would do whatever he could in his power, even if it meant informing the authorities about all of the covert activities that the society had been involved with over the years.

Thomas Blakely was washing his hands of the Malizia Society of Detroit. But with the solemn vows of discretion and secrecy that Blakely had taken and sworn to when joining the Archangels, he knew that "washing his hands" would not be that easy. The older banker knew that he just couldn't walk away.

By vehemently protesting his grandson's 'mortal redemption,' he was blatantly putting his own life in danger. He knew the score when he joined the Archangels. He knew that there would be a price to pay for going against the Malizia Society of Detroit.

Three weeks later, Thomas Blakely's dead body was found sitting upright in his late-model Mercedes on Lakeshore Drive facing Lake St. Clair. He had been missing for over twenty-four hours, and his cold, lifeless body was sitting erect in the driver's seat. Unlike the other Archangel's victims, a black bowler hat covered his face, making it look as though he had used it to fall asleep at the wheel. It appeared as though Blakely may have committed suicide, as a Baretta M9 semi-automatic pistol was found in his hand, with a gunshot wound to his temple.

The Grosse Pointe Police were immediately suspicious when they discovered Blakely's body at the crime scene. Although he had been shot at close range, the gun's ballistics and position did not appear as though Blakely had committed suicide.

Ten days later, Trevor Blakely's rat-infested dead body was found face down in a desolate, vacant field near Sixteen Mile and Dequindre Road. His body had been stabbed several times on his face, legs, and torso and appeared to be dead for more than seventy-two hours.

The grieving Blakely family was given a double dose of mortal redemption, ordered by the Malizia Society.

# CHAPTER FOURTEEN
## A REPORTER'S INQUIRY – SPRING 2021

The sun was shining brightly on that early Tuesday morning as Justine Cahill was settling at her desk. The newspaper room of the Detroit News was already quite busy at seven-thirty in the morning, as several reporters had been up most of the night, frantically working to make their publication deadlines that morning.

Justine winced at the first sip of her hot, freshly brewed coffee from the kitchen, and she couldn't help herself from smiling.

The veteran news reporter was feeling quite proud of herself that morning. After having dinner the Saturday night before with Detective Palazzola, she had still managed to stay below her Jenny Craig calorie allocation for that evening. Justine had been very good over the weekend, watching her calories and working out while staying on track with her diet.

She was now wearing a tight pair of size seven denim jeans that she had borrowed from her daughter. With Justine's significant weight loss over the last six months, she found it difficult to wear her own clothing that didn't look baggy or out of style. She had managed to keep her daily calorie intake at under fifteen hundred calories while going to the gym five evenings a week. Between the intense Zomba classes and doing the elliptical for an hour each day, she had managed to go from a women's size seventeen to a size seven, and she never felt better.

It had taken Justine Cahill a long time to get the attention of Detective Mike Palazzola. She had met him several years ago on a City Hall corruption inquiry that he was investigating, and she could never put the veteran Detroit detective entirely out of her mind. He was a handsome, rugged, classy gentleman trying to raise two daughters on his own, and his kindness and sense of humor had made a lasting impression on her. After trying for several months to get his attention, she was delighted to finally have dinner with him at the Roma Café on Riopelle Street. She watched his eyes study her new, enhanced, shapely figure when he thought she wasn't looking and was grateful for the new, low-cut, black Armani dress that she had worn to the restaurant. She had always been quite smitten with the Detroit detective. She was ecstatic that she had finally gotten him to take her out to dinner. Justine was more than delighted to assist Palazzola in solving the murder investigation of these two small children from St. Clair Shores.

As she sat there at her desk, she began contemplating a significant event that was taking place at the Roma Café that previous Saturday evening. Both she and Palazzola found it strange that several men had entered the restaurant for an exclusive meeting in the back, all well dressed and wearing bowler hats.

*Very odd*, she thought to herself.

Not having a whole lot on her plate regarding any outstanding reporting assignments, she decided to investigate the extraordinary group of men that periodically met at the old Italian restaurant for decades.

Who were these *Archangels*? What did they do? Why the bowler hats and the intense cloak of secrecy?

Cahill decided first to make a phone call to the restaurant and directly dig up some information.

"Roma Café, how can I help you?" a male voice answered the telephone.

"Hello, this is Justine Cahill, and I'm a reporter for the Detroit News. Could I speak with the owner, please? I have some questions regarding a party of men who were meeting at your restaurant last...."

"I'm sorry, ma'am," a male voice immediately responded. "The owner is not here. May I take a message?"

Justine knew that leaving a message with a name and number would only be thrown immediately into the garbage. She was familiar with restaurant owners like this one. The information regarding their guests was usually kept very discrete. This was never given out to just anyone, especially a local reporter.

"I will call back later. Thank you."

She then thought for several moments. Who else in the community would know anything about a group of individuals who go by the name 'The Archangels'? She made several other phone calls to various community centers, including local chambers of commerce and other not-for-profit organizations that regularly accept help and assistance from other charity associations. Most of the inquiries that she had made were only answered by those known to keep such private information of their donors secret, especially those who requested discretion as a prerequisite to their donation. Cahill realized that the community help and donations coming from these Archangels had strings attached, as their charitable assistance came with the designation of 'anonymous.'

After several phone calls with the same result, she encountered a local food pantry located on the East Side of Detroit that was willing to volunteer information.

The 'Saint Malachy Food Pantry' located on Nine Mile and Harper annually receives donations and assistance from the Archangels to the tune of $10,000 to $15,000 annually to operate their weekly food distributions to needy families and spaghetti dinners twice a week.

"Could you tell me a little about these donors who call themselves 'Archangels'?" Cahill inquired.

"Oh yes," an elderly lady responded over the telephone. "They are the nicest group of men. They send us a check between $10,000 to $15,000 every year, which we receive certified mail in a brown envelope with no return address or receipt. They only request that we keep their donations anonymous," she replied.

"But it is such a wonderful thing what they do for us every year. I don't understand why they don't want to be recognized. I've come to understand that they give over $100,000 every year to needy charities and food pantries like ourselves. We are so appreciative of their kindness and generosity. But please, don't publish our name in your paper because we look forward to their donations each year."

"How long have the Archangels been sending your organization money?"

"Probably for over forty years," the elderly lady responded.

"Do you know any of their names or who they are?"

"No. All I know is that they are local community big-shots who enjoy passing out money anonymously to needy charities like ours."

"Thank you."

Justine Cahill shook her head. She just couldn't understand it. Since when does a local group of community leaders get together to anonymously pass out money around to local charities without being recognized? She knew enough of the rich and famous in town, and these people had egos as big as their bank accounts. Most of these local millionaires never donated anything without wanting to get their names in the papers. Were these guys the local Robin Hoods of Detroit? Who were they, and why doesn't anyone want to volunteer any information about them?

Justine had another hunch. Being the experienced investigative reporter that she was, she immediately went on the internet. She looked up all of the haberdashery stores in the Detroit area. With all of those men on that Saturday night wearing not-so-common bowler hats, she figured that she would take the time to track down all of those hat stores and get them to volunteer some information on the customers who purchased black hats. She printed up the list of them and temporarily put that list in her investigative manilla folder titled 'Archangels.'

Cahill then picked up her desk phone again and decided to make another phone call.

Justine now had an excuse to call Detective Palazzola.

---

I was sitting at my desk trying to assemble files for some local car thefts I was assigned to investigate. A big, open bag of Better Made Potato Chips was sitting on the edge of my desk, which I used to bide me over until lunchtime. As my desk phone started ringing, I decided that shoving several more delicious potato chips into my mouth was far more important than answering my ringing desk phone.

"Detective Palazzola," answering with my mouth full.

"Hey Mike, it's Justine. How's it going?"

"Great, Justine, how are you?" I answered, trying to put more enthusiasm into my voice.

"I'm good, Mike. Say, do you remember those guys with the black hats that kept coming into the restaurant last Saturday night? I've been trying to do some investigative work on these guys, but I'm not coming up with a whole lot of info...."

"Really? You haven't found anything on them at all?"

"Well, no...these Archangels seem to operate like Robin Hood and his band of Merry Men. They donate over $100,000 to local charities and food banks every year, with the caveat that their donations be kept anonymous. I got one local food bank to volunteer some information. They said that this group of men are local millionaires within the community who like to pass out their money without publicity."

I shook my head in silence for several long seconds.

"Really? Who are these guys? And why would they want their monetary donations anonymous?"

"That's my big question, Mike."

"Is it dirty money? Is it undeclared cash income that these guys don't want to be disclosed on their books anywhere?"

"Are they drug dealers? Rich gang members? Are they a connected organized crime syndicate?"

I shook my head again, trying to answer my own question.

"Who are these fucking guys?"

More silence over the phone.

"I don't know, Mike. I'm finding more questions than I have answers. I'm thinking of going to my editor and requesting that I do more investigative work on these guys. I'm thinking I can pitch running an article on these local Robin Hood fellas...."

"Hmmm...that may be a good idea. Rat them out, so to speak. Yeah, Justine...I like that idea. Put something in the Detroit News and see if this merry band of do-gooders come out of Sherwood Forest and up for air."

A silent moment.

"But why the anonymity? Why all the secrecy? What are these guys trying to hide?"

"I don't know," Justine responded. "It just doesn't make any sense."

I paused for a moment.

"Maybe a very public article in the Detroit News about these guys is just the thing we need to pull these guys out of that back room of the Roma Café."

I could hear Justine chuckling over the phone.

"That's what I'm thinking, Mike. I will call you back and let you know what else I find out."

There was a short, three-second pause.

"By the way," she continued. "What is your schedule this week? Maybe we could get together somewhere for dinner."

I wasn't initially enthusiastic about hooking up with Justine again, even though she now had a great body and an even greater crush on me. I tried to make up a quick excuse.

"My girls are in dire need of my tutorial talents with their homework this week. Let's talk before the weekend."

"Okay, but my treat this time."

"Yeah, sure. Thanks, Justine," as I quickly hung up the telephone.

I was knee-deep in car theft investigations and gang-banger shootings on that day, so my curiosity regarding Robin Hood and his band of merry men with black hats wasn't exceptionally high on my priority list. I figured I would let Justine take the lead on this investigative story hoping that she would enlighten me with any information that may look suspicious or interesting.

Within a few days, I received another phone call from Detroit News reporter Justine Cahill.

It seemed that the information that she was finding out on these guys with black hats was very interesting indeed.

# CHAPTER FIFTEEN
## FINLEY'S HABERDASHERY SHOP

The old wooden door of the retail shop had loudly opened on that Friday morning, with the charming sound of an old-fashioned doorbell. The clerk in the back of Finley's Haberdashery Shop on Griswold Street looked up towards the front of the store, noticing an attractive older woman waiting to be helped.

"May I help you," the young, well-dressed African American man requested, hoping to make his first sale of the morning.

"Yes. I'm Justine Cahill. I called earlier about some bowler hats that you sell here at your store."

"Yes. We have a very nice collection of those hats in our inventory."

"I see. Do you sell a lot of them?" the woman asked, unbeknownst to the young salesman that he was speaking to a reporter.

"No, not a lot. But we are the only haberdashery in downtown Detroit that sells these unusual men's hats. I believe the only other haberdashery that sells them is located in downtown Mount Clemens."

"Do you have a list of customers whom you have sold those bowler hats to over the last few years?"

The salesman began to look suspiciously at the attractive woman who was asking unusual questions about bowler hats.

"We don't sell a lot of them. But when we do, along with the other men's clothing items that we sell, we include our customers' names into our system," he graciously answered.

The reporter, who was still standing near the entranceway, walked closer to the front counter where the young man was standing. She could see the salesman breathing in her overbearing, expensive perfume scent as she approached him.

"I'm doing an investigation for my newspaper, and I need to know who you have sold these hats to over the last three or four years. Would that be possible?"

The black salesman, now looking skeptical, began to realize that woman he was speaking to was not a customer but probably a detective.

"Can I see your badge?"

"Of course," the middle-aged woman replied

She then opened up her purse and pulled out a crisp, one-hundred-dollar bill, and dangled it with her right hand in front of the young salesman along with her business card.

"My name is Justine Cahill, and I'm a reporter for the Detroit News. I need to know whom you have sold those bowler hats to over the last several years for an investigative story that we're doing."

"I'm sorry. I would have to talk to my boss about something like that. We don't normally disclose such information about our clients," he nervously answered.

Justine then went into her purse and pulled out another one-hundred-dollar bill. She then smiled as she offered the young men's store salesman some cash that neither his boss nor the IRS would ever have to know about.

The young salesman smiled. He then walked towards the back room and went onto the store's desktop computer, located in the back office. Within fifteen minutes, the salesman came back to the front of the store with a detailed list of all the customers who had purchased inventory item numbers H1077-B, H1078-B, and H1080-B for the last five years. These were all the style differences and fabric variations for the bowler hats that they exclusively sold.

He handed the list over to the reporter, who happily tendered the two-hundred-dollar bribe she was offering the young men's store salesman.

"Take your girlfriend out to dinner on me," Justine smiled as she folded the two sheets of computerized information into her purse.

"You mean Eric, my partner?" the young salesman replied, informing the reporter in a very subtle way that he was gay.

"Yes. Please give Eric my regards," Justine smiled broadly, thankful for the information.

Exiting the haberdashery store on Griswold Street, she walked quickly to her late-model BMW parked several yards away from the front of the store. She remotely unlocked her car door and promptly entered, eager to examine the list of customers that the young salesman had printed out for her benefit.

As she sat in the driver's side of her car, she began reading some of the customers' names on that printed clientele list.

Justine Cahill raised her eyebrows in complete and total surprise, shaking her head as she read down the list of customers who had purchased bowler hats at the Finley Haberdashery since 2017. The list included several local business people with very favorable reputations and even larger checkbooks. She was more than familiar with several of the names of the men who were on that list, but one of the purchases completely surprised her.

One of the customers who had purchased a black bowler hat was the current Wayne County Prosecutor.

# CHAPTER SIXTEEN
## ONE HUNDRED YEARS AGO
### THE MISCARRIAGE OF JUSTICE – APRIL 1921

The Federal Courthouse on Fort and Shelby Streets in downtown Detroit was packed with visitors on that bright spring day of April 26, 1921. The courtroom at Room 1002 was starting to fill in with court observers, witnesses, and other interested parties looking to follow the murder trial of a Ford Assembly employee in Highland Park, who was being tried for the brutal stabbing murders of two fellow employees in September 1920.

Mitchell Blackfoot was a native Chippewa Indian. 'Injun Mitch,' as he was commonly referred to, was born and raised on an Indian Reservation near Mt. Pleasant, Michigan. He was now being tried for the recent stabbing murders of two employees of the Ford Assembly Plant in Highland Park. It was quite apparent by the facts of that case that this murder trial was a classic example of self-defense. Blackfoot claimed that he was assaulted in the factory parking lot after work on that autumn day. The two employees were physically beaten before withdrawing a knife and stabbing them to death.

The public defender, Jerome Johnson, who was sitting at the defendant's table with his client, went over trial strategies and reviewed notes regarding any more potential witnesses and their probable testimonies. The public defender, who was assigned to defend Blackfoot, was using a method of defense that was anything but impressive. In his inexperience, the legal counselor was constantly being overruled by Judge George Mulligan, a long-time courtroom judge. The prejudice against Native Indians of the latter was rumored in all of the local papers. No courtroom observer was enthralled with Johnson's method of defense and his poor analysis of this criminal case.

A Detroit Herald news reporter had published an article earlier that week, criticizing Judge Mulligan's obvious courtroom prejudices and the public attorney's less than stellar performance.

His legal defense methods in that murder case were considered shoddy, unprepared, and unsophisticated. He was constantly making presentation errors and courtroom mistakes in front of the presiding judge. It was pretty evident that the Wayne County prosecutors easily had their way with the defendant and his poor legal representation.

'*The defendant in this murder case would have probably been better served to represent himself, rather than allowing the public defender to handle his legal defense,*' was the quote in the previous day's papers.

The inexperienced legal defense team was expected to rest its case on that third day of the trial proceeding. Johnson had called up a witness on that previous day, who had claimed to have seen the defendant being assaulted and bullied by the murder victims. But his testimony was rebuked by the prosecutors when challenged in cross-examination.

"Hear Ye, Hear Ye...all rise before this circuit court of Wayne County, State of Michigan, the Honorable Judge George Mulligan presiding," the courtroom bailiff commenced.

As all the attendees began to sit down in their seats after the judge's entrance, he immediately called on the public defender.

"Mr. Johnson, do you have any other witnesses to present before this court on the defendant's behalf?"

"No, your honor. The defense rests its case," the public defender answered.

It was apparent to everyone within the courtroom that the defendant's lawyer had done an inadequate job in proving 'murder by self-defense' regarding these victims.

"In that case, this court will refer this trial to the jury," the judge proclaimed.

He then gave specific instructions to the jury:

"As the jury in this case, and your duties are to consider the facts and evidence of this case and how they have been presented before this court in an unbiased and in an impartial manner. As you deliberate, it will be your duty to weigh and evaluate all the evidence received in the case and, in that process, to decide the facts on the evidence and the law before you. You should not be influenced by any person's race, color, religious beliefs, national ancestry, sexual orientation, gender identity, gender, or economic circumstances."

In the judge's instructions, he left nothing to chance. Judge Mulligan specifically stated that the jurors should only consider the facts and circumstances of this trial without bias. But all of the observers of this murder trial thought otherwise. With the apparent rulings that Judge Mulligan made against the defendant, it was almost certain that a mistrial would be declared.

The twelve jurors consisted of only white men, chosen from the limited pool of potential candidates, then sequestered for deliberation. The murder trial had taken a total of two-and-one-half days. When the jurors returned with their decision two hours later, their courtroom decision was more than apparent.

"We, the jury, your honor, in the multiple homicides of these victims, find the defendant, Mitchell Blackfoot, guilty *of two counts of first-degree murder.*"

Judge Mulligan then moved to immediately sentence the defendant to two consecutive life sentences without any possibility of parole. The now-convicted murderer, Mitchell Blackfoot, stood there, mute and emotionless, and was without comment or reaction. The bailiff, along with two other officers, handcuffed Blackfoot and escorted him out of the courtroom. There was no declaration of a mistrial, despite the rampant bias and prejudice within those proceedings.

As all of the courtroom observers began to file out of the chamber, a middle-aged attorney sat stoically in the back of the room, holding his coat and hat. He had observed the two days of the criminal trial with complete and utter disgust. It was more than obvious to him that there had been a total miscarriage of justice. With the defendant's inept legal representation, he knew that this poor Native Indian never had a chance.

The attorney rose from the back of the room and stood there stoically, staring at the judge and jury as they began to exit the court. He waited for everyone to leave, as he was now the last person standing in that empty federal chamber.

Standing there for several long minutes, the experienced legal counselor was now glaring at that empty bench, unable to comprehend the total failure of justice that had just been passed onto that poor, minority defendant.

As he proceeded to leave, he then put on his black bowler hat.

# CHAPTER SEVENTEEN
### SIX YEARS LATER
### BIRTHDAY PARTY FOR VITO TOCCO
### BOOK-CADILLAC HOTEL - FEBRUARY 12, 1927

The large snowflakes that were falling that evening were quickly melting as they hit the ground, as the February snowfall was now accumulating on Washington Boulevard. The weather reports in the Detroit Herald called for several inches of snow that evening. Still, the inclement forecasts didn't put a damper on the evening's events. The upscale, swanky Cadillac-LaSalle's and Rolls Royce's were lined up in front of the newly constructed Book-Cadillac Hotel, as the valets were hustling to park all of the cars that were arriving with its guests.

Judge Anthony Siracusa and his wife, Elizabeth, were well dressed for the formal dinner party for the guest of honor, William Vito 'Black Bill' Tocco, and the occasion of his thirtieth birthday party.

The judge was a tall, handsome, first-generation Italian in his late forties who worked hard his whole life and played by the rules. His slicked back hair and dashing good looks greatly resembled the silent movie star, Rudolph Valentino, whose movie 'Son of the Sheik' had just been released. He graduated from the University of Michigan School of Law in 1907. He excelled successfully as a state prosecutor for several years before joining a prestigious law firm in downtown Detroit in 1912. A judicial vacancy was available with the sudden death of Judge Randall Barnett three years ago, and Governor Alex Groesbeck appointed him to fill the vacancy.

A lifelong Republican, his seat was up for re-election in 1928, and he needed to start putting together some 'political friends.' To that end, he knew he would be obligated to attend more dubious parties and occasions like this one.

Wearing a cashmere coat, black tuxedo, and a black bowler hat, both he and his wife, Elizabeth, entered the grand hotel. Adorning a long, beige satin gown, both she and her husband were looking forward to this formidable occasion. It was a social event planned for several months. All three hundred of the arriving guests were the 'who's who' of the Motor City's most influential politicians, businessmen, and socialites.

The notable dinner guests expected at this upscale social event included Henry Ford and his wife, Clara, Harvey Firestone and his wife Idabelle, politicians John Lodge and James Couzens with their wives, and several other prominent, influential people of that day.

The judge pulled up on Washington Boulevard in front of the Book-Cadillac Hotel. Several photographers were taking pictures of all of the guests arriving on that evening. He also noticed several Detroit Police Department detectives near the doorway taking photos and notes, and he wasn't surprised.

At the age of thirty years old, Don William Vito 'Black Bill' Tocco was one of the most powerful men in Detroit. Born in Terrasini, Sicily, on February 12, 1897, Guillermo Vito Tocco was the oldest child of seven children. His poor family immigrated to Detroit, Michigan, in early 1912. Tocco became a naturalized citizen after serving in the United States Army during World War I. Along with his cousins Giuseppe 'Joe' Zerilli and Angelo Meli, they began bootlegging operations during that Prohibition Era. They were involved in smuggling operations across the Detroit River from Windsor. The three men became involved in the 'Unione Siciliana' in Detroit and were the most influential organized crime figures in the Motor City during the Roaring Twenties.

In 1920, Tocco was arrested for the murder of Antonio Badalamenti, a rival Vitale Gang leader killed in retaliation for an attack on Giuseppe Manzello and Angelo Polizzi, respected gang members of the Eastside-Giannola Gang. For some strange, unknown reason, the charges were immediately dropped against Tocco two days later. Along with Meli and Zerilli as his associates, Vito Tocco took over the Giannola Gang, renaming it the Eastside Mob.

Vito 'Black Bill' Tocco was engaged to Joe Zerilli's sister, Rosalia (first cousins), and planned to be married within the following year. He had just purchased a large tract of land in Grosse Pointe Park, and he and his lovely bride-to-be were going to build a spectacular mansion off of Lakeshore Drive.

At thirty years old, Don Vito 'Black Bill' Tocco had earned a dangerous reputation as a violent, ruthless gangster who had no problems making his rivals disappear, usually in Detroit's River Rouge. When Tocco decided to throw himself a thirtieth birthday party at the elegant, luxurious Book-Cadillac Hotel, his unique invitations did not include a response for 'regrets only.' Everyone who received an invitation to this party was expected to be there, as Tocco was standing at the entrance doorway taking attendance.

Judge Siracusa and his wife immediately checked their coats. They then entered the grand ballroom where Don Vito (which he preferred to be called) Tocco and his fiancé immediately welcomed their guests. Since it was Prohibition, several personal bodyguards were standing guard at the door to ensure that the evening of free-flowing alcohol would not be interrupted.

"Judge, it's so nice to see you this evening," as he and Rosalia kissed the couple on both cheeks.

"So glad to be invited, Don Vito. It's an honor to be a part of your wonderful birthday party."

"So sorry about that murder verdict last week, Judge. It's too bad that damn murderer got off," the gangster immediately commented at the door.

Siracusa was utterly taken by surprise. He didn't expect to be assaulted at the door regarding that violent murder case he had just presided over.

"Me too," the judge immediately replied, not wanting to discuss that violent murder case with either Tocco or anyone else at that party.

Truth be told, that murder case Tocco referred to was a very sensitive topic for Judge Anthony Siracusa. He had presided over the murder trial of Thomas Michael Shifflett, a career convict accused of the murder of two sisters on the East Side, Susan and Anna Licata, ages twelve and ten years old.

The two little girls had been found stabbed, raped, and molested, with their young bodies dumped off near an abandoned house in an alley on Fordham Street just off of Seven Mile Road. The two girls had been last seen getting into their neighbor's car, Shifflett, before being kidnapped and taken to the abandoned house on Fordham Street.

The case should have been an open and shut conviction, as the accused killer would have quickly been sentenced to the death penalty in the State of Michigan. But the Detroit Police detectives handling the case made some unfortunate mistakes in managing the evidence. The crime labs had tainted the blood evidence found on the discovered murder weapon, and the prints on the knife had been compromised.

No one was willing to make a testimony against the alleged killer, who had initially stated that they had seen the little girls get into his vehicle. The Wayne County prosecutors couldn't get any other additional testimony from other witnesses. The jury ended up handing a 'not guilty' ruling. There was no doubt that the police and the

Wayne County prosecutor's office had done a sloppy job prosecuting that case.

The Detroit Herald splashed the headlines the next day:

**Accused Child Murderer Goes Free**

This was a horrific criminal case that tugged at the heartstrings of everyone in the city. The newspapers had extensive news coverage of the murder trial Judge Siracusa had presided over. Several reporters published scathing editorials regarding how the criminal case was grossly mishandled.

On that night, Judge Siracusa and his wife were out to enjoy their evening at the luxurious, upscale gathering, and he was in no mood to answer to anyone regarding the murder trial's misplaced ruling. But deep in his heart, the judge felt responsible. Two innocent little girls had been brutally murdered and were void of justice on his watch. As Siracusa sat and presided on that bench at the Federal Building on Fort Street, he could not acquire equity and fairness for their pointless, brutal deaths.

The judge and his wife sat at the table with several other influential guests, including two other prominent attorneys and another federal judge along with their wives. They all made small talk throughout the evening as toasts were being made to Tocco by his friends and family. Before the entrees were served, everyone was asked to take a picture, holding their glasses in the air as if to make a birthday toast to the infamous Mafia gangster.

"Everybody loudly sing Happy Birthday," the photographer from the upper balcony directed, as several camera flashes went off. In contrast, all of the guests sang to Don Vito 'Black Bill' Tocco. The dinner included a 'surf and turf' entrée of lobster tails and filet mignon, along with minestrone, orecchiette pasta, and other Italian specialties.

As the dinner was concluding, Joe Zerilli, Tocco's first cousin, family underboss, and future brother-in-law, approached the judge at the table.

"Judge, Don Vito would like to have a word with you."

Elizabeth looked at her husband with a worried look on her face as he grasped her hand, assuring her that he would be okay.

Siracusa excused himself in front of the rest of the dinner guests at the table and followed Zerilli to a small parlor located adjacent to the grand ballroom. It seemed that several men, all of Tocco's proteges, were sitting around the smoking room in large, velvet red chairs. They were enjoying their illegal brandy and smoking cigars after dinner.

"Judge Siracusa," Don Vito Tocco greeted the honorable judge, kissing him again on both cheeks and offering him an imported Cuban cigar.

"It's so nice of you to honor us with your presence this evening," the gangster stated loudly. The Detroit mobster had a slight Italian accent that became more apparent as he indulged in more brandy.

"I wouldn't miss your birthday party for the world, Don Vito," he replied, as an associate cut the judge's cigar and amply lit the end of it for him to enjoy.

"You know, Judge, that jury verdict broke my heart for those two little girls," Tocco immediately said to the judge.

"That trial was a travesty of justice," the mobster summarized as he was pointing his cigar at the judge as if to admonish him for what had happened in his courtroom.

"I know this, Don Vito," the judge immediately responded, as no one ever addressed Don Vito Tocco as 'Black Bill.'

"The Detroit detectives and the prosecutors should be fired for the way they mishandled the evidence in that case," Tocco editorialized.

"I agree. The DA's office just couldn't tie all of the evidence together. The defense lawyers were unable to convince the jury of Shifflett's guilt beyond a reasonable doubt," Judge Siracusa explained. At the same time, another associate offered him a crystal glass tumbler filled with two fingers of imported brandy.

"So judge, now what?" Tocco asked.

"What do you mean?"

"You know...now what?"

The judge was silent.

"Two innocent little girls from a hard-working Italian family get murdered by some deviant pervert, and the courts can't get a damn conviction," Tocco commented.

"Now we are all supposed to stand around with our thumbs up to our asses while this fucking pervert walks around free and gets away with murder?"

As the judge glared at him, his face was expressionless. There were a few moments of silence in the room as everyone realized that the Detroit mafioso was putting the judge on the spot.

"We can't try him again on the same case, Don Vito. That would be double jeopardy, and the evidence presented was inconclusive. We don't have enough to try this bastard again."

Tocco took a long drag from his cigar and practiced blowing his smoke circles in the air in front of his friends in the parlor.

"Then perhaps, Your Honor, this fucking bastard needs to be given a hard dose of Sicilian justice."

Siracusa looked at the Mafioso, not saying a word. The last thing he wanted to do was to order up the death sentence of a murderer and child molester to Vito Tocco. He knew that there would be other ramifications and obligations to consider.

Several years ago, Vito 'Black Bill' Tocco's arrest for the Badalamenti murder years before was dismissed and thrown out of court for one very good reason: Judge Vincent Daudelin was obligated to Vito Tocco and his family for various favors granted and other rendered personal benefits.

The judge never wanted to be indebted to Tocco for anything. The last thing Siracusa wanted was to give Tocco a 'get out of jail free card.' He already knew that Tocco, Zerilli, and the rest of their family could get away with just about anything in Detroit, and the last thing he needed was to have an additional obligation to the Detroit mob. The judge knew that if he agreed to have the East Side Mob take care of this child molester on their own, the judge would always have to look the other way to the Unione Siciliana's deplorable crimes.

"It's not your place to be the executioner of justice, Don Vito," the judge brazenly replied.

Everyone within the room was shocked at the judge's response. Very few people stood up and talked to the Detroit capo in such an audaciously bold tone of voice.

Don Vito momentarily glared at the judge, and a cocky smirk came over his face.

"Well, obviously, your brand of justice doesn't work, Your Honor. And now, this fucking bastard goes free to run the streets, looking for more of our little children to rape, molest, and murder."

A moment of silence.

"Our justice system isn't perfect, Don Vito," the judge reminded the gangster.

Tocco suddenly rose from his chair, yelling,

"OUR JUSTICE SYSTEM IS FUCKED UP," Tocco loudly screamed, slamming his empty drink glass up against the wall. Pieces of crystal glass went scattering everywhere as the dozen or so well-dressed men in their tuxedos stood there in silence. It was a miracle that none of them were splashed with chards of broken glass or the contents of his drink. Every person in that room was more than familiar with Don Vito Tocco's violent, brutal temper.

There were several minutes of silence as Don Vito 'Black Bill' Tocco sat back down in his red velvet chair and tried to calm himself down.

"Look, Judge, I know none this is your fault. But there needs to be some justice and morality served here for the Licata family and the loss of their two little girls. They have already approached me and demanded vengeance for the lost lives of their daughters," Tocco revealed.

"We cannot allow this fucking pervert to continue to roam our streets."

Judge Siracusa, still holding his cigar and his glass of brandy, suddenly made a very bold statement:

"There will be justice, Don Vito. That I can promise you."

Everyone in the room looked at the judge, not understanding how he would directly be able to deliver justice to the local community now that the courts had released this alleged murderer.

Don Vito Tocco glared at Siracusa.

"And how do you expect us to believe that justice will be served, especially by you, after that despicable comedy show that occurred in your courtroom, Judge? How in the hell can you bring justice to this family now?"

The judge didn't have an answer.

And he certainly didn't have a plan.

The only thing that he did know was that he didn't want to be obligated and indebted to Vito 'Black Bill' Tocco and his family of bootleggers, thugs, and murderers. He didn't need the city's crime syndicate to undermine every verdict from the federal building on Fort Street. There must be other ways and means to acquire justice, Siracusa thought to himself.

Direct actions and measures should never include the Unione Siciliana or the Detroit Mafia.

"That will be my problem, Don Vito."

Vito Tocco smiled as one of his associates brought him another fresh glass of brandy, then relighting his cigar. He then glared at the judge for several long seconds.

"Then your problem it will be, Judge. I should hope to hear about your dispensing of justice against this killer on behalf of the Licata Family sometime soon."

Taking a long drag from his cigar, he then began blowing more smoke circles in the air.

"Or else, you and I will have a serious problem."

At that moment, everyone raised their glasses to make a toast to the judge.

"Salute, Judge Siracusa."

---

It was just past eleven-thirty, and the messy drive home from the Book-Cadillac Hotel was a long one. Siracusa maneuvered his new 1927 Cadillac-LaSalle around the ice, snow, and traffic on Cadieux and Lakeshore Drives. He and his wife Elizabeth had purchased an upscale home in Grosse Pointe Woods several years before. They needed to relieve their babysitter for their two little girls, ages eight and ten years old.

He couldn't get that failed murder trial out of his head, not just because Thomas Shifflett had gotten away with murder, thanks to the incompetence of the Detroit Police detectives. And not just because of the brutal murder of the Licata sisters themselves. But because every evening, as he tucked his little girls in bed, he would say a prayer to himself, hoping that the fate of those little Licata girls never became the fate of his two young daughters.

At about two o'clock in the morning, Anthony Siracusa couldn't sleep. He got up from his bed, put on his bathrobe, and went downstairs to his study, where he maintained an extensive library of law books, case law, and judiciary rulings. The judge sat at his desk, lit up a cigarette, and pondered his situation while gazing at his bookshelves stacked with law literature. Siracusa then spent the next three hours delving through his law books, trying to figure out how to get Shifflett back in his courtroom for a second murder trial.

He then stumbled upon some Italian law books in his library, a volume series of six titled 'The Renaissance Laws of Florence.' These books were given to him by a fellow law partner from his previous law firm. He pulled a few volumes out and began perusing them for over an hour. Buried inside one of those Italian law books, he discovered something interesting:

Back in Florence in 1539, the Medici Family formed a special judicial committee out of disgust for how the courtrooms of that era were handling the cases of several abhorrent juvenile murders. That committee consisted of thirteen local statesmen, church elders, bishops, local judges and lawyers, to hand out justice to those perpetrators who were able to escape the local laws of justice. That committee was only dedicated to dispensing justice for those criminals who so deservedly needed it, and they met on an annual basis. They would make a death sentence ruling against those criminals, then seek out 'hit men' to brutally stab and kill those accused criminals. They were a chamber of judges, a jury of men who also served as executioners.

That committee was called the 'Societa Della Malizia', or the Society of Malice. They consisted of thirteen upstanding citizens within the Tuscan community. Every September 29th, on the feast day of Saints Michael, Gabriel, and Raphael, the Lord's angels of justice, the men of this secret society gathered to dispense the proper sentences against all those demons of evil.

The local vendors within the town square knew when these local committee members would meet. They would dress in long black garments and black hats and meet at the judicial chambers in the town hall basement, near Florence's Basilica di Santa Croce.

The judge smiled, then got up and made himself some coffee on that Sunday morning. He later went to eight o'clock mass with his wife and two children at St. Paul of the Lake Church.

Later that Sunday, he sat back down at his study and pulled out a large pad of paper and a fountain pen.

Siracusa drafted a set of by-laws, corporate resolutions, and articles of incorporation. He then made a list of thirteen names, including his own. These were the names of men that he knew he could trust with his life.

He pulled out a stack of blank cards from his bottom desk drawer and sent private formal invitations, using his best cursive and black fountain pen. These invitations were addressed to each individual as to where they would meet and the matters that would be discussed. 'Formal Attire Preferred' is said on the bottom of each invitation.

All these invited men were established, upstanding citizens of society whom he knew he could recruit to seek justice for those criminal cases where the civilized judicial system had miserably failed. These would be men who would stand up against all those murderous criminals who ruthlessly escaped the laws of justice, who beat the system, thanks in part to their cunning, malicious lawyers. These would be respected, honorable men

133

who would dispense proper death sentences to those brutal, violent demons that the criminal courts could no longer touch.

And on that Sunday in February 1927, the Malizia Society of Detroit was born.

# CHAPTER EIGHTEEN
## AFTER THE FIRST MEETING – MARCH 1927

The all-night Cadieux Café smelled like stale cigarettes and cigar smoke, as Judge Anthony Siracusa, wearing a mohair overcoat and a black bowler hat, was comfortably seated next to the window. After taking off his hat and coat, the judge lit up his cigarette and looked at his watch. It was just past one o'clock in the morning. The Malizia Society of Detroit had just finished its first official meeting in the exclusive, private meeting room of the Roma Café on Riopelle Street.

It had been a long but productive gathering. All of the invited attendees were respectfully there to assist the judge in creating this non-for-profit organization dedicated to doling out justice to those unpunished criminals. They have taken advantage of a broken federal judicial system. Judge Siracusa received a tremendous amount of vocal support from the various community leaders that he had invited sit-in at the first charter meeting of the Society. The prospective members realized the need to administer the kind of eye-for-an-eye justice currently lacking in the federal judicial system. There were too many criminals, especially murderers, beating the system and taking away innocent lives in their murderous wakes.

To that end, the crime syndicates of that era served a purpose to those in the community who were less fortunate. To the many Italian, Polish, Irish, and Croatian immigrants who could not afford expensive lawyers, they helplessly watched their children and loved ones get raped, beaten, and killed for no reason. The crime syndicates of that era served as alternatives to the police and the broken judicial system. They were paid to provide justice to those murderous few who took advantage of the court system and escaped prosecution with little or no jail time. Those were the people who

135

turned to the Mafia and requested help, who asked for criminal recourse.

After attending Vito Tocco's birthday party a few weeks ago, Judge Siracusa knew that there had to be an alternative to Detroit's East Side Mafia or the Eastern Market's Purple Gang. A formal, more sophisticated means of administering justice had to be derived without being beholden to the criminal elements of the Sicilian and Jewish crime syndicates. For Judge Siracusa, there should be no contracts, no motive of profit or extortion in upholding the ancient, rightful laws of the Old Testament.

It was a matter of honor. It was a matter of justice. It was a matter of right and wrong.

Siracusa believed that enlisting the likes of Vito 'Black Bill' Tocco was not a viable alternative to upholding justice. He contrived and reasoned that the innocent victims of society should not be obligated to the Mafia or the Purple Gang.

Detroit's good, law-abiding citizens needed an alternative, a 'big brother' if you will, to oversee the federal judicial system within the Great State of Michigan and uphold justice to those who so greatly deserved it. These were the purposes and the sociological mandates that the judge so intensely believed in, and he didn't need to preach to his fellow Malizia members of their newly formed society's manifesto.

There needed to be justice. There needed to be retribution. There needed to be vengeance.

Thirteen men now had a common purpose. The new members of the Malizia Society of Detroit had also decided, as a means of covering up their covert operations, to call themselves 'The Archangels' publicly. They would be a community-based organization dedicated to serving those less fortunate individuals and organizations in dire need. The Archangels would go on to charitably fund hospitals, build children's wards, raise money for soup kitchens, and fund any charity in need over the next century. The members all knew at the time that they couldn't hold themselves out as public assassins, so they needed a community purpose that was more conforming. They needed to stay under the radar yet conspicuously contribute to those charitable causes which would be grateful for the Society's financial assistance.

The name 'Archangels' was a perfect moniker for their community cause. In the years to come, the organization would anonymously donate millions of dollars, benefiting numerous local Detroit charities but never disclosing their identities over the years. They would help those within the community in need and slay all those who greatly deserved God's divine wrath. They would model themselves to the holy archangels of Raphael, Michael, and Gabriel, the angels of justice. They were the guardians of paradise who slew the dragons of evil and Satan with their mighty swords. They would serve the community in need and oversee their purpose to ensure that the Lord's will is done.

Each new member in their written invitation was required to wear formal wear to the meeting. Most everyone arriving at the Roma Café was well dressed for the first meeting, wearing formal tuxedos, black ties, and stylish black bowler hats, which were all the rage in 1927. The initial charter meeting was opened with the Lord's Prayer, with Judge Siracusa reading several passages from his family bible that he had brought along:

*"And a man who injures his countryman as he has done, so it shall be done to him, namely, fracture for fracture, eye for an eye, tooth for a tooth. Just as another person has received an injury from him, so it will be given to him." (Lev. 24:19–21).*

And then, after an elaborate meal of crab cakes and lobster brisk, pasta primavera, and porterhouse steaks, the general meeting was called to order.

Each member took a lifetime oath. Each Archangel took a solemn promise of secrecy and swore on the bible and their God that their covert, secret manifesto would never be revealed to anyone outside of Detroit's now secret society. Each individual who attended the meeting pledged one thousand dollars in cash as start-up members' dues, with capital calls to be made by the executive board to members whenever money would be needed in the club's coffers. Initial elections were called upon, and an executive committee was immediately voted in.

Judge Anthony Siracusa was unanimously elected as the club's first president, with criminal attorney Thomas Cleaver as Vice President. The Assistant Police Chief of Hamtramck. Stanley Kolkowski was elected as Secretary and Manufacturer's Bank Senior Vice President Michael Wilcox as Treasurer. The other members who were in attendance were tax accountant Samuel Jenkins, retailer David Hudson, jewelry store owner Arthur Talarico, Detroit Assistant Chief of Police Jonathon Borkowski, wholesale food distributor Benjamin Feldstein, Michigan State Representative John Amari, Detroit City Council Trustee Patrick O'Conner, another criminal attorney Robert Marcus, and medical physician Andrew Grant.

These thirteen upstanding individuals of society, whom Siracusa personally trusted with his life, were invited to join. The number thirteen had a tremendous amount of significance, modeled after Jesus and his twelve apostles. All thirteen invited members were in attendance, and all had the same common goals and purpose of the Malizia Society of Detroit, with all in agreement: To uphold justice and deliver vengeance to those malicious criminals who have successfully escaped the legal justice system.

"Coffee, sir?" the middle-aged waitress asked the judge as he sat at the table, patiently waiting for his party to arrive.

"Yes, please." The judge lit up another cigarette.

"Would you like a menu?"

"No, thank you. I will just have some toast with butter for now, please."

The waitress gave him a dirty look as she scribbled something down on her ticket pad, then ran directly to the kitchen to provide the chef with his simple order.

He agreed to meet with Thomas Cleaver and Stanley Kolkowski at the all-night diner on Cadieux Road and Harper Avenue to finish discussing some of the details that had come out of the meeting. With all of the intricate details that had been discussed, there was one major issue that still needed to be resolved.

Cleaver and Kolkowski entered that late-night diner within twenty minutes after the judge was seated, as the loud jingled ring from the entrance door loudly announced their arrival. They were both still wearing their black bowler hats along with their cashmere coats, which they had decided earlier as their new society dress code. The three men shook hands once again, complimenting each other on the success of their first charter meeting. All agreed that the by-laws would be promptly drafted after being voted on, and the minutes of their first meeting would be recorded.

All of the attendees of that first meeting agreed that the minutes of the meetings would be sectionalized in two parts. The first half of the meeting would be recorded appropriately, which addressed the society's not-for-profit business that was conducted. The second part of the meeting, concerning the society's acts of mortal redemption and vengeance, would be written and recorded in Latin. The executive board would be the only ones to review the private minutes and then deposit them in Siracusa's personal safe. Judge Siracusa chose the Latin language, which he had studied proficiently in college. He knew that it would not be a common language that could be easily understood and translated. Kolkowski had also studied it in parochial school many years ago and stated that he would have no problem recording the meeting's course of business in that ancient, medieval language.

The three of them sat down, and the waitress politely filled all of the coffee cups with fresh coffee, hoping that someone at the table would put in a large, late-night food order. After several minutes of more discussion, the subject that was on all of their minds was finally brought up by Cleaver.

"So, Judge, who is going to be our executioner?" he quietly asked.

Siracusa was visibly stumped, as he did not have an immediate answer for the criminal attorney.

As the three of them slowly sipped on their fresh black coffee, there was a very long, deafening period of silence.

"Where are we going to find a hitman to do the job? It's one thing to sentence a dangerous street criminal to death. It's another matter to find someone who is going to carry out that sentence," Kolkowski pointed out.

"Do you have any thoughts?" Siracusa asked the other gentlemen.

All were without any answers or solutions, as neither of them knew of who they could appoint as their executioner. Because of the noise and ballistics issues that go with using a firearm, the members of the Society agreed that their would-be assassin had to be proficient at committing murder using a knife. A butcher's knife or a hunting knife could be easily cleaned and reused. It would be more difficult for police detectives to locate and associate a knife as a murder weapon.

As the waitress took Kolkowski and Cleaver's late-night breakfast order, Siracusa remembered a criminal case several years ago in which a Native American Indian had been wrongly convicted of a double homicide at the Ford Assembly Plant in Hamtramck. The convict was assigned a court-appointed attorney who knew little about criminal law and was sentenced by a well-known prejudiced judge who openly didn't care for Native American Indians. He had difficulty recalling his name at that moment, but he remembered the criminal case very well. He also recalled the incident vividly because the homicide was committed using a large bowie hunting knife.

"Perhaps, Lizzie Fucking Borden is still around. Maybe we could hire her?" Cleaver joked.

Siracusa was still deep in thought as he tried to recall the criminal case.

"I recall a criminal conviction of a Native American a few years ago that was prosecuted in Judge Mulligan's courtroom. I remember it well because it was a stabbing death, and his counsel was a public defender who didn't know shit about criminal law," the judge stated while sipping on his now cold black coffee.

At that moment, the older waitress brought over their food orders as the judge pushed his coffee cup to the edge of the table so the waitress could see that he needed a refill.

Cleaver was now deep in thought.

"Are you thinking about that injun from Mount Pleasant that worked for Ford several years ago? The guy that got jumped after work and killed those two white guys in self-defense? Yeah, I remember that case."

141

"He got two life sentences for those murders, Judge. He's rotting at the Milan Federal Prison right now. What good is he going to do us?" Cleaver asked.

Siracusa softly smiled at the criminal attorney.

"As a federal judge, I can petition Governor Groesbeck for an early release of the prisoner on probation, based on the facts of the case and federal judge's prejudice during the court trial."

"Are you going to be able to get the governor to go along?"

"I think so. I will have a meeting with him in Lansing. Presuming he's in favor of his early release, I can approach the prisoner and have him released on probation under my supervision."

Cleaver and Kolkowski both smiled.

"It's a great idea if the injun goes along with our program," the Hamtramck Assistant Chief of Police remarked.

Several more moments of silence.

"What if he refuses?" Kolkowski asked.

"Then he will stay in Milan, rotting for the rest of his life."

Another silent moment.

"He would be stupid to refuse," Cleaver stated, talking with his mouth full.

"He's not going to do it for nothing. How much can we compensate for this hired murderer?"

The judge was now thinking out loud.

"Providing him with room and board, a cash bonus, along with a job at an auto factory nearby, might be incentive enough to keep him permanently on our payroll."

The three of them finished their late-night breakfast, all of them in agreement. As Cleaver recalled his name, the federal prisoner, Mitchell Blackfoot, would be approached by Siracusa after the proper channels of the convict's jail sentence were reduced to time served and paroled by the governor. They all knew that although this was a long shot, they realized that they needed an assassin who was motivated enough to murder on behalf of the Society's manifesto.

He had to be motivated. He had to be trusted. But most of all, the Society's new killer had to be very good and talented with a long, serrated knife.

Judge Siracusa put a ten-dollar bill on the table for a late-night breakfast totaling $3.54. They all then stood up and shook each other's hands as if to make a sacred pact. Their assassin had been chosen and agreed upon. It was now up to Siracusa to ensure that the incarcerated Native Indian followed along with their ambitious, discrete plans.

The judge then smiled at his new fellow society members.

An offer would be made that he couldn't refuse.

# CHAPTER NINETEEN

It was a chilly weekday evening in March 1927, as the large guard tower of the federal prison in Milan, Michigan, cast a large shadow on the entranceway of the penitentiary campus. The barbed wire encircled the red brick wall around the bordering prison property, as the well-guarded correctional institution encased some of the country's most dangerous criminals.

The sentry at the prison gate opened his reception window as the 1927 Cadillac LaSalle pulled up to the entranceway, handing the jail guard a piece of paper.

"I'm here to see prisoner number 731-59," the well-dressed driver only said. Although he looked to be on official business with his Brooks Brothers dark suit, hat, and overcoat, this was a personal task. This trip was a personal mission that he needed to do. He had driven over an hour after his last court proceeding to visit the federal prison.

The sentry guard read the documents and mentioned the prisoner's name out loud along with the prisoner's number. He then directed the driver to park his newer model Cadillac off to the side parking lot and began the entrance process.

Judge Anthony Siracusa was here at the federal prison on his own personal time. He had completed his last court session at four o'clock. He then mentioned to his wife Elizabeth that he had some official business at the prison that he needed to attend.

He would be home late; he reminded her.

It was a rare occasion when the judge went to a federal prison to visit a prisoner. The last time he had done this was several years before when he was a practicing criminal attorney for the law firm that he was associated with, Herzog and Silverstein, in the Penobscot Building in downtown

144

Detroit. There were numerous prisoners in that federal penitentiary that he had personally sentenced there to serve their time. He was more than aware that his presence at that prison campus could possibly present a safety concern.

"Thank you, Judge," the prison guard pleasantly said to Siracusa as he frisked and padded down the federal judge before entering the conference room of the penitentiary, located at the end of a very long, dark hallway.

"Please have a seat here, Judge. We will retrieve the prisoner you wish to visit shortly," the guard said, as the judge sat down at a long wooden table, surrounded by old, rusty steel chairs in a drab, lime green room that looked like it had seen a fresh coat of paint in years.

The purpose of Judge Siracusa's visit to the federal penitentiary was a mystery to the federal prison's warden, Randall Scott. The judge had scheduled this visit at the prison to see this particular inmate a few weeks ago. He only stated that some new evidence had been uncovered regarding the inmate's current life sentence for first degree-murder charges he had been sentenced to. The federal judge requested that the private conference room be void of other inmates or visitors and requested the utmost discretion regarding the informal prison visit.

Federal Prisoner Mitchell Blackfoot, Inmate Number 731-59, had been sitting in his prison cell that early evening, anxiously awaiting his visit with the federal judge. 'Injun Mitch' had been informed several days earlier by the warden that he would be receiving an unusual visit from a federal judge. Still, he had no idea what the subject of the meeting was regarding.

Injun Mitch had called the Milan Federal Correctional Institution his home for the last six years, spending each day staring at the drab, gray walls of his ten by a twelve-foot prison cell. He hadn't had many visitors during that long period of his serving time, which was two life sentences without parole. He had not spoken to his attorney in several months, and he no longer had any relatives or family to speak of who would claim him as their own.

In 1919, Mitchell Blackfoot, a very large man of Chippewa Indian descent, was an autoworker on the Ford Motor Company assembly line. At six feet, five inches tall, he towered over most of his fellow employees and mostly kept to himself. He had been honorably discharged from serving the Army in World War I. Blackfoot was happy to be gainfully employed at the Highland Park Ford Plant.

Because of his native Chippewa Indian roots, the quiet auto worker was constantly being bullied, stalked, and teased by the other Ford employees.

It was a fair assessment that Blackfoot was a lifelong, constant victim of Native American prejudice. Born and raised on an Indian reservation in Isabella County in Central Michigan, he was constantly defending himself because of his Indian race. He was a quiet, Indian reservation victim of an American society that had just recently won the Indian Wars that crippled the country and the wild west frontier during the prior one hundred years.

One evening, after being continuously harassed by four other workers at that assembly plant, he waited for the four of them to punch out and finish their shift on that late evening. After being physically provoked again by the four of them, a violent fight ensued. While being held by two auto workers, he was physically beaten and punished by two other employees. When Blackfoot broke free of the two men holding him down, he suddenly withdrew his weapon. Blackfoot managed to butcher and kill the two with only a serrated knife while the other workers ran for safety. He left two of them for dead, face down in the middle of the Ford Assembly parking lot.

This case would have been an involuntary manslaughter incident provoked and sustained out of self-defense in any federal court of law. Blackfoot, being relatively poor and without any immediate family, was without a competent attorney. The court-appointed an inexperienced, public lawyer to his defense. With the outcry of the two Caucasian victim's local families, and because of the prejudice of native Indians at the time, he was sentenced by a jury to two life sentences at the federal prison without the prospect of ever being eligible for parole.

"He didn't have to kill them with a knife," was the prosecuting attorney's mantra, as he was disappointed that he couldn't secure a death sentence against the native Indian.

"He could have just walked away," was the district attorney's consistent claim.

To that end, Mitchell 'Injun Mitch' Blackfoot quietly began serving his two life sentences in April 1921 at the Federal Correctional Institution in Milan, Michigan.

The Milan Federal Prison was a miserable place to be incarcerated. It was full of gangsters, drug dealers, rapists, murderers, and life-long hardened criminals who only knew how to live from the wrong side of the law. The single mattress situated within the middle of his jail cell was his only piece of furniture, next to an old, dilapidated toilet and a dirty sink stained with dirt that hadn't been cleaned or scrubbed in years.

Blackfoot was trying his best to survive mentally. He never had any visitors, knowing that his quiet existence in the jail cell was his only lifelong reprieve. To pass the time, Blackfoot became a ferocious reader. He read the Bible several times to the point of quoting the old and new testaments by scripture. He read other books, novels, and anything that he could get his hands on in the prison library to pass his time.

But deep down, Blackfoot was a very angry man. He knew that those factory employees had set him up, and his killing of those assembly victims resulted from his violent temper and his making the mistake of bringing along a serrated knife to work. Despite how the jury had ruled against him at his trial, he knew that he wasn't a cold-blooded murderer.

At the time, Judge Anthony Siracusa, a criminal defense attorney, had heard about the Blackfoot murder case and how he was a probable victim of the jury's prejudice. He was very familiar with the murder case that was brought against Blackfoot in 1921. Having had other experiences with the federal judge associated with that case, he knew that his being of Chippewa Indian descent was a significant factor in the prevalent injustice in his trial.

Being a federal judge, Anthony Siracusa now had the power to commute Blackfoot's sentence and grant him an early release due to the blatant discrimination and unfair trial proceeding against him. The judge was seriously considering an early release for this Milan federal penitentiary prisoner.

For a price.

It was almost five o'clock in the afternoon when the corrections officers came over to open his jail cell.

"You have a visitor," the large, oversized prison guard said.

Blackfoot followed the guard over to the large conference room, bearing an old wooden table and some very worn-out steel chairs. As he entered, he noticed a well-dressed man sitting alone at the large wooden table, his black bowler hat and cashmere overcoat neatly folded and placed on the other side.

The man stood up and introduced himself to the prisoner, shaking his hands while still handcuffed.

"Mr. Blackfoot, I'm Judge Siracusa, from the Federal Circuit Court in Detroit."

Blackfoot graciously shook the judge's hand.

"Guard, could you remove the handcuffs off of this prisoner, please. I don't believe he will be a dangerous threat here."

The corrections officer begrudgingly removed Blackfoot handcuffs, still allowing him to wear the heavy chained shackles around his legs.

"Please allow us to be alone. You may stand guard outside," the judge ordered the prison guard as he exited the conference room and stood outside the large, steel exit door.

The judge and the prisoner sat across from one another at that long wooden table. For the first initial moments of their meeting, they did not say a word to each other.

Mitchell Blackfoot looked to be in his early thirties, with dark native skin and very long, dark black hair. It was combed and slicked back with a hair product of some kind, its scent resembling the distinctive smell of Vaseline. The judge was initially surprised, taken off guard by the towering physique of this Native American, as he loomed over the judge.

"How are you doing here, Mr. Blackfoot?" Siracusa asked.

"Trying to survive," the inmate responded in a deep, low voice. The loud, guttural sounds coming from his throat resulted from the prison inmate not talking very much to anyone within his immediate surroundings.

There was another moment of silence.

"I am sorry for the circumstance and the trial results of your being here," the judge began to speak, making eye contact with the prisoner.

Blackfoot only sat there, nodding his head.

"You are probably wondering why I am here," Siracusa began the conversation.

"The thought has occurred to me, yes," Blackfoot stated, again in a very low, deep voice.

The federal judge continued to make eye contact with the prisoner, ensuring he would not miss his reaction while making his proposition.

"I represent an organization that reviews the severe injustices that have been inflicted on federal prisoners such as yourself, and your case falls under the category of our review," the judge began.

"You were given a bad rape in court, Mr. Blackfoot. It is quite obvious by the court documents and the lack of evidence that was presented in your defense."

Several moments of silence.

"You were unfairly judged by your peers, Mr. Blackfoot."

The inmate leaned closer to the judge while responding,

"I was fucked," Blackfoot softly said.

Another long moment of silence.

"Yes, Mr. Blackfoot. You were indeed."

The two of them continued to study each other in several long, uncomfortable moments of silence.

"How would you feel about an early release from prison?" the federal judge suggested to the prisoner.

Blackfoot looked at him in silence, his facial expressions practically motionless. He did not initially respond to the judge's suggestion, as though he were being teased and ridiculed.

He then suddenly got up from the long wooden table. While the judge was still sitting there, he began to take several short paces around the room, his leg shackles preventing and limiting him from pacing the room faster. He then approached the judge.

"Are you here to fuck with me?" he loudly demanded to know, now standing over the table where Siracusa was sitting. Mitchell Blackfoot's towering presence resembled the recent silent King Kong movie, with his giant gorilla stature overshadowing the tiny, miniature occupants of New York City.

"I can assure you, Mr. Blackfoot. I am not."

The prisoner sat back down at the long wooden table and continued to stare at the judge.

"What's the catch?"

A moment of silence.

"What do I have to do for this freedom?"

As Judge Siracusa sat there deep in thought, a long moment of silence came over him. It was as if he was searching for the words to define the prisoner's new objective.

"Are you interested, Mr. Blackfoot?"

"Of course I'm interested. I will do anything to get out of this hell hole."

Another long moment of silence.

"Anything, Mr. Blackfoot?" he asked again as the federal judge raised his eyebrows, making sure that the prisoner was willing to accept the penance that he was about to propose.

The judge then reached into his pocket, pulling out a Lucky Strike from his platinum cigarette case, lighting it with his silver lighter. He then offered one to the prisoner, who refused. Siracusa took several long drags from his cigarette, exhaling the smoke from his nostrils. They were both silent for several long moments. The prisoner, now even more suspicious, glared at the judge, then slowly nodded his head.

Judge Anthony Siracusa then leaned closer to the prisoner while still sitting comfortably at the table.

"We desire the services and abilities of a professional hitman, and you have been selected to fulfill those services."

"A professional hitman?" he asked.

Siracusa continued to stare at the prisoner as Injun Mitch looked shocked at the mere suggestion of his having to commit another murder for his freedom.

"Are you serious?"

The judge slowly answered the prisoner.

"You are being asked to serve our organization without question discreetly."

"Who is this organization?"

A silent moment.

"The Malizia Society of Detroit. We call ourselves 'Archangels'".

The prisoner looked dumbfounded as if to now be confused.

"And who are you people?"

The judge now glared at the prisoner.

"That isn't important for you to know right now, Mr. Blackfoot. As you come to know us, you will understand our devout mission down the road. For now, you will take orders from only me."

Another silent moment.

"There will be nothing in writing, and there will be no evidence of this or any other conversation regarding this subject. You will do as you are told by me and my me alone. You will not ask any questions, and you will not do anything other than what you are ordered and expected to do."

A long pause.

"The only weapon that will be available to you will be the same kind of knife that you used to kill those auto assembly plant employees six years ago."

A pause.

"There will be no guns, no explosives, and no other weapons will be used. We do not want the burden of any ballistics or traceable guns involved in these professional hits."

Another moment of silence as Injun Mitch was listening intently.

"There will be no discussion with anyone regarding any mission that you are asked to perform. Your only directive will come from me and no one else."

Another silent pause.

"There will be total anonymity in your mission assignments. You will be expected to perform your assignments like any other professional. Should you have the unfortunate circumstance of being caught or captured by the authorities, we will have total deniability to that regard."

"Total deniability?" Injun Mitch questioned.

The prisoner briefly stood up from his chair. Confined by his ankle chains, he briefly paced the floor behind the table as if trying to absorb the information this stranger was proposing to him physically. This was all too good to be true, he kept thinking to himself.

"You guys sound like a bunch of fucking right-wing extremists," Mitch observed.

"I can assure you," Siracusa stated loudly. "We are not."

A silent moment, as the judge took another hit from his Lucky Strike cigarette.

"We are an organization of upstanding citizens within the community who are righting the wrongs of our errand justice system. we need your services."

Another pause as the judge exhaled the cigarette smoke from his nostrils, then took a very deep breath.

"...and your loyalty."

Siracusa then pointed his lit cigarette at Injun Mitch.

"In other words, Mr. Blackfoot, if you rat us out, you'll be back here in this god-forsaken prison so goddamn fast it will make you fucking Injun head spin," the judge curtly responded.

He took another drag from his cigarette.

"And this time, Mr. Blackfoot, I can assure you," the judge proceeded to say, getting his point across. He exhaled another stream of cigarette smoke from the side of his mouth.

"There will not be another guardian angel sitting here in front of you, offering you your freedom."

The Native American glared at the federal judge for several long moments, completely speechless and without words. He swallowed hard, knowing that he was now about to make a deal for his freedom. Injun Mitch was about to make a moral exchange and physically escape these federal walls of purgatory in return for the performance of another cardinal sin.

It was the most forbidden commandment of the Lord's Ten Commandments.

"And what if I refuse?"

Another long pause, as the judge, now getting angry, momentarily glared at the prisoner. He quickly extinguished his cigarette on the wooden table, then flicked the cigarette butt onto the dirty prison floor.

He then grabbed his folded cashmere coat, put on his black bowler hat, and began to dress before proceeding to leave.

"Perhaps this was a mistake, Mr. Blackfoot. I apologize for taking up your precious time to discuss this proposal and this ultimatum for your freedom."

Blackfoot suddenly rose from the table.

"Don't fuck with me, Judge!"

"I can assure you, Mr. Blackfoot. This proposal is completely on the level. Nobody is here to 'fuck' with you," Siracusa said loudly.

The judge then walked up to the prisoner, his presence dwarfed by Blackfoot's large stature.

"You have been unfairly condemned to two consecutive lifelong prison sentences, Mitchell. I am the only judge in the federal court circuit who

154

recognizes the deep prejudice and discrimination that was more than apparent at your trial," Siracusa explained.

"I was present at your court proceeding, and I saw the miscarriage of justice that was carried out against you."

Siracusa then raised his voice again, affirming his point.

"I'm your only ticket out of here. But your freedom is a conditional one, and only on my terms. There is no room for options. There is no room for other considerations or second guesses here, Mr. Blackfoot."

A long silent moment.

"There is no negotiation," Siracusa reiterated as the two of them made direct eye contact.

"This is your ticket out of here, Mitchell. I can arrange to have you released by the end of next week," the judge promised.

"I will coordinate an apartment for you in South Bend, Indiana, and you will be working at the Studebaker plant there. You will receive a monthly cash stipend of $500 per month, plus a large cash bonus fee of $5,000 for every mission that you accomplish."

Another pause.

"We will make the need for your services well worth your while, Mr. Blackfoot."

He took another step closer to Blackfoot.

"But again...you will work for me. And you will do as you are told without question. And suppose the moment ever arrives that you do question or not perform your expected services. In that case, you will be back here in Milan, finishing up your two consecutive life-long sentences without any possibility of parole."

Injun Joe stared intently at the judge. Siracusa was now speaking in a very loud, stern whisper.

"I will make sure that you spend the rest of your life rotting here in this fucking jail cell, do you understand?" Siracusa boldly stated.

The two of them continued to stare at each other in silence for what seemed like an eternity. The judge, while still wearing his coat and hat, then extended his hand to the prisoner.

"So, Mr. Blackfoot…do we have a deal?"

It was a moment that the Native American thought he would never see in his lifetime. Being condemned to a life sentence in prison, he never thought that he would ever see the light of day beyond the tall, red-bricked prison walls, surrounded by large coils of thick, barbed wire and supervised by correctional officers patrolling the grounds with automatic rifles.

Inmate Number 731-59 was now smiling, realizing that his once-in-a-lifetime hall pass to freedom had finally arrived.

Mitchell Blackfoot then grasped the judge's hand.

"Yes, Your Honor. We have a deal."

# CHAPTER TWENTY
## A DISCOVERY – APRIL 1927

Susan Shifflett Rowan was worried. Extremely worried.

It had been five days since she had seen or heard from her younger brother Thomas Shifflett, and she now needed to drive over to his house on St. Patrick and Gratiot Avenue to do a wellbeing check on him. The middle-aged woman had called his home several times without an answer. Her brother didn't show up at their house for dinner that Sunday before, and it was now late Monday evening without a single word from her younger brother.

Susan Rowan lived on Woodland Street on the East Side of Detroit near Harper Avenue with her husband and two teenage sons. They usually had Sunday family dinner together, but she knew something was wrong when her brother was a 'no-show .' she knew something was wrong. They usually got together every Sunday afternoon as a family. Her younger brother, 39 years old and divorced, had no other family to look after him.

Susan was well aware of her younger brother's legal problems, as she had just endured the longest, most dreadful sixteen months of her life. He had been picked up on the rape and murder charges of those two little girls, Susan and Anna Licata, on Fordham Street two years ago. After spending all of her life savings on acquiring a criminal attorney to defend her brother in those murder indictments, it had left her family struggling financially. Her husband, Milo Rowan, worked on the auto assembly line at the Chrysler Plant on Jefferson Avenue. After securing her brother's freedom, his steady job, and their house on Woodland Street were the only things her family now had.

Mrs. Rowan was indeed worried. She had to wait for her husband to come home from his auto assembly shift at six o'clock so that they could take their only car to St. Patrick Street off of Gratiot Avenue to her brother's house and do a well-being check. Susan had not heard from him, and she now had a nauseous, sick feeling in her stomach. She knew that something was wrong. Very wrong.

Milo and Susan Rowan took the thirty-minute drive to his house at 12061 St. Patrick Street. As she pulled up in front of the house, the sun was setting, and it was starting to get dark. The lights in the house were all off, and there didn't seem to be anyone home. They both rang the doorbell and knocked hard on all of the windows. It didn't look like there was anyone in the house. They then walked back into the garage of the alley and noticed that the garage door was opened. Her brother's 1924 Ford Model T was still parked in the garage. By all indications, she knew that her brother had to be home.

After knocking on the back door, they both tried to enter even though it was locked. Milo then forcibly kicked the door, breaking the deadbolt and pushing the wooden door open.

"Tom, Tom...are you home? Where are you?" the older sister continued to inquire in a loud voice, as the two of them now scoured the kitchen, family room, and both bedrooms of the house. They went upstairs to the attic bedroom. There was no sign of him.

They then went downstairs to the basement. A sudden, dreadful odor began to overcome them as they pushed open the basement door. The basement was pitch black and dark. Milo pushed the two-button switch on the side by the basement entrance door, and a single bright, sixty-watt light bulb lit up the low ceiling, musty old basement.

Suddenly, Susan Rowan began loudly screaming at the very top of her lungs.

"OH MY GOD, OH MY GOD!"

In the middle of the basement was a body of a naked man, hanging from his neck by a rope tied up from the rafters. He had several stab wounds across his torso, and his neck had been slit open. His hands were tied together, and his genitals had been cut off and mutilated. His body was soaked and covered with dried-up blood. The man's eyes had been gauged out and bleeding. A sharp, long broomstick was impaled into his body and crammed inside of him from behind. Judging from all the blood and the body's position, it looked like he had been killed first before being hung up and filleted like a porterhouse steak. Flies and other large insects were buzzing around the dead carcass as if it had been dissected at a slaughterhouse and ready to be carved.

A large pool of blood was underneath the victim. Blood everywhere around the body was splashed across the walls and around all sides of the basement. It was as if the killer decided to decorate the brick-constructed, white painted basement walls with red, crimson blood.

Susan continued screaming, now running upstairs hysterically at the top of her lungs, running out the back door of the house, and frantically banging on the neighbors front door.

"MY BROTHER'S BEEN MURDERED!" she continuously screamed, over and over and over again.

Milo Rowan ran outside to chase after his wife, who startled all of the other neighbors on St. Patrick Street. She flagged down passing cars, begging someone to call an ambulance or a police car to assist them.

Within several moments, two police patrol cars arrived. Several patrolmen had ascended down the house's basement to inspect the murder scene. Four more police cars arrived at the murder scene at St. Patrick Street, with a large, black truck labeled 'Detroit Coroner' on the outside in large, white letters.

As the investigators inspected the crime scene, they put the time of death at more than seventy-two hours ago. The brutally stabbed victim was beginning to decompose hanging there on the rafters, and they had counted more than forty-eight stab wounds across Shifflett's body, face, arms, and legs.

"Who the fuck kills like this?" said one of the Detroit detectives, as he walked outside of the basement with a cloth over his nose and face. He then ran over to the side of the house and started throwing up.

Susan was still in a state of shock, uncontrollably crying as she was being comforted by her husband, Milo. She couldn't believe it. Her brother had just been acquitted in a murder trial in February, and he had only been out for two months. She and her husband had spent their life savings securing her brother's freedom, and now, he had been brutally murdered.

Who would commit such a gruesome murder on her brother? Susan Rowan continued to shake her head in disbelief.

"THEY KILLED MY BROTHER," she kept loudly screaming. Although Susan was hysterical, she already had a few suspicions about who would have wanted her brother dead. She wasn't stupid. Susan Rowan knew from the minute her brother was released from jail that his life would be in jeopardy.

Her husband, Milo, still holding his wife as they sat on the curb while surrounded by more than fifty on-lookers from the neighborhood, wasn't surprised. He had spent his whole life growing up on the East Side of Detroit. He was well aware of the neighborhood vendettas that the local syndicates were capable of inflicting. The East Side was ruled by several well-known Mafia gangs and self-proclaimed hoodlums, and Milo had a suspicion who the killers might be.

But Milo also knew that an accused killer like his brother-in-law Thomas Shifflett, who got off in a murder trial scot-free from the rape and murder of the two little Licata girls, would not be safe in Detroit. He had advised Shifflett to immediately move out of state and escape any potential danger that a dangerous vendetta against him could possibly have.

But after the trial, Shifflett felt invincible. Knowing that he had legally defeated that vile murder rap, he could now go on without any repercussions to his safety or his life. Milo knew this was a vendetta murder, and it didn't matter to him who had done it anymore. Although he had doubted Shifflett's innocence from the very beginning, he went along with his wife's requests and financially subsidized his brother-in-law's criminal defense. Milo also knew that Shifflett's problems would be far from over once he was released from jail and acquitted on the murder charges of those little girls.

It seemed as though the whole City of Detroit was out to get Shifflett, and it was only a matter of time.

---

Judge Anthony Siracusa was sitting in his judge's chambers the following day when his legal clerk placed the morning newspaper on his desk. The headlines read:

### Exonerated Child Killer Found Dead & Mutilated

The judge read the whole article in detail several times and was discretely smiling to himself.

161

He then took a long deep breath and reviewed his court calls for that morning. He knew he would have to lay low for a while. The judge didn't want to communicate with Injun Mitch, Kolkowski, Cleaver, or any other of the Archangels on his executive board right away. He knew that he had to go about his business as a federal judge and pretend that he had no idea what was going on.

But deep down inside, Siracusa was gloating. The word was now out that justice had been rightfully served on Shifflett. He smiled to himself, wondering deep inside what was going through Black Bill Tocco's head. He wanted to be a fly on the wall when Vito 'Black Bill' Tocco read the morning newspapers that day. His eye-for-an-eye society of justice had accomplished its immediate task. Siracusa now had to keep their Malizia Society's manifesto under wraps until the investigation into Shifflett's murder had well subsided.

But another thought began to run through Judge Anthony Siracusa's head. What would Vito 'Black Bill' Tocco's reaction now be? He gave him his word that he would take care of the alleged killer of those two little girls, but did he really expect the judge to accomplish that task?

Siracusa had taken the task of judicial vengeance and 'legitimized it' in the eyes of the local Detroit syndicates. The poor victims of heinous crimes of the Motor City were no longer beholden to the East Side Mafia or the Eastern Market's Purple Gang. There was now a powerful, respected, discrete secret society of civilized heavyweights who will now call the shots on which felons will or won't receive rightful justice. It was no longer up to the local syndicates to enforce the Old Testament's Eye For An Eye. The Malizia Society of Detroit would now make a name for itself. The judicial system within Detroit's federal courts would now have an alternative to releasing any criminal who rightly deserved to die for their crimes.

Judge Siracusa wasn't worried about the police investigation. He wasn't concerned about his twelve fellow Archangel members. And he certainly was not worried about Injun Mitchell Blackfoot in this investigation. He now had a new concern:

William Vito 'Black Bill' Tocco.

# CHAPTER TWENTY-ONE

It was a chilly Sunday morning for May, as Judge Siracusa was getting his family ready for Sunday mass at eight o'clock. He and his family typically went to mass every Sunday morning. It was a rare occasion when the Judge and his family didn't attend Catholic services at St. Paul of the Lake Church on Lakeshore Drive.

The judge prided himself on being a good Christian and an exceptional Catholic. He observed all religious holidays abstaining from eating meat on Fridays. He went to confession on Saturday afternoons once a month. The sins he typically confessed to were the trivial ones, those in which he had taken the Lord's name in vain or had spoken maliciously of a brethren out of anger, spite, or jealousy.

He believed, however, that his sins did not include the ordered, contracted death of any perpetrator who had broken the 'thou shall not kill' commandment and gruesomely terminated an innocent life. The judge believed that his creation and oversight of the Malizia Society of Detroit was his contribution to his community. Keeping dangerous criminals off the streets and ordering the death of those offenders who escaped justice was his donation to society, and Siracusa felt rather proud that Sunday.

The Archangels had organized, assembled, and carried out the death sentence of Thomas Shifflett. Mitchell Blackfoot had performed and executed their order professionally and without any problems or suspicion.

---

Mitchell Blackfoot had waited for Shifflett to arrive home on the evening of April 26, 1927. He

164

picked the backdoor lock and entered his home around four-thirty that afternoon.

He went down the basement, shut off the lights, and sat down against the white painted wall of bricks and mortar behind the coal stove in the corner of the dark, damp room. He was patient. He was quiet. And he made sure that Shifflett would not detect his presence while he was in the house.

At about six-thirty, Shifflett had arrived home from work. He had just started a job several weeks before as a dock operator at the Eastern Market. His job duties included loading and unloading trucks that arrived early every morning that delivered fruits and vegetables, meats, poultry, and other food products to the popular wholesale distribution port.

Shifflett entered his house and began making himself dinner in the kitchen. He then walked into his living room and turned on his large, walnut Zenith radio standing in the center wall of the room. Shifflett had received it as a gift from his older sister Susan when he was released from jail. He enjoyed listening to the music and news programs typically broadcast every evening.

At about seven-thirty, Shifflett heard a thunderous noise coming from the basement. Blackfoot accidentally knocked over a glass jar lying on the cement floor while waiting downstairs to make his move. Shifflett curiously went down the basement stairs, holding nothing in his hands. He believed that it was probably a rodent of some kind lurking down his basement. He pushed the two-button light switch. Shifflett curiously looked around his basement, initially noticing that nothing was amiss or out of place. Only a broken glass jar, with glass scattered near the coal furnace.

Suddenly, Shifflett felt a hand across his mouth, and a cold, sharp object instinctively pressed up against his throat.

165

It was pretty apparent that Judge Siracusa was quite pleased with Injun Mitch and his initial job assignment. He had met with him the night before last in the parking lot of the local speakeasy near Woodward Avenue. He parked his Cadillac-LaSalle in the back of the lot. He patiently waited for Injun Mitch to arrive, which he usually did on foot.

Nothing was said as the two men met in the darkness of that vacant parking lot that evening. No words were exchanged. He paid him their agreed-upon price, tendering a small brown envelope of five thousand dollars in large, unmarked bills. The judge handed his professional assassin the envelope and nodded his head to Injun Mitch. They both knew that they would be meeting at that exact location again for his next secret mission in a few months.

The Siracusa family was all dressed up and ready to attend Sunday mass that bright, chilly morning. It was barely forty degrees, as all of them had their winter overcoats on and were getting into the family car. As the judge was locking the front door behind him, he noticed a black, long Rolls Royce limousine pull up on the driveway of his home on 415 Lakeland Street. The newer model four-door luxury car looked brand new. Its shiny black lacquer paint reflected the morning sunshine off of its long, extended front hood. The chauffeur opened up the driver's side of the door and exited out, walking around to let one of its two occupants out of the luxury limousine.

"Good morning, Judge," said a short, well-dressed man in a loud voice.

It was Joseph Zerilli, one of 'Black Bill' Tocco's associates.

"Good morning."

"Don Vito would like to have a word with you this morning, Judge."

A long moment of silence, as Judge Siracusa's family was already seated inside the family car, waiting to go to Sunday morning mass.

"I'm sorry, but we are getting ready to church this morning."

Another awkward moment, as Zerilli continued to stare at the well-dressed judge, wearing his dark cashmere coat and black bowler hat.

Then the passenger window rolled down, and a man inside began to speak directly to Siracusa.

"I'm sure there is a later mass you can go to. We need to speak with you, Your Honor."

A moment of silence as the judge recognized the passenger in the back seat of the car. It was Don Vito 'Black Bill' Tocco.

"Immediately," he reiterated loudly.

The judge then walked over to the family car and turned to his wife, Elizabeth. She was already seated in the front passenger side of the Cadillac-LaSalle.

"Go ahead with the kids, honey. I will meet you at church when I'm through," he loudly said.

They both looked at each other as Mrs. Siracusa had an alarmed look of concern on her face. There was a short husband and wife moment when the two of them locked eyes as if he was telepathically reassuring her that everything was going to be okay. She moved over to the driver's side of the car and started the vehicle. She then slowly backed out of their driveway and onto Lakeland Street, driving towards the direction of Saint Paul of the Lake Catholic Church on Lakeshore Drive.

When the Cadillac was well down Lakeland Street, the judge approached the Rolls Royce limousine.

"Now that you've interrupted my time with my family, Don Vito, what is it that you want?" Judge Siracusa was annoyed as he loudly vented his frustration at the Capo-di-Capi.

"Get in, Judge. Let's have a little talk this morning."

The judge hesitated.

"Don't worry, Your Honor. We'll have you back at church in time for communion," Tocco smiled as Zerilli opened the passenger door for their Sunday morning guest.

The judge begrudgingly got into the black limousine along with Zerilli and Tocco as the chauffeur closed the passenger doors and then pulled out of the judge's driveway.

A few silent moments as Siracusa was sitting in the back seat facing the two Mafiosi.

"Well, gentlemen, to what do I have this honor, now that my family time has so rudely been interrupted?"

Don Vito Tocco smiled, then started the intense conversation.

"So you've kept your word regarding that child killer that was released from your courtroom...huh, Judge?"

Another silent moment.

"Complimenti, Your Honor," Zerilli snickered.

Siracusa glared at the two crime bosses sitting across from him. The long, black limousine began traveling southbound on Jefferson Avenue.

"I have no idea what you are talking about."

"Really?" Zerilli responded coldly.

"I wasn't aware of you having your own hired assassins and starting up your own crime family in the process, Judge. I figured you were going to find some legal excuse to throw this sick bastard back in jail on some trumped-up charges. I didn't think you had the balls to rub this guy out."

"What makes you think that I had anything to do with rubbing him out?" Siracusa lied. "His sister found him sliced up down his basement, hanging by his neck."

Don Vito Tocco laughed aloud while lighting up a Cuban cigar, then arrogantly blowing cigar smoke in the judge's face.

"Come on now, Your Honor. You must think we are all pretty fucking stupid!" as Zerilli joined in on the laughter.

"You must really think that we don't know what is fucking going on in this town? This secret society of yours that you call 'The Archangels'? Come on, Judge. Let's cut all of the bullshit."

Judge Siracusa was silent as Zerilli rolled down the back window to let some of the stale cigar smoke out of the back seat of the limousine.

"You managed to recruit some heavy hitters here in Detroit to meet and pass judgment on this bastard. You guys met at the Roma Café and had your little meeting two months ago. You had the life sentence of some Injun bastard doing time in Milan prison commuted through your connections in Lansing. Then you put this convict on your payroll and rubbed this son-of-bitch out by slicing him up like an overweight pig from the Eastern Market."

Anthony Siracusa was silent as the three of them sized up each other while the car was traveling southbound towards downtown.

"To tell you the truth, Judge, I'm a little insulted. You asked every other 'spaccone' in this town to join your little fraternity except me."

A long moment of silence.

"Don't I have a say here, Judge? Don't I get to vote on which criminal you all decide to execute and which one you don't?"

"You have your little fraternity, Don Vito. You don't need to be a part of ours," the judge replied.

Tocco laughed out loud again while relighting his cigar.

169

"You forgot one little detail, Judge. I'm the 'Capo di Capi' in this town, and I decide who gets rubbed out on the East Side and who doesn't."

He then blew more cigar smoke in Siracusa's face.

"I don't like the idea of your little fraternity going around behind my back and 'deep-sixing' criminals that should be getting the death penalty. I don't like the idea of competing with another gang of executioners."

"We are not executioners, Don Vito. We assemble to decide justice on those who have skirted the legal system and were wrongly released back into society. We pass judgment on those who neglected to receive the judicial death sentence that they deserve."

"Really? That's a joke, Judge. And you fucking guys call us criminals? You are all taking the laws of society into your own hands," Zerilli interjected.

"Something that your family is more than familiar with doing," Siracusa arrogantly stated with a smirk on his face.

The expression of Don Vito Tocco's face suddenly changed. He was not pleased with Siracusa's sudden condescension.

The was a ten-second silence as the three men stared at each other.

"Look, Don Vito. We are not looking to chime in on your bootlegging, loan sharking, or prostitution business. We only assemble when there are alleged convicts or murderers that get wrongly released from the courts."

They both sat there, listening intently to Siracusa.

"We will operate as a not-for-profit organization and will always strive to do good things for the community. What happened was a rarity, Don Vito. We are not going to go around executing alleged killers or rapists unless the federal judicial system fails."

The judge paused for a moment.

"Besides, Don Vito...I would think you would be pleased."

"Why?"

"Because you and your family don't have the pressure now of inflicting justice to those who escape the judicial system. That is our responsibility now. Should a criminal escape justice in this town and suddenly be found dead, you now have the perfect alibi."

Another long silence, as Vito Tocco kept inhaling and exhaling his long, Cuban cigar.

"You can't get convicted for a hit or murder that you didn't order or carry out, right?"

Vito Tocco and Joe Zerilli looked at each other as if they were communicating subconsciously.

Zerilli then looked at the Judge.

"I don't like it."

"Look, Don Vito. If you want to go around 'whacking' other rival gang members and knocking off other mobsters whom you feel greatly deserve it, we will look the other way. We don't care what your family does or how you do business in this town. We only want to take care of those who make a mockery of our judicial system, the way Thomas Shifflett did."

He knew that the two crime bosses were listening intently to his reasoning, as they were now his captive audience.

"You and your family have bigger fish to fry, Don Vito. You now don't have to get involved with those criminals who should be getting the death penalty. That will now be up to the 'Archangels.'"

"So you want us to turn a blind eye?" Tocco responded.

A silent moment.

"You don't rat on us, and we don't rat on you," the judge replied.

Don Vito then reached over to the small bar that was enclosed behind the back seat of the Rolls

Royce limousine. He pulled out three crystal tumblers, grabbed a hand full of ice, and deposited a few ice cubes into each glass. Joe Zerilli then uncorked a bootleg Canadian Club Whiskey bottle and poured two fingers full into each tumbler, handing a glass to Siracusa.

Then Tocco held up his glass.

"We will make a toast to your Archangels, on one condition."

"What would that be, Don Vito?"

"As a courtesy, out of respect, I want you to let me know BEFORE you go off whacking any more alleged or accused criminals or killers."

Siracusa smiled. "Wouldn't that make you an accessory to murder?"

"You let me worry about that, Judge. I still run this fucking town, and I need to know everything that's going on," Tocco emphasized.

"I want to be consulted. It's about respect, Judge."

He then held up his glass tumbler, clinging their glasses as he made a toast.

'Salute, Your Honor. Here's to your Archangels," as they all took a sip from their glasses.

At that moment, the limousine pulled into the long drive leading up to the St. Paul of Lake Catholic Church. Siracusa finished his drink as the chauffer exited the driver's side of the vehicle and opened the door for the judge to leave.

"See Judge? We got you back here just in time for communion," Tocco observed as Zerilli sat there, both of them holding their drink glasses.

"Thanks, Don Vito."

The three of them shook hands as the judge began to exit the car. As the limousine was about to pull away, Tocco rolled down his window and made his last directive to Judge Siracusa.

"Remember our deal, Judge. As I said, nothing goes on in this town without us knowing about it."

"You have my word, Don Vito."

The judge solemnly walked towards the church that Sunday morning. As he opened up the grand wooden entrance doors, he found his family sitting five pews away from the church's altar. The mass was almost over as the parishioners filed out and walked towards the priest distributing communion in front of the church. At that moment, he looked at his wife, Elizabeth, as she had a relieved look on her face.

He declined to get up and follow his wife and children up to receive Holy Communion. Siracusa felt tainted as if he had committed a mortal sin. He pulled down the kneeler within the church pew and made the sign of the cross.

As he knelt in church, his mind immediately began to wander.

How did Don Vito 'Black Bill' Tocco acquire so much information about the Archangels? Who leaked this information out, especially to the Tocco Family? It had to be someone within the Malizia Society.

But who?

Siracusa turned it over in his mind over and over again. There was obviously a 'snitch' in the group of twelve other 'Archangel Disciples'. There was one person in the group that he undoubtedly couldn't trust.

But who could that be?

Judge Siracusa said several long prayers to himself. He silently asked for the Lord's forgiveness, for taking the law into his own hands. Anthony Siracusa didn't feel very good about himself or his vengeful deeds on that morning after making yet another deal with the Detroit Mafia.

Kneeling before God, Siracusa prayed. He felt guilty and ashamed. By sitting in that Rolls Royce limousine with the likes of Vito Tocco and Joseph Zerilli, he was no less a criminal or a killer than they were. He could still smell Tocco's cigar smoke

173

on his cashmere coat. Siracusa was kneeling before God in that pew, trying to absolve himself for participating in breaking the Lord's most coveted commandment.

By taking an eye-for-an-eye, had he created a society of executioners? Were they assuming the Lord's role in passing a death sentence on those only reserved to be judged by God himself? Were they any better than the Tocco crime family, rubbing out those who receive the exact retribution performed by the crime syndicate families in this town?

Siracusa had just made a deal with the capo of the Tocco family. It was as if they were operating a crime syndicate of their own, hiding behind the right image of the Lord's coveted archangels. He had created and set into motion an assembly of men who would now pass judgment on those who skirted the laws of society and escaped conviction. The wheels of retribution and self-justice had been set into motion, and there was no stopping them.

As his wife and daughters arrived back to their pew to say their final prayers, Anthony Siracusa had tears in his eyes. Had he created an organization of zealots, who were no better than the demons they were trying to destroy? He was drenched with guilt and self-doubt on that Sunday morning, kneeling before that large, oversized crucifix hanging from the rafters of that church.

Judge Anthony Siracusa realized at that moment that the Malizia Society of Detroit was, in reality, no more than just another organized crime syndicate.

# CHAPTER TWENTY-TWO
## TWO YEARS LATER
### REGRETS – FEBRUARY 13, 1929

The traffic on Woodward Avenue was getting congested on that dark, cold winter's day. Judge Siracusa was on his way to the Roma Café on Riopelle Street after his court session, and he was utterly exhausted.

The Malizia Society of Detroit had been in existence for two years now. The 'Archangels' were developing quite a philanthropic reputation in the Detroit area. They had assisted St. John's Hospital on Moross Avenue with the purchase of an iron lung and some cardio equipment for their new surgical wing that previous summer, at the cost of a whopping $7,500. They had provided several scholarships for some deserving students to attend the University of Michigan, who would not have otherwise been able to attend. They had written a check to Sacred Heart Church on St. Antoine Street for food and assistance for their weekly 'soup kitchen,' providing meals to the poor.

The charitable organization was fast becoming quite a humanitarian not-for-profit association of local Detroit businessmen. They gathered several times over the last twenty-four months, deciding on which organization or religious organization was in the most need and desired their help. Each of the members of the Archangels was required to contribute several thousand dollars each to fund the society's charitable efforts, and membership to their charitable organization was becoming an expensive one indeed. Several members on the board compared the Archangel's membership to that of a very expensive country club, without the privileges of playing golf or having upscale social events that go with it.

But it was the darker side of the Archangels activities that was beginning to wear down

175

Siracusa. The organization had passed put out 'mortal redemptions' and executed six violent offenders over the last two years. One of those offenders was a serial killer, who had been preying on local children on the East Side, who had successfully beat out the judicial system and had escaped conviction. Another assassinated victim was a murderer who had willfully preyed on several senior citizens, pretending to be a contractor before robbing and then killing his victims.

In all of these instances, Injun Mitchell Blackfoot performed his assassin's duties flawlessly. He patiently waited for each one of his preyed upon victims, catching them either alone at home, in a parking lot, or in another secluded place where he was never seen. Blackfoot would approach all of his victims from behind, amply slitting their throats and stabbing them several times before leaving them to die. The authorities within the city were beginning to ask questions, and investigations with the Detroit Police Department were initiated several times.

But with the Society's influential membership, each investigation was thwarted, never receiving the proper attention or newspaper publicity to alert the public of their secret activities. Except for William Vito 'Black Bill' Tocco and his crime syndicate, no other outsiders were aware of the Archangels and their murderous stealth endeavors.

Behind the shield of their charitable activities, the Archangels were getting away with murder.

All of this was beginning to take an emotional and psychological toll on Judge Anthony Siracusa.

Still calling himself a devout Catholic, he prayed during mass each week with his family for each condemned soul of society's victims. He spent many hours awake at night, sometimes sleeping only a few hours, feeling guilty for the executions that his society was extolling on these violent criminals. The judge was beginning to understand the numbness and the lack of mercy that the Malizia Society was extolling on its criminal victims. The thirteen Archangels had now become judges without forgiveness or compassion. They were closed-minded jurors without any afterthought or remorse.

They were now heartless executioners.

The Archangels were now ordering the death of any violent criminals who had successfully invoked the rights to a legal defense and a fair trial. The Archangels had found and employed a cunning, skillful butcher to exact the executions needed to destroy their prey. To that end, the Malizia Society of Detroit was now a thriving, dark association of self-proclaimed judicial members who could now pass life or death sentences on any alleged criminal that it so chose and selected.

The Malizia Society of Detroit was a prosperous secret society indeed.

The extreme guilt was beginning to take a toll on Judge Anthony Siracusa. It seemed as though that when the judge prayed, he had conveniently excluded himself from the 'thou shall not kill' commandment. He felt at first that the eye-for-an-eye passage from the Old Testament was a convenient excuse to exact the proper sentencing to those violent criminals who were allowed back on the city's streets. They used the 'Swords of St. Michael' to input their revenge on those criminals deserving justice for those innocent souls they mercilessly killed.

But by doing so, who were they now?

As righteous, self-proclaimed executioners, were they any better than the alleged murderers they will killing and taking off the streets?

As Judge Siracusa stopped his Cadillac-LaSalle at the corner traffic light on Woodward Avenue, he looked into his rearview mirror. For

**177**

several long seconds, Siracusa looked into the reflection of his own eyes on that cold afternoon, and he didn't like what he saw. He looked as though he had aged twenty years, probably from all of the stress and guilt of being an Archangel. His appearance at that moment startled and scared him. He no longer resembled the handsome, dashing silent film star Rudolph Valentino.

Judge Anthony Siracusa had created a monstrous association of slayers and assassins, and the guilt afflicting him was taking an emotional toll. It was becoming apparent on his face. He was noticeably more wrinkled, and he was rapidly aging beyond his years. He was no longer the handsome, youthful judge of Italian descent that was the pride of his associates, his peers, and his immediate family.

Within his dark chestnut eyes was now the mirror image of a self-proclaimed executioner.

Siracusa parked his Cadillac-LaSalle in the first available parking space on Riopelle Street. He put on his bowler hat and walked into the Italian restaurant wearing his dark, pinstriped Brooks Brothers suit. He briskly entered the back meeting room. His other associates were patiently waiting for him to begin the dinner meeting and attend to their schedule.

"Good evening, Judge," he was greeted by each archangel who attended that meeting. They all spent the next hour enjoying their dinner entrées of minestrone, linguini and clam sauce, chicken Caesar salad, raw oysters, and a specially prepared salmon entrée, with capers, onions, and a light pesto sauce.

The meeting was called to order. Several resolutions were passed, including a large donation to a local charity providing schoolbooks to impoverished children in the city.

Afterward, the Society began their deliberation for the mortal redemption of an

African American convict, who had escaped conviction for killing a local grocer during an attempted robbery during that prior year. At that moment, Judge Siracusa, the meeting chairman, stood up and made an unusual request.

"Gentlemen, I would like to make a motion that we, as the Malizia Society of Detroit, discontinue our redemption activities and cease our endeavors in inputting justice to those who have escaped legal conviction."

Everyone around the table, while still wearing their bowler hats, gasped at the chairman's proposal. A long silence of several minutes encircled the room as if everyone at the table was afraid to speak.

Finally, the assistant chief of police from the City of Hamtramck, Stanley Kolkowski, rose to question the board chairman.

"Mr. Chairman, what has brought about this motion, and why are you suddenly withdrawing this activity from our society?"

"I think the time has come to halt these execution activities, gentlemen. We have taken the role of ruthless executioners, passing judgment on those unworthy souls who have escaped the legal system, only to be amply terminated by our society of death angels."

Everyone looked at each other around the room in a total state of shock. There were several long moments of silence. Each of the Archangels struggled to put their heads around what was being proposed by their society's founder.

Finally, a board member stood up and voiced his opinion while the others silently listened.

"Isn't that why we were incorporated, to begin with, Judge? Isn't this the reason why we are gathered here together? To pass execution on those who have killed their victims without any mercy or remorse?" asked Samuel Jenkins, the tax accountant on the board.

"Yes," the judge slowly replied. "But now, I must confess, my conscience has been bothering me. Are we now a table full of killers, no better than those felons who have committed murder and escaped justice?"

There was then intense, loud commotion at the table. Several board members began to voice their disapproval of Siracusa's motion, and his guilty feelings associated with the Society's covert activities. Siracusa banged his gavel several times but to no avail. All twelve other members sitting at that table voiced their displeasure and disagreement at the judge's suggestion.

"We are here to invoke justice," retailer David Hudson loudly proclaimed.

In response, Siracusa loudly raised his voice.

"But what if we invoke our justice on someone who indeed is truly innocent? What if we choose to execute someone who isn't a criminal and was entirely innocent of the crime that they had been indicted for?"

There was even more commotion during the meeting. Several of the board members began voicing their opinions of disapproval out loud.

"These killers are NEVER innocent, Judge. They are criminals who beat the system, and we are the ones who will invoke justice," Jenkins replied loudly, speaking over the loud voices of the others at the judgment table.

"This is why we are here. We could all join any other philanthropic organization that we choose if our only goal was to give back to the community. But our specific activity of mortal redemption serves as a special service within our community. We are now in charge of taking those criminals off of the streets and making our city a safer place," Hudson reiterated.

"And at what cost?" Siracusa loudly answered. "By invoking an eye for an eye, are we no better than the violent murderers we are taking off the streets?"

There was a long silence in the room.

"At some point, we will have to answer to God for our redemption activities?" Siracusa asked.

He then fixated his eyes on everyone sitting at that table at the Roma Café.

"WE ARE PLAYING GOD," the judge loudly declared in anger, screaming those four words with abhorrence.

Everyone looked at each other around the table, and at first, no one said a word.

"My conscience is not letting me sleep at night," the judge now professed in an almost silent voice, finishing his declaration and staring at everyone around that table.

There were more silent moments around the room.

And then, a member stood up and vocalized his opinion. Detroit Assistant Chief of Police Jonathon Borkowski loudly exclaimed his displeasure with Siracusa's proposal.

"I sleep just fine, Judge," Borkowski loudly stated.

"And if you now have a problem with what we are doing here, then you should have considered this *before* incorporating this Society. We are here to serve justice, Mr. Chairman. And we will continue to do so, with or without your guilty conscience or approval."

There were more loud voices of dissent.

"You're getting soft on us now, Judge," Cleaver loudly accused Siracusa, as the others loudly agreed.

"Here, here," several other members agreed while banging their open hands on the long conference room table.

It was pretty apparent that Judge Siracusa's motion to cease the Archangels' mortal redemption activities had miserably been defeated. He received no support from any one of its members. They were all there for one definitive purpose. They all recognized their charitable donations were only a clever cloak to disguise their criminal execution activities. They were all there to invoke judgment on those alleged murderers who killed innocent citizens without remorse. And they were there to pass sentencing.

Judge Anthony Siracusa regretfully retracted his motion, and the Archangels meeting continued. An assignment was made to the Archangels' hired assassin. The alleged murderer who had killed the grocery store owner in Corktown one year before was sentenced to death by the Malizia Society of Detroit.

The meeting was concluded after midnight that evening. As each one of the members wished each other a good night, the judge dutifully walked to his car to return home.

Siracusa felt defeated. He felt remorseful.

Siracusa now realized that he had created an assembly of emboldened, heartless executioners.

---

It was just after midnight on February 28, 1929, when Elizabeth Siracusa was startled and awakened in the middle of the night. She had heard a loud noise coming from the basement of their Grosse Pointe home and immediately noticed that her husband wasn't in bed. She quickly put on her bathrobe and walked downstairs, calling out her husband's name.

There was no answer.

She looked from room to room, going into the kitchen, dining room, and the study, to no avail. Her husband Anthony was nowhere to be found. Finally, she turned on the light switch and walked down the basement, gently calling out her husband's name.

Upon further discovery, Elizabeth suddenly screamed at the top of her lungs.

"OH DEAR GOD!"

In a pool of blood, there laid her husband's lifeless body, Judge Anthony Siracusa, with a bullet hole to his head. He was face down in his own blood, holding a gun, a .38 caliber Smith & Wesson revolver in his right hand.

When the Grosse Pointe Police finally arrived, it initially looked like an apparent suicide. With all of the judge's guilt and remorse, he obviously could no longer deal with the personal pain and culpability. He had created a larger-than-life society of executioners that was getting out of control. Siracusa had conveniently checked out, realizing that he could no longer stop the Archangels from doling out their own brand of justice.

But upon further inspection, the detectives found no gun residue on the victim's right hand, the one holding the gun when he was found dead. And it looked like, although there was a bullet wound to his temple, that it was not a gunshot at close range. The Grosse Pointe detectives were baffled as to how and why the judge could have been possibly killed by someone breaking into the Siracusa's home without being noticed or heard by anyone else who was sleeping in the house that night.

His wife was interviewed extensively by the police, and she mentioned several times that her husband never owned a gun. She had no idea where the unregistered Smith & Wesson .38 caliber revolver had come from.

After several hours of investigation by the police, the Wayne County Coroner was called. Several neighbors were now assembled around the Siracusa residence in the middle of the night to witness the lifeless body of the respected federal judge, being hauled away on a gurney with a white blanket covering his body. The coroner performed an autopsy the following morning, and the detective's suspicions had been indeed confirmed.

Anthony Siracusa's mortal wounds were not self-inflicted.

His funeral at St. Paul of the Lake Catholic Church three days later was filled with over five hundred mourners, and the forty-eight-year-old's death was grieved by all those in the Detroit area who knew him. His widow, Elizabeth Siracusa, and their two daughters were devastated as they sat there in the first pew, crying inconsolably. As family members sat at that church listening to all of the respective eulogies that day, they could not comprehend the motive that would have brought about the murder of such a well-loved, respected member of their community.

The Detroit Herald published a two-page article on the esteemed judge, citing his accomplishments as a prideful example of a very successful Italian American who had achieved the American dream but whose life was cut short by an unknown assassin. Who could have possibly wanted this well-respected family man, the pillar of the Detroit legal community, shot to death in his own home in the middle of the night?

The death of Judge Anthony Siracusa was ruled a homicide. Unfortunately, this murder case, after an extensive investigation, was never solved by the police. More newspaper articles were speculating on who the judge's enemies could have been and who may have wanted him dead. With the countless criminals that Siracusa had sentenced from behind his bench, the list of potential adversaries was endless.

Siracusa was solemnly interred at Mount Olivet Cemetery on Van Dyke Avenue.

Three days before the murder, unbeknownst to Siracusa, there was an emergency meeting in the basement of Thomas Cleaver's Indian Village home.

The Malizia Society of Detroit had unanimously voted on a special act of mortal redemption.

# CHAPTER TWENTY-THREE
### A FEDERAL INQUIRY - SPRING 2021

It had been a busy, wet Monday morning at the Detroit Police Department's Third Precinct. I only remember being so behind with my investigation reports and inquiries that I barely had any time to break for my usual coffee and bagel with cream cheese. On that spring morning, the only thing that I remember was that it was raining cats and dogs outside. My new leather shoes were utterly soaked from walking in all of the water puddles in front of the precinct.

All of my information on the Archangels and the Malizia Society of Detroit came from my Detroit News reporter and girlfriend wanna-be Justine Cahill. She had been investigating this covert organization through her news reports, and she was pretty much feeding me all of her information. I had no idea at the time whether she was genuinely interested in cracking a great story or using the investigation as an excuse to call and correspond with me. By that point in our relationship, she called my office or cell phone at least three times a week, starting each conversation with 'guess what I found out about our friends with the black hats.'

I would admit that I was warming up to her. We had been on a few more dinner dates since the Roma Café, and I could tell that she was primed and ready to make our next date a very intimate one. Although I entertained the thought of sleeping with her, there was just something inside of me that just wasn't ready. Being a devout Catholic since my wife's death, I felt as though I needed to respect our wedding vows, even though Laura had passed on. I just wasn't ready for a roll-in-the-sack with Justine Cahill.

When my partner's half-brother, Anthony Carleton, and another agent stopped by the Third

Precinct, it was almost eleven-thirty. At first, they came to visit my partner, Johnny Valentino, and they talked in his cubicle for about twenty minutes or so. I was busy with whatever I was occupied with at the time, so I wasn't really paying any attention to what they were discussing, even though our cubicles were adjacent to each other.

Then, Johnny called me in to join their meeting. I greeted Anthony with the usual man-hug, and then he introduced me to his friend.

"Mike, this is David Arnett. He is a good friend of mine from the FBI."

"Forever Bothering Italians," I joked, although no one was laughing.

There were only two other chairs in Valentino's cubicle, so I walked back to my office and grabbed another folding chair.

We exchanged a few pleasantries about the weather, baseball, and specifically, the Detroit Tigers and their deplorable bullpen. Then my partner quickly changed the subject.

At that moment, the Third Precinct Commander Anthony Ambrose came into Valentino's cubicle, and he was introduced to the two federal agents.

"So what's going on?" Ambrose inquired.

"David would like to ask Detective Palazzola some questions regarding those Archangels he had been investigating," Johnny mentioned.

"What can you tell us about them?" Arnett eagerly asked.

"Not much, other than they're some discrete, non-for-profit organization that pass out a lot of dough to a lot of needy people."

A silent moment.

"Oh, and they like their black bowler hats with their veal parmigiana," I said sarcastically.

Arnett smiled. "That's not all that they like."

"Really?"

Arnett sat there for a moment, making sure that he had our undivided attention.

"They're called the Malizia Society of Detroit, and they've been around since the 1920s, back when Black Bill Tocco and Joe Zerilli were running this town. They're a clandestine organization that consists of a lot of heavy hitters from the community. They call themselves the Archangels because they pass a lot of money around to many needy organizations. But behind closed doors, these guys are putting out murder contracts on felons and perps who cut a break with the courts and are back on the streets," Agent Arnett explained.

"They've been on our radar for many years, but we have never been able to get inside of their inner circle."

I sat there and nodded my head, listening intently to Arnett's information.

"Putting out murder contracts? Who has been taking these guys out?" I ignorantly asked.

"It's usually one of three killers. That's where the 'Archangels' name comes from. They go by the codes name of the three Archangels, Gabriel, Raphael, and Michael. Right now, they use strangulation as their method of choice. Years ago, they used almost any method to destroy their prey."

"Hmm, the Boston Strangler college course 101, huh? I wonder why?" I said out loud.

"Maybe since these guys are so well dressed, they don't want to splatter any blood on their Brooks Brothers suits," Valentino joked.

"Strangulation, if done right, is a much cleaner method of murder," Commander Ambrose pointed out.

Another silent moment.

"Lately, the killers have been brazenly leaving their black bowler hats at the crime scene. Years

188

ago, they were much more discrete," Arnett explained.

I had heard bits and pieces of some of this, and it was clear that we were dealing with a professional, convert organization.

"These guys are judges, lawyers, doctors, businessmen, and just about every other profession you can think of over almost one hundred years of history. They take a solemn oath, and these guys are members for life. There have been only five chairmen of the Malizia Society since its inception in 1927, and they are extremely mysterious and secretive. We've been trying to infiltrate these guys for the last fifty years."

I sat there in silence for several more minutes. The way this FBI agent was talking, it was as though he was describing the Mafia.

"They meet every three months at the Roma Café. We have had agents parked outside of the restaurant and have even tried to bug the place. Because there are so many lawyers, judges, and even prosecutors involved, we haven't been able to get a court order to allow us to get surveillance on any of them. This break is the closest we have been able to get to them."

"The Roma Café is a tough place wire up," I replied out of knowledge and experience.

"We know. The Detroit crime families have been having their little 'cenetta' meetings there for years. The owners there are now pretty tech-savvy, and they regularly comb the place," Anthony observed.

I smiled to myself, knowing that whatever information that I had gotten from Justine was pretty much spot on to what these federal agents were telling us.

"I'm here with Agent Carleton to let you know, off the record, that you need to back off of your investigation into these guys."

I was stunned, maybe even a little insulted. I didn't know if I should be angry or upset and whether I should be taking this guy's request personally.

"Oh really? Why?"

Another silent moment.

"One of their members has flipped and is now working for us. We've had this guy wired for all of their secret meetings at the Roma Café for the last six months."

I was a little shocked. For starters, how did the FBI even know that we were investigating this group? And secondly, how did they know that I was involved?

We all sat there silently for several long minutes until Agent Carleton broke the silence.

"The member who is wearing the wire has been with the group for several years, and the Feds have had a hard time getting one of these guys to flip in the past."

"How did you manage it this time?"

"One of the Archangels is a stockbroker, and he was busted on an embezzlement charge recently. He copped a plea to drastically reduce his sentence if we could get him to wear a wire."

Arnett suddenly sneezed.

"Salute," Johnny replied.

"Thank you."

The FBI agent then continued. "These guys are so embroiled in secrecy. Getting into this organization has taken a tremendous amount of work and effort just to penetrate them."

I smiled. "I suppose you're not going to tell me who it is, right?"

"I'm sure we could figure it out, especially if you got him on a white-collar crime charge," Valentino said.

Both agents smiled, knowing that whatever information we found out underhandly behind their backs would be classified information.

"In any case, we know that you and your reporter girlfriend have been snooping around," Arnett added.

"Justine Cahill? She's not my girlfriend," I quickly corrected the FBI agent.

"That reporter broad?" Valentino asked.

"Yes," I replied.

"She's got quite a reputation for cracking a story," Chief Ambrose commented.

"Yeah, she has a lot of information on everyone," Valentino observed.

"She's like the yellow pages, only with large breasts," Johnny added.

"Well, whatever she is, you need to put a leash on her. She's been snooping around the prosecutor's office asking a lot of questions," Arnett stated.

"Well yeah, she thinks the Wayne County Prosecutor is involved with these guys. He seems to like wearing his black bowler hat too," I interjected.

Then I got 'the look' from all four of them.

"You need to get her to back off of her investigation. Justine Cahill is the most aggressive reporter at the News, and you have to get her off of this story," Arnett sternly suggested.

"And how in the hell am I supposed to do that?" I asked.

Agent Carleton smiled.

"Take one for the team, Mikie."

I looked at the four of them, now realizing that they were all fucking whacked.

"You're not suggesting that I...."

"Do whatever it is that you gotta do, Mikie. But this investigation can't get any publicity. Otherwise, a lot of people's lives will be in danger."

Then IRS Treasury Department Agent Anthony Carleton looked at me intently.

"You will need to put the brakes on whatever you're doing regarding this case. And you need Ms.

Cahill to do the same. We can't have this federal investigation compromised."

I looked at my partner, Johnny Valentino, who seemed to be as surprised about all of this as I was. At that moment, the two agents got up and shook our hands.

"We'll be in touch, Mikie," Carleton said.

Then within minutes, the two of them left our cubicles and were out of the Third Precinct.

"I have some other business to attend to," Ambrose said. "You two have a lot of investigations to clean up, right?"

We nodded our heads as Commander Chief Ambrose left Valentino's cubicle.

The both of us just sat there for several long minutes in silence. We were both trying to absorb what had just happened. I then looked directly at my partner, knowing that I could count on him to be straight with me and tell me the truth.

"What do you know about this?" I asked him.

"My brother called me this morning and told me that he and this FBI dude were going to stop by and talk to us about this case. The guy they have wired up was under investigation by the Treasury Department, and Anthony was their lead investigator. They only happened to get tipped off because they had a phone tap on Campana's line?"

"Campana?"

"Yeah, that's the Archangel that's working for the Feds."

I was silent, trying to absorb Johnny's explanation.

"His name is Michael Campana. This guy is a stockbroker with Barrett Investments downtown. He had a Ponzi scheme going with his clients, to the tune of over ten million dollars."

"Really?"

"Yeah. This guy was living pretty large. Besides the new cars and the house on Marco Island, he had purchased a new Sea Ray

Sundancer yacht in Fort Meyers, paying over $450,000 in cash."

"That's a nice boat," I exclaimed.

"Yeah, well, that's the transaction that did him in, according to Anthony."

I smiled to myself. The stupidity and arrogance of some of these white-collar criminals never ceased to amaze me.

"It's kind of like that executive from Chrysler who secretly embezzled all that money to bribe the unions, then went out and bought a Ferrari," Valentino said.

"That will get the IRS's attention," I said.

"The Justice Department isn't announcing their investigation into this guy until they can get him to 'rat out' his Archangel buddies in the Malizia Society. The Feds are figuring they can get a clean sweep on all of these guys. This case could be a huge bust," Johnny explained.

I smiled. "Why catch one rat when you can catch a whole nest of them in one clean swoop?" I replied.

"Yeah, that's what they're figuring."

Another silent moment.

"But we gotta keep all of this under wraps until the Feds finish up their investigation. This means you gotta get Cahill to 'dummy down' and lay off of these guys. She needs to stop snooping around."

I thought about it for a moment.

"That's not going to be easy."

"Well, do whatever you gotta do. We don't need the Feds making our lives miserable, even if Anthony is my half-brother. When it comes to shit like this, 'my bro' is 'Dudley Do-Right of the Canadian Mounties.'"

I then thought about it for a few minutes.

"Did I tell you that I saw your brother Anthony at the Roma Café a few months ago? I was with Justine, and he was having dinner with his wife."

"Really?" Valentino replied.

193

"Yeah. I thought that was a little unusual. Maybe he was checking out the place?"

"Yeah, he probably was. Maybe that's how the Fed's got wind of you and Justine too," my partner added.

I shook my head and laughed to myself.

"What a fucking rat."

"You know, my half-brother is a nice guy and all, but I believe he's a federal agent first," Johnny observed.

"I think you're right."

I sat there for a moment and thought about what my partner was saying. Although I had not been able to get a lot of information regarding the Malizia Society, what little information I did receive was on the count of Justine's intense legwork. She was the one who had done all of the 'heavy lifting' on this investigation, and I knew that I was just along for the ride.

Being that Justine was such an intense, headstrong reporter, getting her to put the brakes on this investigation was going to be difficult at best.

I went back into my cubicle. I then swallowed hard and dialed Justine's phone number.

# CHAPTER TWENTY-FOUR

The afternoon sunlight on that Friday afternoon in August 2018 reflected its bright rays off of the sparkling white deck of his new boat, a 2018 Sea Ray Sundancer 450. It was sitting in a boat slip on Jefferson Harbor off of Lake St. Clair, as its owner was proudly washing off the front bow with a garden hose. The wealthy stockbroker was quite proud of his recent boat purchase, having purchased it brand new in Fort Meyers for the discount price of $450,000 in cash.

Michael Campana was extremely pleased with himself. In this stage of his life, he was on top of his game. He knew that he had gotten a great deal on this new, luxury yacht, having it shipped directly to Detroit from Fort Meyers. Luxury vessels of this make and model usually sold for $750,000 or more, and there was a long waiting list of boat owner wanna-be's who were looking for such an excellent, elaborate investment like this one.

At the age of 41, Michael Campana was flying high on life. He had 'the world by the ass,' he would tell his wife. Campana had a beautiful trophy wife, Lisa, and two lovely children he sent to a private school in West Bloomfield. He lived in a formidable, 6,500 square foot mansion in Auburn Hills with a long circular driveway and several collectible cars in his six-car garage.

His stock brokerage firm, Barrett Investments, enjoyed a long string of profitable years, with several associates and a beautiful, upscale office in downtown Woodward Avenue. He had purchased a gorgeous home on Marco Island, Florida. He tried to get away as often as possible with his wife whenever they could find a sitter for their children.

On that sunny afternoon in August 2018, Campana was detailing and cleaning his new boat. He and his wife were getting it ready to entertain several couples joining them later that evening. Campana turned on the Bose stereo, and Dean Martin's greatest hits were now blaring from his boat slip in Jefferson Harbor.

Michael Campana was a man of many secrets and many significant faults. He was usually very boisterous, extremely loud, and very energetic. Campana bragged to all of his friends about all of his significant asset purchases and was not afraid to tell anyone who was interested what he paid for them. Having lost his father at a very young age, Campana believed in living large, realizing early on that every day was a gift, and he enjoyed living life to the fullest.

Several years ago, Campana's lifestyle and significant asset purchases surpassed his investment firm's substantial income. And so, as several intelligent, dishonest stockbrokers have done in the past, he created a 'Ponzi Scheme' where a pyramid of investors infused large amounts of money. He made false brokerage statements and disbursed funds to his old clients from new investors' new funds.

Campana initially wasn't worried about the IRS audit that was currently being conducted in his brokerage office. His controller had assured him that all of his financial affairs were in order and that any and all financial transactions were well documented. According to his CPA firm, all of his corporate and personal income tax returns were well prepared. His tax preparers had legally taken any and all of his deductions.

Campana's best friend, Kevin Scanlon, was also the Wayne County Prosecutor, and they were significantly close. Having a best friend like Scanlon was like being 'Superman,' with superpowers to deflect bullets, bend steel with his bare hands and leap tall buildings in a single bound. Campana figured that no matter what kind of trouble he would get himself into, that Kevin Scanlon would fix it for him.

But having this kind of a friend came with a price. Scanlon had asked him a few years ago to be a part of the Archangels, the Malizia Society of Detroit. The group had a vacancy at the time and needed someone with a diverse background in finance who did not have a legal background. Because of their close relationship, Scanlon and Campana trusted each other with their own lives. They both knew that nothing would ever come in the way of their intense friendship. They had gone to the University of Michigan together and were Sigma Phi Epsilon fraternity brothers.

At about three o'clock, Campana was down below the deck of his boat when two men in dark suits and black ties boarded.

"Mr. Campana?" one of the gentlemen said.

"Yes?"

"We need you to come downtown with us. We have some questions to ask you."

Michael Campana looked at both men, now realizing that they were both federal agents. He was wearing a black tee-shirt, Nike shoes, white shorts and was hardly dressed to go downtown.

"What is this regarding?" he asked.

"We have a warrant here for your arrest. We've discovered that you have been operating a Ponzi scheme with your investment clients, and we need you to come downtown to answer some questions."

"Can't this wait until Monday?"

"No, sir. You need to come down with us immediately."

The Treasury Department became involved in the investigation because several of his clients complained about the disbursements from their investments that weren't available to them.

Knowing that the worst thing he could do was panic, Michael Campana informed both agents that he needed to contact his attorney. When the criminal lawyer agreed to meet him downtown at the federal building on Fort Street, he went below, got dressed, and proceeded to go with the federal agents downtown.

Michael Campana was arrested and spent that whole weekend locked in a jail cell. During that period, the lead Treasury Department investigator, Anthony Carleton, summarized the serious charges about to be leveled against the wealthy stockbroker.

David Arnett, the lead investigator with the Federal Bureau of Investigation, had been asked to join the team of federal agents who had become aware of Campana's illicit activities. They had also been tipped off that Campana was a member of the Malizia Society of Detroit.

With all of Campana's criminal activities, even after the eventual sale of all of his liquid and other assets, Campana's Ponzi scheme would have a shortfall of over ten million dollars. These funds were obviously used to finance Campana's lavish lifestyle, to buy expensive houses, collectible antique cars, and the Sea Ray Sundancer, which he paid for in cash. The attorney general's office was looking to put away Campana for a period of twenty-five years in federal prison.

But his criminal attorney, the federal prosecutors, the Treasury Department, and the FBI all came up with a clever plan.

For years, they had all been trying to infiltrate the Archangels and needed specific information that tied the 'Black Bowler Hat' murders to the Malizia Society. With Michael Campana as a secret society member, they've now been presented with an opportunity for the Feds to collaborate discrete information about the covert organization and its membership.

If all went as planned, Campana would still be forced to liquidate all of his assets, except for an allowance of $350,000, which he could use to purchase a modest, three-bedroom home. He would be under house arrest for two years, forfeit his broker's license, and would be banned from investment trading for the rest of his life.

Michael Campana had absolutely no choice but to go along with the Federal Government's terms. He knew that he had screwed enough of his clients and investors that he would be locked up in some federal prison somewhere and never see the light of day. As much as he hated to, he knew that he would have to wear a wire whenever he was around the Archangels. He also knew that if they were ever tipped off of his disloyalty and betrayal, that his life would be in danger.

On that August weekend, Michael Campana's world came crashing down. When he returned to his home in Auburn Hills, he knew that he now had a new employer:

It was the Federal Bureau of Investigation.

# CHAPTER TWENTY-FIVE
### A HOT DATE

"Hey, baby!"

She probably didn't let her cell phone ring even once, as the Detroit News reporter immediately answered.

"Hey, Justine. How are you doing?"

"I've just been fantasizing about my favorite Detroit copper."

"You have? Well, you can't be getting very much work done," I replied.

"When I think about you, Mikie, who needs work?"

"Be careful what you're saying, my dear. I don't want you getting yourself so worked up that we can't even have a constructive conversation."

She started to laugh.

"So...did you call me up for a hot date? Or are you just going to talk dirty to me?"

I just smiled to myself. When it came to flirting and verbally rubbing my leg with her tantalizing chatter, Justine Cahill could win a blue ribbon.

"Well, let's start with dinner and go from there," I suggested. "Are you free tonight?"

"For you, darling? I'm always free."

I smiled and figured I would give some of it back to her.

"Come on, honey. I know you're not that easy."

She giggled out loud.

"Okay, I'll give you a little bit of a fight."

We both laughed at each other and our enticing afternoon conversation.

"Tonight would be a great night for pizza," I suggested. I hadn't had pizza in a while, and the thought of a great, cheese-laden, thick crust pizza suddenly consumed my mind.

"You know, the best way to a girl's heart is through a great pizza. Do you have a favorite place?"

"Well, my girls and I happen to enjoy Buddy's Pizza on Van Dyke and Twelve Mile Road," I suggested. "We go there every Friday."

"Hmmm...I've never been there. Is that like New York-style pizza?"

"No, not at all. We've been going there for years. It's definitely Detroit-style pizza."

"Well...to tell you the truth, I've heard about this place, Louie's Pizza on Dequindre and Nine Mile Road. I've heard that place is pretty good too," Justine replied.

"Now that is Detroit-style pizza!" I exclaimed. I remembered going there several years ago with Laura and the girls.

"They serve deep-dish, square pies with lots of cheese and tomato sauce, and then loaded up with pepperoni mushrooms onions or whatever else you like. It has an old-fashioned Italian ambiance, with the fiaschi bottles wrapped in straw baskets hanging over the walls. It's a lovely place," I excitedly described in detail.

A moment of silence.

"Okay...what time are you picking me up?"

"I can be at your house by six o'clock."

"Perfect. You know I live in Birmingham, right? I'll text you my address."

"Great. See you then."

---

Justine Cahill's opulent home at 550 Henrietta Street was a recently renovated, 3,725 square foot brick house with four bedrooms and four full bathrooms. Justine was a divorced mother of two grown-up girls, both with productive careers in something other than journalism. Her comfortable home in suburban

Birmingham was probably why her youngest daughter was hesitant to move out.

It seemed to be a rather large house for a mother and her working daughter to live in, as she complained that her youngest daughter spent very little time at home with her.

I was wearing a new blue Tom Ford sport jacket, with a crisp white shirt and Calvin Klein dress jeans. I immediately received some compliments when Justine answered the door.

"My my, don't we look handsome this evening?" she immediately exclaimed as she put her arms around my neck and gave me a long, flavorful wet kiss.

Justine had a black, Armani low-cut blouse, which discretely covered her enticing large breasts and great figure. She had on a pair of tight jeans that looked like she had them spray-painted on and a black pair of Zanotti shoes.

She came down the front porch stairs, and I opened the door for her before entering my late model, Ford Escape, which I seldom ever drove.

"I can't wait to go to Louie's. Their thick-crust pizza is to die for!" she exclaimed.

"Is Detroit-style pizza your favorite?"

"I've never met a pizza that I didn't like, so I would be a very biased judge. I've had New York-style pizza a few times. But I can certainly say that Detroit-style pizza is much better," I replied.

I glanced at her sitting on the passenger side of my vehicle, crossing those gorgeous legs, wrapped tightly in denim.

"Pizza is positively the way to a girl's heart," she repeated.

Louie's Pizzeria is a small, quaint pizzeria on Dequindre Road in Hazel Park that had all the makings of a memorable, intimate dinner date. It has been around the Detroit area since the 1950s, with its checker cloth tables and old-school ambiance.

Louie's was one of those Italian restaurants where you would expect 'Angelina the Waitress' to be serving your table while Louie Prima was singing love songs in the background.

There was already a long line when we got there, just past six o'clock. It was usually crowded almost every night there, as it was practically six-thirty when we were seated at a small, checker cloth table.

We had a lively conversation on the way over as she talked about her job, her friends, and her healthy lifestyle. Justine told me a little about her nationality and background, as her father was Irish, and her mother was Italian. Justine was always very proud of her Irish-Italian roots. She explained that her mother was Sicilian, so she learned her mother's great Italian recipes. She was also a great cook, which was partially why she had so much trouble controlling her weight for so many years.

"Well, it looks like you're doing well with that now," I complimented.

"Yes, but controlling my calories and my appetite is so difficult for me sometimes."

A moment of silence.

"You do realize, Mikie, that I will need an extra hour at the gym tomorrow for this pizza tonight."

"And this is my problem, how?"

"It is your problem because I don't think you'll want to be dating a fat Irish-Italian girl."

I smiled to myself, thinking that she was actually considering being my steady girlfriend.

"It will be well worth it. The deep-dish pizza is to die for, and I promise you, the dough will melt in your mouth," I assured her.

We ordered a couple of Corona beers. The waitress brought some freshly baked bread and some baked garlic, chopped into a small dish of virgin olive oil mixed with some parmesan cheese.

"So, Justine, what's new with these Black Bowler Hat murders?" I began to inquire. I was trying hard to change the subject as I couldn't take my eyes off her cleavage.

She started to give me a progress report on the Malizia Society news investigation. Justine recited the organization's history since the 1920s and all of the various members that had been involved over the years. She had researched and found a considerable amount of information about its founder, Judge Anthony Siracusa, and how he was suddenly found dead in his home in Grosse Pointe Woods in 1929.

After 'Angelina the Waitress' took our pizza order, I decided to ask her more detailed questions.

"Doesn't any of this make you suspicious, Justine?"

"How so?"

"Well, these guys have been discretely putting out contracts on all of these exonerated felons for almost one hundred years. Don't you think the Feds would be getting wise to all this by now?"

"That's a good question," Justine replied. "I think that because of all these high-powered judges and politicians that have been members over the years, they have been able to quash any impending investigations that the Feds may have initiated."

I looked at her after taking a long drink of my Corona and lime.

"Well, that's a good assumption for murder contracts that may have occurred in prior years. But how long do you think it will take before their luck runs out?"

She looked at me intently. At that moment, I think she suspected that I knew something that I wasn't telling her.

There was a long moment of silence.

"What have you heard? Why isn't the Detroit PD pushing their investigation into these murders?"

I then looked at her attentively, knowing that I now had to show her my cards.

"We've been asked to step back."

"Really? By whom?"

Another silent moment.

"The Feds."

"You're kidding?"

"Nope."

She was silent for a while, peeling off the label of her beer bottle while assessing this new information.

"Mikie," she then said. "Don't hold back on me. Who asked you to step back?"

I made sure that I made eye contact with her while I answered her question.

"The FBI is watching them."

She then laughed. "The FBI has been watching them for the last fifty years. They haven't been able to get anyone of the Archangels to roll over and rat them out."

I was reserved for a moment, knowing that I had to tell her just enough information to discourage her from pushing this news story.

"They've got a rat now. One of the Archangels is all wired up."

She was suddenly quiet, and a severe look of disappointment came over her face. We were both silent for a while as the deep dish, square pan pizza with pepperoni, onions, and red peppers, arrived at our table. I cut her a piece first and placed another fabulous slice of pizza onto my plate. I took out my fork and knife and started enjoying my pizza.

Justine looked as though she had lost her appetite, as she only stared at her slice of pizza, getting cold on her white ceramic dish.

We were suddenly having a very quiet and tranquil dinner, as she only studied her untouched slice of pizza while I was enjoying mine.

"Eat your pizza, Justine. You said you were hungry."

She looked at me and began shaking her head.

"Let me put two and two together here, Mike. You want me to hold off on my news story on these guys, don't you? The Feds asked you to get me to back off, didn't they?"

I patiently waited to finish my mouth full of pizza before I answered her question.

"You may not have a choice, Justine. The Feds want you to hold off on any publicity on these guys until their investigation has been concluded, and they can indict these guys."

"Mike, do you know how long I have been working on this story? Even my editor has been pushing me to write up and publish something next week."

"Justine, do you know who you're fucking with? Not only do you have the most powerful, most clandestine organization in the city to expose, but the FBI is now asking everyone to back off and not blow their investigation until they have enough evidence to bust these guys," I replied sternly.

"They now have an Archangel wired up and ready to help expose them. No one is going to allow you to publish a news story on these guys until their investigation has been concluded."

"I'm not sure I'm going to do that, Mike. This is one of the biggest stories to come out of our city since that Mayor Kwame Kilpatrick scandal. I'm not going to just roll over and throw this whole investigation under my pillow just because the FBI says so. This is a great fucking story, Mike."

"Is it worth putting your life at risk? These guys have a history of making people disappear. There have been a lot of questionable deaths and suicides of prior members who have ended up dead in the past." I was trying hard to make my point, as I was now talking in a very loud whisper.

"What makes you think that the FBI is going to allow you to put out a front-page news story on these guys, knowing that you're going to compromise their investigation?"

Justine then looked at me as the disappointment of our conversation was now overtaking her demeanor. Her large, deep blue eyes were moistened, and she looked like she was going to cry.

"I've tangled with the Feds before, Mike. I'm not afraid."

At that moment, she started eating her now a cold slice of pizza.

"Well, Justine, I would be afraid if I were you. You're not just fighting some corrupt politicians in City Hall here. This is much, much bigger."

Another quiet moment.

"These guys are the 'black knights of fucking darkness,' Justine. And that's bad enough," I firmly stated.

"But now you're fucking with the Feds, and they have more or less told everyone to back off until they're through with their investigation. They're not going to sit back and watch all of this go down the toilet. I understand that it has taken the Feds years to get one of these Archangels to flip. They're not going to let some newspaper reporters fuck it all up for them."

"If I backed off every time I felt like I was being threatened in a news investigation, the paper would have had me writing lifestyle food articles and obituaries years ago."

I then looked at her intently, making direct eye contact.

"Is it worth it, Justine?"

We were both quiet at that point, and it was evident that Justine was now eating her pizza out of frustration. I decided not to mention anything more about it, and I tried in vain to change the subject of our conversation.

"How about those Tigers?" I said.

She looked at me and smiled.

"I've never been much of a baseball fan," now working on her second slice of pizza.

Justine Cahill was one of the most powerful, most successful news reporters in the Detroit media. This wasn't her first rodeo. In the past, she had been threatened by some very powerful politicians and power brokers, and I am sure that she was used to being pressured off a story.

But her trademark was usually to flip her middle finger off to all of the higher-ups who tried in vain to influence her news reporting. She was always focused on breaking her news story, and Justine was very mindful of the influential people in this city who tried in vain to stop her.

We finished the rest of our dinner in silence, and the waitress brought the check to our table, which I gladly paid.

I opened the door for her as she entered my Ford Escape. At that point, the tension between us had built up to where she was completely silent on the way home. I couldn't tell if she was furious at me for suggesting that she back off on this Archangel investigation or whether she was contemplating killing this news story.

I pulled up in front of her house, opened the car door, and walked her up to her front doorsteps.

"Thank you for the pizza and the wonderful evening," she said with a smile.

"Really? I know you don't mean that. I'm sorry that you're so disappointed."

She shook her head, then gave me a long, wet kiss. As she turned around to unlock her front door, I made one last statement:

"Please be careful, Justine. I don't want you to get hurt."

She smiled and gave me one last kiss on the cheek.

"Good night, Mikie," she said. She then opened her front door and closed it behind her.

I'm confident that she probably would have invited me inside for a nightcap, which perhaps would have ended up with my spending the night with her until morning.

But our Archangel conversation killed any prospect of that happening. I stood there on her front porch as she closed the porch light and left me standing there all alone. I stood there in the darkness for several long minutes, then proceeded to return to my parked car on the street.

At that moment, I was very remorseful about even saying anything to her regarding this investigation. But I was trying to warn her. I was trying to protect her. I was trying in vain to inform her that the Feds and those ruthless Archangels were far more potent than her strong-willed pen, her ambitious newspaper, and her Microsoft laptop.

That evening was the last time I saw or heard from Justine Cahill.

# CHAPTER TWENTY-SIX
## THE CHAIRMAN – EARLY SUMMER, 2021

The misty summer morning of Lakeshore Drive was dense with Lake St. Clair's heavy fog, as runners were darting along the historic drive to get in their morning workouts.

Judge Ryan O'Conner had just laced up his running shoes and began his morning five-mile trek, carefully crossing the busy boulevard to begin his daybreak workout. The middle-aged judge was religious about getting in his early morning runs. They started in front of his house in Grosse Pointe Woods on Hampton Avenue, along Marter Road to Lakeshore Drive, then south to Moross Avenue, and then back to his home, all before seven in the morning. If all went well, he would get in his morning run and be home in time to shower, change, and be ready for his early court calls, which commenced at nine in the morning.

Judge O'Conner enjoyed his early morning runs, which he did six days a week, regardless of the weather. His brisk, ten-minute mile pace helped him deal with the stresses of his judicial position at the Federal Courthouse on West Lafayette Boulevard, a position to which he was appointed five years ago at the Eastern Michigan United States District. His morning workouts helped him deal with the tremendous pressures of his court appointment, which occupied his time from early in the morning until late every evening. He dealt with many federal cases, including criminal and civil trials, while doing his best to reason with many of the overzealous federal prosecutors and conniving attorneys who appeared before his bench. His court-appointed position was a very stressful one indeed.

But on that early morning run, his mind was engrossed in another activity later that evening that would preoccupy most of his thoughts and concerns that day.

Judge Ryan O'Conner was the current chairman of the Malizia Society of Detroit.

His great-grandfather, Judge Anthony Siracusa, was the founder and chairman of 'The Archangels' until he died in 1929. The next society chairman, Stanley Kolkowski, who later became the Hamtramck Chief of Police, succeeded his great-grandfather. He oversaw the Archangels operations and 'deliverance of mortal redemption' for the next twenty-eight years, until his death from lung cancer in 1957. During the Great Depression and the Second World War, his quiet leadership was pivotal in the Archangels' success within the Detroit community. Chairman Kolkowski began the tradition of anointing each new member of the Malizia Society with a gold medal of Saint Michael The Archangel. Every member of the society, including its 'black angels,' wears a gold medallion and chain of the revered saint around their necks.

Although not a society member, Ryan's grandmother, Trust Attorney Janet Siracusa O'Conner, became aware of her father's discrete activities in founding the organization after becoming a practicing attorney in Dearborn in 1949. She then encouraged her husband and his grandfather, shoe store retailer Patrick O'Conner to become a covert board member in 1955. He remained so until he died in 1973.

After Kolkowski's s death, Circuit Court Judge Anthony Cuomo controlled the reins of the Malizia Society of Detroit, overcoming several close calls of investigations by the Federal Bureau of Investigation during the turbulent 1960s. Several orders of mortal redemption were delivered to several violent criminals and convicts. They had typically escaped local justice during that tumultuous time for rapes and juvenile murders, while the homicide rates within the Motor City exceeded those throughout the country.

The Archangels during that time developed a strong, benevolent reputation of contributing to many of Detroit's local charities, soup kitchens, and poverty-stricken families in need. They worked closely with San Francisco Church and Holy Family Church Parishes to locate those financially needy families. They also reached out to Detroit's Children's Hospital, and in 1975 made a significant, anonymous donation to the tune of half a million dollars.

Judge Cuomo was later succeeded by Ryan's father, Federal Judge Marcus O'Conner, in 1977 until he died in 2019. At his father's urging, while he was a trial lawyer some twenty years ago, Ryan O'Conner became a member and was elected as the new Archangel's chairman upon his father's death.

When the chairman position was later passed from Judge Cuomo to his father, Marcus O'Conner, the federal judge began grooming young Ryan into the organization. His father made him understand and embrace the sanctity of its manifesto until his death from prostate cancer two years ago.

The stewardship of the Malizia Society, along with its thriving membership, has always been a sacred position and a part of a family legacy. Members of the society had to be recommended and thoroughly investigated by the current board, long since his great-grandfather founded the not-for-profit organization.

Every elected archangel chairperson takes on the position for life, swearing their allegiance and loyalty to the secrecy of the club and its discrete activities. All new members who are initiated and brought into the organization are sworn to a lifetime of secrecy. Each new member is sworn in, with their right hand on the bible and holding an ancient relic of St. Gabriel with their left hand. It

212

has always been kept in their possession and locked in a vault for safekeeping.

Their community activities and charitable contributions are always made discretely. While helping many local organizations and charities, their activities required their recipients never to disclose the source of financial assistance. And of course, the 'Archangels' required all of its members to remain discrete and check their egos at the door. They had always done business in a distinct, anonymous manner.

All of their after-hour meetings are still held at the Roma Café, conducted in secret. With the Archangels closely now approaching their one-hundredth year in existence, their contribution to society has and will always be the same. Their benevolent purpose to the Detroit community would always be to take out and eliminate those criminals who have managed to beat the judicial system and returned to the streets.

Judge O'Conner, having been elected as the fifth person to hold that office in the history of the Archangels, was well aware of the enormous amount of power and responsibility holding such a position brings. Every three months, the Archangels have their secret meetings at the Roma Café, deciding on which local charities to assist and donate money to, which organizations required their monetary assistance, and of course, the society's most important function:

Which recently released criminal felons would live or die.

On that morning, O'Conner's mind was zoned out and elsewhere during his fifty-minute run. He was thinking of the recently released convict who another judge had granted probation after sexually molesting and murdering two children on the East Side. O'Conner knew what he had to do, and it was as though the newly elected chairman relished the new power that he now had within the palm of his hand.

As long as the Malizia Society of Detroit was around, no convict or criminal would ever get away with any unconscionable crime without paying the price.

And rest assured, that price would always be death.

O'Conner finished his morning five-mile run in under fifty minutes. He looked at his Nike running watch and was extremely pleased with himself, keeping a pace of under his usual ten-minute miles.

"Not bad for an old man," he loudly said to himself as he entered his home at 5239 Hampton Avenue through the installed door opener of his three-car garage.

At the age of 51 years old, Ryan O'Conner could hardly be considered old. He inherited his brown eyes and dark complexion from the maternal Sicilian side of his family, still sporting a full head of salt and pepper hair and striking good looks. Most people were always taken aback by his distinctively Irish name. His Mediterranean dark features could probably get him into any Italian coffee bar. He even studied Italian while attending college at Michigan State University. He became fluent in the language before graduating magna cum laude from the University of Detroit Law School.

Along with his beautiful wife, Chiara, and their two teenage sons who attended Grosse Pointe South High School, O'Conner was living a charmed life. His Greystone, five thousand square foot mansion was purchased for 2.8 million dollars several years ago. It was an older-built mansion, constructed in 1938, with a large, neatly landscaped back yard and a newly installed lap pool with an outdoor jacuzzi. He had recently purchased a 1964 Aston Martin convertible. Along with his black 1963 Corvette Stingray with the split-back window, he covered his classic toys and parked inside his heated garage.

His $145,000 federal judge's salary could never support the kind of opulent lifestyle that Judge O'Conner currently lived. Even though O'Conner sold his interest in his private, lucrative criminal law practice downtown and had inherited a significant amount of money from his family, the judge was conscientious not to flaunt his upscale affluence.

He drove a 2017 Ford Escape to work every morning and made sure that his boys attended public school. Although they were part of the St. Paul of the Lake parish community, they chose to regularly attend mass at St. Matthew's Catholic Church on Cadieux Boulevard. They kept to themselves within the community, never participating in the annual summer block parties that their neighbors on Hampton Avenue sponsored. He and his family lived a quiet life, ensuring that they never got too friendly with the immediate neighbors who lived around his home. When he and his wife attended their son's football games at Grosse Pointe South, they always made sure that they sat far up on the bleachers so that no one would notice them. They never went out socially, only occasionally attending restaurants far north within the Detroit suburbs.

Ryan O'Conner worked diligently to keep his family and his career in the federal court under the social radar. He wanted to remain nameless, both in his federal career as an associate judge and now, as the powerful head of the very discrete Malizia Society of Detroit. He shunned publicity, even to the point of periodically signing up for local 5K races under a fake anonymous name. He had no social media presence on the internet. His mention as a federal judge within the Eastern Michigan Federal District was without a personal picture.

But as a federal judge and chairman of the most discrete, most powerful not-for-profit organization in Detroit, his powers and abilities to do whatever needed to be done were endless. He could sentence ruthless criminals to the federal penitentiaries. He could authorize large, monetary donations to needy organizations currently struggling to serve the Detroit metropolitan area. He could help the oppressed. He could assist those who desperately needed his help.

But most of all, he was in charge and had the power to execute any hardened criminal who got away with murder in his city.

It could be said that O'Conner while living his life from both sides of the street, was probably more formidable than any local syndicate capo or any Mafia wise guy. His judicial hammer pounded the legal and illegal benches of both sides of the aisle. He was powerful from both sides of the law, having the ability to pass judgment on anyone for almost any reason, and he guarded his significant powers surreptitiously.

As O'Conner arrived at his judge's chambers on West Lafayette Street that morning, he still had a lot on his mind. He had two pending criminal trials on his docket that the federal prosecutors couldn't settle on with the defense lawyers with a plea bargain. He had a significant amount of court procedures and legal precedent that he needed to research before continuing with both cases.

But most significantly, he had a meeting later that evening at the Roma Café. The Archangels were assembling to decide the fate of that recently released convict, Isiah Walker, a young African American who another judge had released after murdering and sexually molesting two local children on the East Side. Those deplorable crimes went unpunished due to the non-admissible DNA evidence that the judge refused to allow in court. Those blood and hair samples of his young victims collected at the perpetrator's home were not allowed in as evidence, and after the defendant's lawyers elected to have a bench rather than a jury trial. The judge ruled that there wasn't enough evidence to sustain a conviction of first-degree murder.

O'Conner had studied that court case and reviewed all of the court records of the murder trial of Isiah Walker. The judge had already formulated his judgment. He now had the task of presenting the court evidence to the Archangels that evening. Ryan O'Conner was angry with the judge who presided over that criminal case. It was a travesty of justice, he said to himself. He should have been sentenced to life in prison without any possibility of parole. But because the critical DNA evidence that directly tied the victims to the place of their murder inside of Walker's home was not admissible, justice was not served.

O'Conner was angry. He was outraged. He was beyond furious. A black murderer who had killed two small little girls on the East Side of Detroit was now walking free on the streets, without any retribution for what he had tragically done to those small, grade school, little girls. They're now suffering, grief-stricken families.

Judge O'Conner had a job to do. He took his powerful positions from both sides of the legal scales of justice very seriously. He would make sure that the right decisions were always made, regardless of any insignificant judicial ruling regarding evidence or court procedure. The Archangels were there to ensure justice would be served, and Ryan O'Conner was now in the driver's seat. He had the responsibility of making sure that the proper judicial sentences of 'an eye of an eye' would always be carried out on those criminal bastards who greatly deserved it.

Judge Ryan O'Conner was currently the most powerful man in Detroit.

And on that evening at the Roma Café, the Malizia Society Chairman would make sure that justice would be served in the form of mortal redemption.

# CHAPTER TWENTY-SEVEN
## ROMA CAFÉ MEETING

It was a perfect summer evening in June, as several motorists were driving around Riopelle Street looking for a convenient place to park their cars. The arrival of summer seemed to come early to the Motor City, as the recent weather jumped from the mid-thirties in May to the low eighties in June. The tulips and other spring flowers were well in bloom around the old, antiquated restaurant, as several patrons were hurrying to get a table at their favorite Italian eating place.

The Roma Café was one of the oldest and most popular Italian restaurants in Detroit. It was established as a popular gathering place for many businesspeople and political leaders looking for an excellent menu to complement their meeting itineraries. There was an old-fashioned, classic meeting room located in the restaurant's back, with turn-of-the-century woodwork, crystal light fixtures, and paintings along the walls that could have passed for a meeting chamber in a European renaissance museum.

Jeffrey Leonardi was early that evening. He took his time parking his late-model Mercedes along Riopelle Street. The attorney casually walked to the restaurant with his new hat in his hand. Leonardi wasn't a hat person, and he felt ridiculous wearing his new black bowler hat into the restaurant.

He stopped at the restaurant entrance and hastily put on his new hat.

As he entered, the restaurant hostess immediately knew who he was and what his business purpose required that evening.

"You're an Archangel. You're here for the meeting," the hostess said.

"Eh...yes, I am."

"You're a half-hour early. You can follow me to the back room."

Jeffrey Leonardi looked at his watch, noticing that he was indeed early. The meeting didn't start until 7:00. He walked towards the back room, along a darkened hallway past the restrooms. Two men were already seated at the long table with ornate chinaware, crystal wine glasses, and fancy silverware.

As he entered the meeting chamber, one gentleman sitting at the head of the table rose to greet the new member.

"You must be Jeffrey Leonardi. I'm Ryan O'Conner. Pleased to meet you," as he rose to shake his hand. He was still wearing his black bowler hat.

Leonardi shook his extended hand and initially went to remove his hat.

"No!" O'Conner stopped him. "We keep our hats on during our dinner and our meetings."

Leonardi looked uncomfortable.

"I'm not used to wearing hats," he tried to explain.

"To tell you the truth, I'm not either. But it's a tradition that my great-grandfather started many years ago."

"Really? Who was your great-grandfather?"

"Anthony Siracusa. He established 'The Archangels' back in 1927. We've been meeting here several times a year ever since then."

Scanlon shook his head.

"Wow...that's quite a tradition."

O'Conner smiled. "We are very selective about who we allow into our society."

"Society?"

"Well, yes. The Malizia Society of Detroit. We call ourselves 'The Archangels.' We do a lot of charitable fundraisers and events for worthy organizations around the city."

Leonardi thought about what O'Conner had just said, and he recalled his conversation with

Prosecutor Kevin Scanlon two months before. He didn't remember him saying anything about charitable fundraisers or benevolent events that the organization sponsored. He didn't immediately say anything and decided to sit back and listen. Leonardi wanted to get his head around all of this before making any kind of judgment about this new, clandestine organization that he was asked to join.

He was then introduced to the other gentleman sitting alongside him at the head of the table.

"This is Pastor Jonathon Albright. He is the pastor of the Old Second Episcopal Church on Woodward Avenue."

"I've heard of your church, Pastor," Leonardi graciously responded.

"Thank you. I've heard of you as well, Mr. Leonardi. Your reputation precedes you."

The pastor was wearing a dark black suit and his white-collar, matching his black bowler hat.

Jeffery Leonardi was once the assistant prosecutor with Macomb County and now had a five-person staff office on Cass Avenue in downtown Mount Clemens. He had also worked for another small law practice downtown and been a practicing criminal attorney for over ten years. Leonardi had tried more than his share of high-profile cases.

But unlike many criminal attorneys who practiced in the Metropolitan Detroit area, Leonardi had a conscience. He refused to defend anyone accused of first-degree murder unless the charges were so egregious that he had no choice but to defend them. He was considered a 'do-gooder' by many of his legal constituents and contemporaries. While he was probably not the wealthiest or most successful attorney in Macomb County, he was undoubtedly the most ethical.

Leonardi had been a devout Roman Catholic his whole life, having graduated from DeLaSalle

High School and attended the University of Detroit for undergraduate and law school. He lived in a modest home in west suburban Troy and was married to his college sweetheart, Denise. They had three teenage sons that kept them very busy with their football, track, and baseball schedules. He was looking forward to taking his wife on a Caribbean cruise vacation that summer to celebrate their twenty-fifth wedding anniversary.

Leonardi had been approached by the prosecutor Kevin Scanlon two months ago about becoming a lifetime Archangels member. He had numerous conversations with the prosecutor about several criminal cases he had unsuccessfully tried before the Macomb County courts. He felt that many of the judges within that suburban county were corrupt and had made several wrongful rulings on several criminal cases that were being tried.

At that moment, an older member of the group, Judge William Ellis, entered the room, wearing his dark Canali pin-striped suit and black bowler hat, looking as dapper as ever.

"Good evening, Gentlemen," he exclaimed, shaking hands with the other two gentlemen present before settling himself next to Scanlon.

Judge William Ellis, at the age of 76, was an esteemed member of the Archangels. He was well respected and was considered by many as the 'consigliere' of the group. His knowledgeable opinions and the mutual regard that he enjoyed from the other members were obvious. Ellis was often consulted during their meetings and after hours. His recommendations carried a tremendous amount of weight with the other members.

"I see you have all met Mr. Leonardi. He is the new member I was telling you about at our last meeting."

"Yes, we've met," the pastor said.

The four men sat down at the long table. They continued to talk about the summer weather and local politics as other men started to arrive for the meeting. They all greeted each other, giving man hugs and customary kisses to those who seemed amicable enough to do so.

It looked as though the men arriving in their well-dressed dark suits and ties were a small fraternity of sorts and seemed very friendly with each other. It was as if they were a family of brothers. Each of them introduced themselves to Leonardi, and he was having difficulty remembering every one of their names and professions.

A waitress came into the room and brought red and white wine to the long table. Each of the 'Archangels' was filling their glasses and enjoying their camaraderie.

At seven o'clock, the meeting was called to order.

"The Chairman will call this meeting to order," O'Conner said as he rose from the head of the table with his hands folded. He then temporarily removed his hat. Everyone put their right hands over their breast and said the 'Pledge of Allegiance,' facing the American flag displayed at the far corner of the room. He then asked Pastor Albright to say the prayer before dinner.

"Oh dear Lord," he began. "We ask that you bless this bountiful food and wine that we are all about to enjoy. We ask that you bless our brotherhood of Archangels, the love and camaraderie that we all share, and to bless us one and all with good health and prosperity to every one of us here this evening," Albright loudly said with his hands folded.

"We also ask that you grant us your will, along with the swords of the Archangels of Michael, Gabriel, and Raphael. Guide us in our decisions for the mortal redemption against the dark souls of evil. We ask that we may be guided in your humble wisdom towards our battles with the malice of Satan. In Jesus' name, we pray...."

All answered, "Amen."

At that moment, the food entrées began being served, as everyone, still wearing their black bowler hats, placed their napkins across their laps while preparing to enjoy their dinner. At that moment, the Chairman rose again and made an introduction:

"My dear brothers, it is my pleasure to introduce to you our new Archangel brother, Jeffrey Leonardi. As you all may have heard, he is currently a practicing attorney in Mount Clemens and was an assistant prosecuting attorney with Macomb County for several years. It is a pleasure and an honor to have him here at our meeting this evening."

Leonardi stood up and nodded his head in acknowledgment to everyone there present. They all applauded, and then they all started standing up one by one and introducing themselves.

"As I mentioned, my name is Ryan O'Conner, and I am the chairman here this evening. I am a circuit court judge, and I've been an Archangel since 1997. My great-grandfather, Anthony Siracusa, was the founding member."

And then the next member stood up and introduced himself.

"My name is Thomas Cleary, and I am also an attorney. I've been an Archangel since 2005."

And then the next member stood up:

"My name is Dr. Peter Iacobelli, and I am a physician. I have been an Archangel since 1998."

"My name is Dr. Edward Whitestone, and I am also a physician. I specialize in oncology, and I have been an Archangel since 1993."

"My name is Paul Calcaterra, and I am a mortician. I have been an Archangel since 1996.

224

My grandfather was also a founding member, and my late father Louis was also a member."

And then the next one:

"My name is Frank Trocchio, and I am a dentist. I've been a member since 2000, and both my father and my grandfather have all been Archangels."

Then four more Archangels introduced themselves:

"I'm Michael Campana. I am a stockbroker and a financial planner. Been a member since 1994...."

"I'm Matthew Rubino. I am a businessman and investor, and I have been a member since 2015."

"I am Stuart Caravello, and I am a contractor and have been an Archangel since 2012. My father was also an Archangel."

"I am Pastor Jonathon Albright, and I have been an Archangel since 2010."

Then Judge Ellis introduced himself:

"I'm Judge William Ellis, and I have been a proud Archangel since 1989."

And then the last one at the end of the table:

"My name is Kevin Scanlon, and I am also a prosecutor with Wayne County. I've been an Archangel since 2017,"

Twelve others were sitting at the table besides Leonardi, which totaled to thirteen members. He came to realize that many of the current participants were legacy Archangels, whose membership to the Malizia Society of Detroit has been handed down from older generations, some being descendants of the founding members.

This organization was an exclusive society. It required approval and intense background checks before being invited to join. Leonardi learned that he had been investigated by others on the board and had been approved for membership well in advance of his arrival that evening.

Their entrées for dinner that evening included minestrone, Caesar chicken salad, fried calamari, rigatoni pasta with ricotta cheese, New York strip steaks with baked potato, and a medley of vegetables, espresso coffee, and tiramisu deserts.

Leonardi couldn't remember the last time he had eaten so much food, as their extravagant dinner concluded by nine o'clock.

Then the Chairman called to order the meeting again. Everyone discussed a charitable golf outing that the Archangels were sponsoring for a local orphanage in Oakland County. After other matters were discussed, that portion of the meeting was concluded.

"Gentlemen," the Chairman then said, "I ask that you put your hand on our bible and repeat the vows which we are all about to take this evening."

The chamber doors were closed and locked. There was no one else in the room as a large, antique bible was withdrawn and placed at the front of the table. The chairman put his right hand on the bible, while Brother Thomas Cleary, seated to his left, put his left hand on the bible. The members then removed their black hats and held hands, forming a circle around the table. It was as if a ring of devotion was created, starting with O'Conner's right hand and encircling around the table to the last thirteenth member. They all then recited the Archangel's solemn oath of secrecy together loudly; their bowler hats placed neatly in front of each member at the table.

"We, as devout lifetime members of the Malizia Society of Detroit, will not divulge nor disclose, nor ever betray the actions and directives of this society upon our souls to all the Archangels in heaven, all of the heavenly saints, and the Lord our God. We do solemnly swear this upon our hearts and souls. In Jesus's name, we pray...."

"Amen."

Everyone sat back down again and, putting their hats back on, tended to the real business that was now at hand.

"Do we have a candidate for mortal redemption this evening?" the Chairman asked.

The words 'mortal redemption' was used in place of the phrase and description of vengeance that society called upon.

"Yes," Brother Thomas Cleary declared. "We have a candidate named Isiah Walker; a 29-year-old African American. He was tried in Oakland County on the first-degree murder of two young ten-year-old little girls, Tammy Bergman and Tracy Richards of East Point. The girls were maliciously killed after Walker sexually molested and raped his poor victims last year. He was found not guilty due to the incompetence of the Oakland County prosecutors during that trial. Walker has now been released and is still living in the Wyandotte area."

Leonardi had heard of that recent case in Oakland County and began shaking his head. He recalled the courtroom situation in which an important witness, who had described Walker as the last person seen with the ten-year-old boy, was not allowed to testify. The middle-aged woman had received improper service of her subpoena in court. Isiah Walker, a local gangbanger from the far west side area, had gotten off on a legal technicality. The local papers were critical of Oakland County's legal team of prosecutors for not properly introducing such an important witness in their legal pursuit to get a conviction.

Everyone at the table discussed the case at length for about ten minutes. Everyone at the table agreed that Walker was a perfect candidate for their declaration of revenge. The Chairman then called for a motion:

"May I have a motion and a call for the mortal redemption of Isiah Walker for the murders of Tammy Bergman and Tracy Richards of East Point.

"I make that motion," Brother Trocchio said.

"I second that motion," Brother Whitestone replied.

"All in favor?"

"Aye," everyone said in unison.

"All opposed?"

There was a moment of silence at the table.

The Chairman then hit his wooden gavel on the table, declaring the redemption of Isiah Walker be administered within the next sixty days.

"Brother Calcaterra, would you inform our brother Archangel Raphael of the Society's board decision to uphold and perform the mortal redemption of Mr. Walker, please?"

Brother Paul Calcaterra served as the Sergeant of Arms. It was his duty to make the arrangements for the mortal redemption of whose final judgment had been decided upon by the Society. His primary responsibilities were to uphold and execute the decisions of the society's actions of vengeance.

"Aye, oh worthy Chairman."

The redemption procedure was that there were three 'hitmen' or 'black angels' on staff to perform the act of murder upon the order of the Malizia Society of Detroit. These three men, whose code names were 'Michael,' 'Raphael,' and 'Gabriel,' had their criminal sentences for first-degree murder recently reduced for time served at the Milan Federal Prison in exchange for working exclusively for the Malizia Society of Detroit. They were convicted killers and professional assassins, who were very good at upholding the Society's orders for murder. Their identities were kept secret from the other members of the Society. The Sergeant only knew them of Arms and the Society's Chairman.

"Do we have another candidate for mortal redemption this evening?" the Chairman asked.

"Aye, oh worthy Chairman," replied Brother Frank Trocchio.

228

"We have another candidate, named Derek Talcott, a 25-year-old white male who resides in Hamtramck. He was tried in Wayne County on the first-degree murder of a young, pregnant 29-year-old woman named Susan Lynch. She was assaulted and killed after her unborn fetus was cut out from her body by Talcott, who sold the newborn baby for drugs to another woman, Heather Finch of Livonia. The newborn, premature baby eventually died, and both Finch and Talcott were initially arrested and held on first-degree murder."

Leonardi shook his head again, taking a deep breath and then loudly exhaling. He had personally known one of the assistant prosecutors. They tried to get a first-degree murder conviction on both perpetrators. Several weeks ago, the judge had declared a mistrial due to some late, inappropriate evidence introduced by the defendant's lawyers in the trial. The prosecutors had to release the defendants on bail until they could formulate a new case against the alleged killers.

There was some discussion regarding the murder case and the tainted evidence that led to the mistrial declaration. Leonardi was silent throughout the discussion, even though he was familiar with the prosecutors who tried to obtain a conviction against Derek Talcott.

The Chairman then again called for a motion:

"May I have a motion and a call for the mortal redemption of Derek Talcott for the murder of Susan Lynch?"

"I make that motion," Brother Ellis said.

"I second that motion," Brother Trocchio replied.

"All in favor?"

"Aye," everyone said in unison.

"All opposed?"

There was more silence at the table.

The Chairman then hit his wooden gavel on the table, declaring the mortal redemption of

Derek Talcott be administered within the next sixty days.

"Brother Calcaterra, would you inform our brother Archangel Michael of the Society's board decision to uphold and perform the mortal redemption of Mr. Talcott, please?"

There were no other candidates for the redemption offered by other board members that evening, as the Chairman called for the meeting's adjournment.

It was just past 11:15 pm, and the restaurant had already closed for the evening. Several waiters and bus staff were hanging around waiting for the meeting to be finished. When the chamber doors were opened, several restaurant staff gathered and cleaned the respective tables. All of the Archangels hugged and exchanged farewells to each other, as several other board members shook hands and said goodbye to the new board member.

As Leonardi was gathering himself to leave the restaurant, his sponsor, Kevin Scanlon, put his arm around the former Macomb County prosecutor and escorted him outside. The two of them were initially silent.

Scanlon was waiting for some comments or discussion from the former prosecutor as they started walking to their parked cars. Finally, Kevin Scanlon broke the silence.

"So, Jeff, what are your thoughts?"

Leonardi looked at the prosecutor, his tired, blue eyes gazing intently at the county magistrate.

"Do you think the forefathers of our country had the redemption rituals of the Archangels in mind when they drafted the Constitution?"

Scanlon looked at the former Macomb County prosecutor.

"Come on, Leonardi. Don't be so naïve. Our society's means for justice is now a broken system. Due to the rampant incompetence and the increased crime rates, the Archangels have been able to fix a lot of the problems that have been wrong with our courts."

Leonardi glared at the prosecutor, still standing there without words.

"We, the Archangels, have been carrying out our form of justice for almost one hundred years," Scanlon reminded Leonardi.

"We're fixing a broken legal system, and we're carrying out righteousness," Scanlon loudly stated.

A moment of silence.

"Then why do I feel like some kind of immoral derelict, administrating justice and death behind the lock doors of an old Italian restaurant instead of a federal courtroom?"

Kevin Scanlon smiled, then gave his naïve legal protégé a brief hug.

"Think of it as correcting the horrendous injustices within our judicial system. Think of it as passing judgment on those felons who have managed to ruthlessly escape it."

"Good night," Scanlon added, and he walked to his parked car several hundred feet away.

Leonardi only stood there in the dark, still standing in the middle of Riopelle Street. He took off his black bowler hat after gazing at his reflection on the driver's side window of his black Mercedes. He unlocked his car door and sat inside for several long minutes with his hands glued to the steering wheel.

Jeffrey Leonardi was motionless. He was deep in thought.

The former Macomb County prosecutor knew he was going to have trouble sleeping that night.

The Detroit News on West Fort Street newsroom was especially loud on that Wednesday afternoon. Everyone was trying to make their news article deadline for the morning addition. There was a plastic Tupperware container of cut carrots and celery sitting on the corner of Justine Cahill's desk as she was busy working on her latest news assignment. Since following her diet and losing over fifty pounds since last year, she made it a point to stay away from the junk food that she usually ate while trying to make her new deadlines.

She had been covering some of the recent union negotiations between Fiat-Chrysler, now Stellaris, and the automobile union mandatory buy-out offering to its senior auto workers. The maker of Jeep SUVs and Ram pickup trucks had been negotiating with the union, offering buyouts to pension-eligible salaried employees as part of its transition toward an electrified vehicle lineup.

Assistant Editor Dave Stover had a considerable amount of faith in his 'roving ace reporter.' She originally got her job with the newspaper as a copy girl in the summer of her junior year at Wayne State University. She had never looked for another job since. As a long-time investigative news detective, she had been a veteran reporter for the Detroit News for over thirty-two years and never worked for another paper.

The attractive, Detroit News reporter wore her red, horn-rimmed glasses on the edge of her nose most of the time, letting everyone in the newsroom know that she meant business.

Stover's confidence in Justine Cahill was not without merit. She had broken several big stories within City Hall, including the recent sex scandals with the city's former mayor, Kwame Kilpatrick. He was charged with perjury, obstruction of justice, and official misconduct stemming from a sex scandal and his handling of an $8.4 million settlement of a whistle-blower lawsuit against the city. Her tenacity in probing into the financial transactions that evolved from all of City Hall's key players was to her credit for her investigative determination. Many insiders believe that the scandal would not have been uncovered if not for her persistence and resolve to get the facts in that case.

She also assisted in investigating the auto union embezzlement schemes occurring with the United Automobile Workers and the Fiat-Chrysler automakers.

Cahill was instinctive in following the players involved in upper management's misuse and misappropriation of funds from the UAW's employee training facilities.

The veteran investigative reporter was far too busy to snack at her desk and take a break that day from the fact-finding mission she was working on. On that day, she was particularly absorbed with one current news investigation:

The 'Black Bowler Hat' murders.

Justine Cahill had convinced her assistant editor to allow her to investigate those 'Black Bowler Hat' murders after John Rigoletto had been found strangled in a Wayne County Sheriff's patrol car in March.

Derek Talcott was a 25-year-old white male who resided in Hamtramck, who was tried on the first-degree murder of a young, pregnant 29-year-old woman.

Talcott had recently been acquitted in a murder trial for lack of evidence in the homicide. His decomposed body was found in a riverbank near the River Rouge in South Detroit. The autopsy had revealed that he had been strangled, and a black bowler hat was placed on

his head as if he was wearing it at the time of the murder.

Isiah Walker was a young African American who another judge had released after murdering and sexually molesting two local children on the East Side. Because of non-admissible DNA evidence that the judge refused to allow in court, he too was acquitted. The judge ruled that there wasn't enough evidence to sustain a conviction of first-degree murder. Recently, his dead body was found in a dumpster of an industrial building on Seven Mile Road and Gratiot. He was also strangled, and his dead body was also wearing a black bowler hat.

After extensively researching the evidence at these murder scenes and related homicides, Cahill began to put all the pieces together. The recent strangulation deaths of exonerated murderers with black bowler hats at the crime scene were more than just a coincidence.

There was a serial killer out there, and he was craving the deaths of those felons who had escaped the justice system. It was as though the prosecution was playing 'catch and release.' They were carelessly trying to attain convictions on these perpetrators, only for them to be released and back on the streets, avoiding a life sentence in prison.

Only to be found strangled to death weeks later after their release. All with black bowler hats at their murder scenes.

Cahill found three other similar homicide cases during 1928 and 1929. There were similar circumstances in which the accused murderers were tried in a court of law. Still, they could not be convicted of the homicides they were charged with committing for one reason or another. Within months of their judicial proceedings, they were found murdered, their untimely deaths unsolved by the Detroit Police Department.

The veteran news reporter went back through all of the criminal records over the last one hundred years, tracing back all of the unsolved homicides of felonious criminals in Wayne and its surrounding counties.

While doing her research, Cahill was able to compile an interesting statistic:

There had been 5,743 unsolved murders in the City of Detroit and its surrounding counties since 1920. Of those unsolved murders, 1,823 of those murders were committed on victims who had criminal records of one felony or more. Of those 1,823 homicides, 428 of those killings had been committed on victims who had perpetuated murders themselves but who were acquitted and later released for one legal reason or another.

Of all of those 428 murders since 1920, 424 were committed since the incorporation of the Malizia Society of Detroit in 1927.

Was this just a coincidence? Or was there a direct link between those unsolved vengeance murders and the Archangels?

On that Wednesday afternoon, her desk phone rang loudly, suddenly disrupting her from her intense train of thought. Justine immediately knew who it was.

"Hey Dave, what's up?"

"What's for lunch?"

Justine smiled, knowing that she no longer had to share her fast-food entrees with her boss.

"Chopped carrots and celery sticks."

"Urgh!" he loudly exclaimed. "I think I liked you better before you became a health freak."

"You're just jealous, Dave."

"You're right; I am. Since you've lost all of that weight and now that you're slim and trim, you look fantastic. But I still miss mooching off your pizzas at lunchtime."

Justine laughed out loud.

"Can't help you there, honey."

Stover then quickly changed the subject.

"Could you come in here? I need an update on that 'Black Hat' murder investigation you're working on."

"Sure," she eagerly replied.

Her assistant editor, Dave Stover, was a great boss and a good friend to have on her side. He was a tough, no-nonsense, pull-no-punches kind of guy who always went to bat for his reporters whenever they were jammed up on a story. Stover was a six-foot, five-inch, over-weight former college linebacker who habitually devoured fast food and craved pepperoni pizza as if they were his final meals.

He was always there to push for her and 'pinch-hit' whenever she needed to get something past the editor when covering a news subject. She had worked for him since 2009, and they had developed a mutually respectful relationship over the many years of working together.

She made her way into his office and sat at the black, circular leather chair directly in front of his litter scattered desk. She brought her pen and notebook, attached with several old news clippings stuffed in a manilla folder.

Cahill glanced around Stover's dirty and disheveled desk and shook her head. His desk was just an eye-sore to her, and she could never understand how the assistant editor was able to run a newsroom. It was crowded with papers, files, scattered books, faxes, documents, lunch bags, and a McDonald's drink cup, which was probably from yesterday's lunch.

Justine Cahill, a 'neat freak,' always made it a point to comment on her boss's sloppy working habits.

"The Board of Health called," she casually mentioned to her boss.

"Their sending two men over to rope off your desk and declare your office a health hazard."

Stover smiled at his ace-reporter.

"A dirty desk is a sign of genius," he replied, tongue in cheek. "Besides, I know where everything is here."

"I'll bet you do," as she rolled her eyes in the air. "Just be careful, boss. There's a cockroach on your desk walking away with one of your old French fries."

Dave Stover looked around his desk for a second, believing that just maybe, Cahill was serious. She chuckled to herself, wondering if comic stand-up could possibly be her next career.

"Okay, smart-ass. Where are we at with these 'Black Bowler Hat' murders?"

Justine pulled out her notes and started reciting some of the facts she had discovered in the case.

"They call themselves 'Archangels' and were officially organized as the 'Malizia Society of Detroit,'" she started.

"These guys have been around since 1927. They were formed by a frustrated judge and several other members of the Detroit community. They were assembled to create their own brand of justice against those felons who were exonerated by the court system and whom they couldn't get a conviction."

"Sounds like the 'Star Chamber' from the Renaissance period back in Europe."

"The Star Chamber?'"

"Yeah, I recently did some research on it. The Star Chamber was an English court that sat at the Royal Palace of Westminster from the late 15th century to the mid-17th century. It was composed of privy counselors and common-law judges to supplement the judicial activities of the equity courts in civil and criminal matters."

Justine Cahill looked at her boss, amazed that he had made himself so knowledgeable on the subject matter.

"Really?"

"There was also a similar judicial committee established in Florence in 1539 by the Medici Family. That committee was in charge of dispensing justice to those criminals who didn't receive a death sentence by the courts. They were a committee of executioners, and they called themselves the 'Societa Della Malizia', or the Society of Malice," Stover recited matter-of-factly.

Cahill glared at her boss, somewhat impressed by his current knowledge.

"Google it, Justine. It's on the internet."

There was a moment of silence as Justine absorbed this new information and began scribbling down some notes.

"So, this is a clandestine organization that's been around for a while," Stover continued.

"Apparently. They've been able to stay under the radar all of these years by hiding behind their non-for-profit status and dispensing large amounts of money to the community," Cahill mentioned, still scribbling on her notepad.

The assistant editor looked at his reporter silently for several long moments, trying to drum up the courage to give her some unexpected bad news.

"Justine, I got a phone call on this news investigation this morning. We're going to have to back off on this for a while."

Cahill looked puzzled at her assistant editor, not understanding at first what he was trying to say.

"Who called you?"

"The FBI. They've got an extensive investigation going on these guys, and they don't want us to publish anything until they can make some arrests."

Justine was silent for several long moments, blankly staring at her boss. She then shook her head and slammed her notepad on his desk.

"This is bullshit! Do you have any idea how much work and research I've put into this story?"

"I know, Justine. I'm sorry. But we have to pull this story for now until we get the green light from the Feds. We don't need them coming in here and making trouble for this paper. We have enough problems just trying to stay profitable," Stover explained.

Cahill just started making herself even more upset. At that moment, her Irish-Italian temper started to flare up.

"Oh, come on, Boss. Grow some balls! Since when did you start taking orders from the Feds?"

"We don't have a choice, Justine! These guys have an investigation going on, and we have to take a back seat until they can send out some indictments on these guys," he said, trying not to raise his voice.

"This is bigger than any of the other scandals that we have investigated," Stover explained.

They both sat there for several long minutes, neither of them saying anything to the other. Justine then broke the silence.

"So what am I supposed to do? Shit-can this whole story now? Don't we have some obligation here to report what the hell is going on?"

Another silent moment.

"There is some guy out there killing off convicts and leaving his black hat at every crime scene, and we don't have an obligation to report it?"

"Not when it impedes on the federal government and the FBI!" Stover exclaimed.

Justine then picked up her notepad and rose from her chair. She was clearly upset.

"I'm sorry, Dave. I disagree. We need to report this," she said. "I can't believe that you're abandoning me on this story after all of the hard work that I've put into this."

She started walking toward the door to leave his office when he suddenly called her back.

"Justine, sit back down here and talk to me."

"Fuck you, Dave! I can't believe your caving into these fucking guys. If it were up to them, we would never report on anything controversial in our paper or this fucking town," Justine loudly answered her boss, her temper getting the best of her.

She stood there in front of his office entrance. Just to make her point, Justine was waiting for the opportunity to walk out and slam his office door behind her.

Dave Stover shook his head in frustration. Although he didn't want any trouble from the Feds, he knew that Cahill was right.

"Okay, Justine. Put together some watered-down version of this story. Do not mention the Archangels or the Malizia Society in your article. Merely report the murders and the fact that they are being investigated. Don't give me more than five-hundred words, and keep it short and sweet," he ordered.

"I don't need these fucking guys crawling up my ass."

Justine Cahill shook her head, still not in agreement with her boss. She then walked back to her desk and attempted to redirect herself and her investigation. As her boss ordered her, Cahill wrote and submitted the news story to her boss, knowing that he would probably 'edit the shit' out of it. She was clearly disappointed, knowing that there was so much more information that she wanted to report on openly.

Justine Cahill was obviously bitter, knowing that these community hypocrites were getting away with murder while waiting for the Feds to take their sweet time on getting an indictment on these guys.

*It would be a long, drawn-out federal investigation,* Justine said to herself.

The Detroit News reporter had no idea that she was putting her life in danger by disclosing her name on that news article.

# CHAPTER TWENTY-NINE
## HAPPY HOUR – SUMMER 2021

I was having a difficult time parallel parking my unmarked squad car in front of the Gratiot Bar and Grill, as the two trucks I was trying to squeeze in between were a little too tight. It took me a total of fifteen minutes to maneuver my vehicle, as I could see some of the bar patrons standing around near the doorway and admiring my near-perfect driving abilities.

"Great job, Detective. Let's hope you don't get a parking ticket," said Chris Kaliopoulos, one of the regular bar patrons who probably paid monthly rent to reserve his usual place at the bar.

"Thanks," I said with a smile as one of the others opened the door for me as I entered my favorite gin mill.

It was four o'clock on a Tuesday afternoon, and import beers were only two bucks until six o'clock that day for their three-hour happy hour. I had been under a tremendous amount of stress lately, trying to solve various homicides that had been occurring on the East Side. The racial tensions were beginning to divide up this town again, as the 'Black Lives Matter' protests were causing more violent incidents than we could investigate and to control

I was also inquisitive about the Black Bowler Hat murders, even though I was not supposed to be investigating that case. My partner, John Valentino, was out of the office doing some undercover work that the FBI and the DEA asked us to get involved with, so he hasn't been able to assist me.

My other investigations just weren't progressing, and I was getting frustrated. I felt like I was striking out every time I would come up to bat, as every break I would encounter in these cases kept leaving me empty-handed.

Even though I wasn't officially involved, I was still standing on the sidelines, keeping score. For my own personal reasons, I stayed involved. I followed up on any new leads in this Black Bowler Hat investigation.

My reporter buddy, Justine Cahill, had come up with a few leads in regard to whom some of the Archangels were. But just because she had a list of a few people who had purchased black bowler hats was a far stretch to associating them with being members of the clandestine organization.

The problem was that nobody was talking. Trying to get any evidence or information on the Archangels was probably more difficult than trying to infiltrate an organized crime syndicate. With the Mafia, you had several illegal activities that you could go after them with, everything from loan sharking to drug dealing with extortion and unlawful bookmaking. And of course, their committing homicide or two was usually a significant part of their current social activities.

But with the Archangels, these guys seemed to only concentrate on two things: anonymous, charitable donations and the covert murders of despicable killers and sociopaths who escaped the random wheels of justice. Both activities seemed to elicit the support and sympathies of those who knew anything about them. Both endeavors appeared to justify their covert means of doing and conducting business.

Both accomplishments made them modern-day anti-heroes to anyone who knew anything about the Malizia Society of Detroit.

As I sat down at my usual bar stool and ordered a Corona with a lime, my 'sometimes good friend' walked into the front door of the Gratiot Bar and Grill. He grabbed a barstool next to mine and greeted the bartender.

"Hey, Gina...I'll have a Heineken, please," as he took off his suit coat and loosened his tie.

"Sure, Kevin."

He made himself comfortable and began watching the ballgame, an afternoon doubleheader between the Detroit Tigers and the Minnesota Twins. He looked over at me and smiled, and we both got up to do the affable man-hug.

"How's it going, Mikie?"

"Great, Kevin. How's your life going?"

"No worries. Grabbing and slamming the bad guys. How about you?"

"Just having fun, playing cops and robbers," I said with a smile.

I had known Wayne County Prosecutor Kevin Scanlon for several years. We had more than our share of standoffs when doing our jobs as police detective versus county prosecutor. We had worked together on a long list of capital offenses, spanning from the rapes and molestation of minors up to several gruesome homicides.

We had collaborated on many prior cases, and after butting our heads and exchanging 'F-U's,' we usually came to a compromise regarding the means and methods of how the prosecutor's office would handle a particular offense that I would be investigating. He let us 'collar the perp most of the time, and then we would stay out of his way while he filed the arraignments. The last time I had seen him was at the Rigoletto murder trial.

We sat down and exchanged pleasantries, both of us complaining about how hard we were working and how little appreciation we were getting from Mayor Stafford's office. As we casually talked, I recalled the information reporter Justine Cahill tipped me off a few months ago about Scanlon being one of those black bowler hat customers she had discovered at Finley's Haberdashery Shop.

When there was a lull in the conversation, I decided to be a smart-ass and ask him the question:

"So, I hear you like wearing black bowler hats."

244

I wished I could have taken a picture of his reaction when I asked him that question. At that moment, his face turned three shades of white, and he looked as if he was embarrassed by the inquiry.

"What are you talking about?"

"You know damn well what I'm talking about."

As a talented performer, I received the best actor award at Sterling Heights High School in my senior year. Scanlon looked at me for several long seconds; then, his demeanor started to get very defensive.

"What the fuck do you know about us?"

*Huh? Us? Really?*

At that moment, I played along as if I knew something, which was all a complete and total game of bullshit.

"I know you guys like to wear black bowler hats and enjoy your veal parmigiana entrees at the Roma Café'."

Scanlon actually believed that I knew something about his clandestine organization, and he suddenly became very cautious.

"You can't say anything," he quickly scolded me, as if I knew what the hell I was talking about. At that moment, Scanlon got extremely suspicious, and his blue eyes widened like saucers.

"How did you find out about us?" he immediately asked me.

"Thomas Blakely was a friend of mine. They found him dead on Lakeshore Drive of an alleged suicide. Then later, his grandson was found dead in a vacant lot on Dequindre and Sixteen Mile Road. I talked to the Grosse Point coppers. They all suspect it could have been two related homicides."

It was all bullshit. All I knew about Blakely was reported in the papers and police reports that I had previously read.

Again, I was pretending that I knew more than I really did, and I was now trying like hell to bait him into giving me more information.

"It's such a shame," I said while shaking my head. I then finished the last drop of my Corona beer and placed the empty bottle in front of the bartender so that she would replenish my drink.

"Exactly, what did Blakely tell you?" he sheepishly asked.

"Enough," I lied. I felt like I was in a Tom and Jerry cartoon, dangling a piece of cheese in front of a hungry, desperate little mouse.

"Well," Scanlon said defensively, "Blakely was a sick man. We made the mistake of inviting him into our meetings, and he seemed to be hysterical about all kinds of concocted activities."

"Concocted activities sounds like a stretch, Kevin. Something was obviously bothering him. Thomas Blakely was an upstanding guy. Why else would he kill himself?"

'HOW THE FUCK SHOULD I KNOW!" Scanlon suddenly screamed, banging his almost empty beer bottle on the bar counter.

I was very familiar with Scanlon's very Irish temper, having tangled with him on many other past occasions. I just smiled and looked at him, letting him know, by the expression on my face, that I knew he was full of shit.

"Relax, Kevin. I'm not wearing a wire. And I'm certainly not interrogating you."

There were several very long minutes of silence, as Scanlon needed every bit of that time to lower his blood pressure. He then looked at me, and he had that *'I wanna know what you know'* look on his face. Of course, being a copper, I wasn't about to give him the satisfaction.

"Can we talk off the record?" he openly asked.

"Of course," I responded, sealing our prevailing verbal discussion with a very firm handshake. When I shook his hand, I knew that any information that he gave me in confidence couldn't be used against him.

Kevin Scanlon was about to hand me all the answers that I needed for my personal inquiry on a silver platter.

"Look, Palazzola...we have a very discrete organization that does a lot of good here for the Detroit community," he then admitted, speaking in a very loud whisper.

"An organization that has been around for almost one hundred years."

"A clandestine, secret cult sounds more like it to me," I said, trying to pump more information out of him. I was smiling, about to award myself an Emmy nomination. I was playing Kevin Scanlon like a Stradivarius violin.

"Who's doing your contract hits?" I curiously asked him, knowing damn well that he would never tell me the truth.

"If I tell you, I might have to kill you," he smiled, now on his second Heineken.

"Let's just say that they are named after the three archangels in the Bible...Gabriel, Raphael, and Michael," he said, trying to be as vague as possible.

"To be honest with you, I don't have any idea who they are," as he took another gulp of his beer.

"I've never met them," he added. "They are covertly contacted and given their assignments by one member of our society. Because there is more than one, nobody knows who will get the contract to perform the hit. I wouldn't be able to tell you who they are if I wanted to," he explained, taking another long gulp of his cold beer.

"Any relation to that character that John Travolta played in that guardian angel movie named 'Michael'?" I joked. "Do you guys sit around watching reruns of that movie?"

Scanlon slightly smiled at my feeble attempt at making a joke. I was trying to break down some of the tension in the air.

"Very impressive," I said out loud.

247

We both sat there in silence, trying to absorb the baseball game and ease the anxiety that our current conversation was bringing us. The Tigers were losing to the Twins at the bottom of the sixth inning, 5 to 1.

Scanlon then looked up at me as if a sudden revelation had overtaken him and became engulfed in a new, deranged scheme that he was about to throw in my direction.

"You know, Mike...we now have a vacancy on our board," he said matter-of-factly, quickly taking a swig of his Heineken beer. He mentioned it as if they were some legitimate non-for-profit hospital organization that was appropriately serving the community.

Was this guy drunk? Did Scanlon suck down one too many beers? I was mildly shocked. I looked at him and smiled, first thinking that he wasn't serious.

"I don't think you need a Detroit detective like me on your board of directors, Kevin."

"No...really, Mike. Why not?" he reasoned. "You have the disposition and 'the chops' to handle our society manifesto," he said, with that innocent Irish look on his face.

"I've heard you bitch and complain about the legal system, and especially the erroneous release of several murderers back on the streets when our prosecution couldn't get a conviction," he casually mentioned.

"Are you referring to that Rigoletto murder case? That fucking bastard should be rotting in a jail cell right now," I loudly stated, having a difficult time controlling my anger.

"Those sheriff deputies set him up in front of some donut shop, and Rigoletto was suddenly strangled," I recapped that murder case.

Five seconds of silence.

"That piece of shit got what he deserved," Scanlon smiled, taking another swig of his Heineken.

Another moment of silence.

"You would make a great Archangel, and you would fall right in line with our society philosophy."

"Philosophy? Manifesto? What the hell would that be? Icing murderers and convicts that you couldn't get a legitimate conviction on? What makes you think I would have the fucking stomach to order executions on collared perps that the courts cut loose and released back on the streets?"

Kevin Scanlon then started laughing out loud.

"Shut the switch off on your altar-boy act, Palazzola. We both know it's a load of shit," still amusing himself.

"You've got as much of a hard-on for taking out some of these sick bastards as we do. We're just making sure that they get the punishment that they so desperately fucking deserve. So put your goddamn Bible away, Mikie."

"I didn't say that I disagree with your cause. It's your association's methods that I'm in disagreement with."

"Really, Mike? What would you rather do? Shoot them when they leave the courtroom with their lawyers?"

He then scooted his barstool even closer than he already was and began to speak very softly, perhaps a decibel louder than a whisper.

"If you had the opportunity to sentence to death some perp, some convict, some fucking murderer that you knew would otherwise go free and kill another innocent person again, would you do it? Look at me straight in the eye and tell me that you wouldn't take that opportunity?" he said, his cold blue eyes glaring at mine. They were as wide a saucers, and I knew that he was totally serious.

249

A moment of silence.

I looked at him for several long seconds. I then finished my Corona beer and put a twenty-dollar bill down on the counter, covering both of our bar tabs.

"Keep the change, Gina."

"Thanks, Mikie. Have a great night."

I wasn't going to give Scanlon the satisfaction of telling him a response that he already knew the answer to. And since we were both casually talking off the record, the Wayne County Prosecutor knew that he would burn me at the stake if any of this bar counter dialog ever became public knowledge.

"I don't look good in black bowler hats," I casually said to him out loud.

At that moment, I noticed that my shoes were untied, so I bent over to tie them. As I did so, my gold, shiny, eighteen karat Saint Michael medal was exposed and out of my shirt, dangling for all to see.

Scanlon looked at me intently.

And then, he broadly smiled.

I nodded my head to him as if to say goodbye. I then grabbed my coat and car keys and headed out the front door.

After having an off-the-record conversation with the Wayne County Prosecutor, I quickly put two and two together and figured out exactly what I needed to know.

Scanlon, indeed, handed me a silver platter of complete information. Not only had I solved those open murder cases, but I now figured out who and how those murders and homicides were being executed. Unfortunately, none of these facts or evidence was admissible, especially knowing the Wayne County prosecutor was involved.

Kevin Scanlon was a member of a society of do-gooders who put out murder contracts on released killers who should have received life sentences by the prosecution. They were an association of members who passed judgment on those convicts who were released back on the streets, possibly intending to kill more innocent victims.

As I was battling traffic on Gratiot Boulevard, I thought about our conversation. Here was a society of upstanding members who were repairing and fixing our currently flawed justice system by taking out those criminals who allegedly committed a heinous crime.

But what if those accused criminals were innocent of those crimes? What if the prosecutors got it wrong? What if those alleged killers were not guilty of their accused offenses? The Archangels were in charge of inculcating justice based on the current facts presented by the prosecution. But where was their defense? Where was their trial in front of this society? And would I want to be a part of a clandestine association that passes judgment on criminals for the sake of revenge? Was I really that bitter about the justice system?

His proposal was definitely on the table.

I had been asked to join the Malizia Society of Detroit.

# CHAPTER THIRTY

It was a warm Monday morning in early June. The newspaper stands on the corner of Grand River Avenue and Bagley Street were bustling with customers. Although the story had already broken overnight on all of the local newscasts, there was an unusual number of customers waiting to pick up the latest newspaper edition of the Detroit News.

I had stopped by the Dunkin' Donuts at the corner of Time's Square before going into my office for my usual coffee and bagel. It was only seven o'clock in the morning, so I decided to walk up to the newsstand and pick up the morning paper out of curiosity. I was completely unprepared for what I was about to read on the front-page news headlines:

### Investigation Pending on Black Bowler Hat Murders

Since our pizza date last month, I had not seen or heard from Justine Cahill, and I had hoped that she had wholly abandoned that story. I was juggling my coffee and bagel with the newspaper folded in my hand as I walked over to my car to read the news article.

*"This could have been worse,"* I said to myself.

It was a very diluted news story at best. Considering the amount of discrete information that was out there on these Archangels, I was expecting much worse.

The news headline was a very general one indeed. It stated that several related recent murders had been committed over the last few years. The murder victims had the common thread of being exonerated felons, who were usually strangled. Of course, a black bowler hat was left at each of the recent crime scenes.

There was no mention of the Malizia Society of Detroit, the Archangels, or any specifics of where and how the organization meets or the decisions made on which felons will get a contract on their life.

My immediate reaction to the news article was that someone from the FBI had probably contacted Justine Cahill and her newspaper. I was sure that after a considerable amount of compromise with the Feds, the Detroit News decided to release a watered-down version of the Black Bowler Hat murders and the society that was responsible for them.

A part of me was relieved that all of the information on these covert members had not been made public in the Detroit News article. But the fact that the Black Bowler Hat murders had now been openly publicized made me fearful. There would now be other investigations out there by other news media sources. It would only be a matter of time before someone puts two and two together and figures out who these guys are.

Another fact that scared me was that Justine Cahill's name was tied to the news article. As far as the media was concerned, no one had ever published any information on the Malizia Society or the Archangels. The fact that there was now a newspaper reporter out there who had access to the discrete information on these guys scared the hell out of me.

As I walked into the Third Precinct, my partner John Valentino and my commander, Anthony Ambrose, were waiting for me in my cubicle. As I walked in, the Detroit News article was already sprawled across my desk.

"Good morning," I sheepishly proclaimed.

"Good morning, my ass! I thought you took care of your girlfriend," Valentino said in an accusatory voice.

"I told you, pallie. She's not my girlfriend."

253

"I was under the impression that you had talked some sense into Cahill and that she wasn't going to publish any information on these serial killings," Ambrose said.

"I tried, boss. I haven't seen or talked to her since last month. I tried to convince her back then that the Feds were now involved and that they didn't want any publicity on these murders."

The three of us stood there in front of my desk, pushing the newspaper from one side of my desk to the other.

"Well, I don't think her putting a story out there with her name on it is a good idea, especially knowing the 'M.O.' on these guys," I casually mentioned, as the three of us stood around in my office cubicle.

Because no one in our precinct was involved in investigating these several murders recently, we all had other police business to attend to. They were gang murders and shootings over drug deals, car hijackings, thefts and robberies, and other serious offenses to investigate and deal with. We had been told to step aside, and neither the news media nor the Detroit P.D. had any say in the matter.

The Feds and especially the FBI had their own agenda to capture the 'Black Bowler Hat' killer and get an indictment on the Archangels.

---

It was early on a Friday morning, later that week. I was sitting at my desk trying to get myself settled in to begin my day. I probably had only taken the first sip of my Dunkin' Donuts coffee when my desk phone rang:

"Detective Palazzola," I eagerly answered.

"Mikie? It's Johnny." It was a cell phone call from my partner, who was still on the road.

"I just heard from my detective buddy over in Birmingham. Your friend was killed this morning."

"What?" I recall saying, as I wasn't processing who or what he was talking about.

"Your friend, Justine Cahill, the Detroit News reporter. She was found dead in her car this early morning."

"Oh no," I said to myself, covering my eyes with my hand while still holding the phone.

"I'm sorry, Mikie," my partner said, expressing his condolences.

"The Birmingham coppers found her in her car. It looks like she had been strangled."

There was a long silence, and I tried to process this information that my partner was telling me over the phone.

"I'll let you know if I hear anything else," he abruptly said, then hung up the phone without saying goodbye.

I sat at my desk, completely motionless, for the next ten minutes. I couldn't believe it. The woman whom I was becoming good friends with, who at one point wanted a personal relationship with me, had now lost her life.

It was tragic, I thought to myself, that someone who was so tenacious, so driven in her career and her job as an investigative reporter, had paid for her persistence and her steadfast stubbornness with her life. Her investigative reporting efforts had made a lot of enemies in this town, and she had now paid them back with her last breath.

I came to find out later that she had indeed been strangled. The killer probably broke into her dark blue, late model BMW that early morning and waited for her, staking and killing her as she was about to drive into work that morning.

Although there was no black bowler hat left at the crime scene, it was apparent that the Archangels were likely involved in her death.

I attempted to warn her; I kept telling myself over and over. I advised her to walk away from this investigation.

Cahill's death was broadcasted on the morning news that day, and the Detroit News did a memorial piece on her, with her face splashed all over the front pages that morning.

Justine Cahill was a very talented, hard-working reporter driven by her career and her desire to report the truth at any cost. It was just heartbreaking that she paid for all of that with her life. She certainly didn't deserve to die.

Later that morning, I decided to make a phone call to my Archangel friend.

"Wayne County Prosecutor's Office," the receptionist answered the phone.

"Yes, this is Detective Palazzola from the Third Precinct. Is Mr. Scanlon there?"

"No, I'm sorry. Mr. Scanlon is currently in a meeting right now."

I thought about it for a second and then decided to push myself past his receptionist.

"You will need to interrupt Mr. Scanlon and put him on the phone before I show up there with two other detectives and a set of goddamn handcuffs."

After making my threat, there was a long silence.

"Please hold, Detective."

More silence, as I sat there holding my desk phone receiver next to my ear. I felt my temper starting to get ever more intense as I contemplated how I would go about arresting my friend on suspicion of murder.

"Kevin Scanlon speaking."

"DID YOU HAVE TO KILL HER?"

"What?"

"YOU HEARD ME," I shouted, not giving a shit who was overhearing our conversation.

"DID YOU HAVE TO FUCKING KILL HER?"
I screamed.

"You could have just cracked her around a couple of times. You didn't have to send one of your gorillas to go over there to strangle her this morning."

A long moment of silence.

"Mikie, you need to cool off. I have no idea what you're talking about."

"FUCK YOU, KEVIN!" screaming with contempt.

"You know exactly what I'm talking about. They found Justine Cahill strangled to death in her car this morning. But of course, you're going to deny sending one of your goons over there to kill her," I said right away, making him understand that I was onto him.

Another silent moment.

"Cool off, Detective. I don't have any idea what you're talking about or who you're referring to," he vehemently denied my accusation.

"Call me back after you take your meds, Mike. You're obviously delusional," he loudly said before hanging up the phone.

I sat there for a few seconds, still holding the receiver in my hand. I was so angry and upset with this asshole that I felt like going over to Scanlon's office to take a piece of him with my bare hands.

Justine didn't deserve this, and I knew Scanlon was more than aware of who she was investigating. I felt terrible about her death, and she didn't have to die for pursuing this investigation.

My eyes were now getting moistened by the thought of Justine losing her life. I wiped my eyes off with my sleeve, trying to grasp that she would no longer be around to flirt with me and dangle the possibility of my having amazing sex with her. We were obviously very attracted to each other. Still, this Black Bowler Hat investigation got in the way

257

of having any normal, personal relationship. Perhaps, I was more attached to her than I wanted to admit to myself and knowing that she was now dead truly broke my heart.

This Black Bowler Hat investigation was now starting to get very dangerous.

The drenching rain was soaking Harper Avenue as Jeffrey Leonardi parked his Lexus SUV in the parking lot of Apollo's Restaurant. It was just after one o'clock in the afternoon, and Leonardi had made arraignments to meet with his close friend and fellow Archangel, Kevin Scanlon, for lunch on that gloomy, rainy afternoon. He grabbed his umbrella on the side of his car door and struggled to open it up in the rain, while his blue Canali pinstriped suit got soaked while he walked from his car to the entrance door.

Leonardi was in court most of the morning, handling two DUI charges for two clients and an assault and battery charge that had occurred over the past weekend. Although he seldom defended first-degree murder charges for his clients, he was well versed in the criminal laws of such offenses. He had adjudicated plenty of them in the past. Leonardi chose to focus his law practice on other felony and misdemeanor charges for his clientele. Even though they were less profitable, he felt more confident that he could sleep at night.

The Mount Clemens criminal attorney had been extremely troubled since the last Archangels meeting at the Roma Café two weeks ago. Even though he knew what the organization was all about and felt like something needed to be done, he complained to Scanlon for that reason. There was too much judicial corruption and a considerable lack of justice in Macomb County. He needed to address those problems in some constructive means. But putting out murder contracts on those defendants who escaped justice in Leonardi's mind was a little too extreme.

Leonardi was a good Christian and a very good Catholic. The Macomb County attorney grew up in a spiritual environment in a middle-class family in

Warren. He attended parochial grade school at St. Edmonds before eventually graduating from DeLaSalle High School. His mother ensured that he never missed Sunday mass and made all of his Holy Sacraments in the church. He and his wife Denise were even married at his family parish in Warren. There was no doubt that he practiced his strong Catholic values with his family.

Jeff Leonardi was struggling, both mentally and emotionally. He was having difficulty sleeping since donning his black bowler hat and attending the last Archangel's meeting. He wasn't good with any of this. But Leonardi also knew that there wasn't anyone that he could discuss his personal conflicts with.

He had been sworn to secrecy, which was an integral part of being an Archangel. The whole society's manifesto was based on secrecy, and he knew that he couldn't discuss the Malizia Society's activities with anyone. Leonardi was conflicted, and he was mentally struggling with all of this.

Leonardi was seated at a small booth in the back of the Greek restaurant as the lunchtime crowd was beginning to dissipate. He wasn't waiting for more than five minutes before his close friend, Kevin Scanlon, arrived at the restaurant.

"Hey, Jeff," as Leonardi stood up to man-hug his friend.

"Hey Kevin, how are you?"

"Great. Busy as all heck today. We are putting together the criminal files for a murder trial next week."

"Oh really? Which case?"

"A rape and murder case. Some kid from the East Side raped and murdered a little girl three months ago. A lot of strong DNA evidence, and we have the murder weapon with prints. I offered a plea deal to the defendant's attorney, but he hasn't responded yet."

"Oh really? Interesting."

The waitress approached the booth and brought two ice-cold glasses of water to the table.

"Good afternoon. My name is Cindy. What can I get for the both of you?" the middle-aged blonde server asked, noticing that neither one of them had looked at the menu.

"I'll have a Rueben sandwich on wheat bread, please," Leonardi responded.

"I'll have a BLT, extra mayo," as the waitress wrote down the lunch orders on her green ticket book.

"Anything to drink?"

"Diet coke, please," Scanlon responded.

"I'll have the same."

"Thank you, gentlemen," as their waitress gathered the menus and briskly walked to the kitchen to submit their lunch orders.

Leonardi took off his damp Canali suit jacket and hung it on the attached coat rack adjacent to the booth.

"It's raining like hell out there," Scanlon observed. He had left his suit coat in his car, and his short-sleeve white shirt was still soaked from rushing in from the rain.

The waitress immediately brought their Diet Cokes to the table. There was then a long moment of silence as Leonardi began to fidget with his drink straw while Scanlon immediately attacked his beverage.

The tension was beginning to build at the table, and Scanlon knew that Leonardi had something on his mind. It had to be important, as Leonardi had called him early that morning to meet him for lunch. He studied his friend sitting across from him at the table. He noticed the dark circles forming below Jeff Leonardi's eyes.

"So, pallie? What's up?"

The Macomb County attorney put his drink down and stared intently into Scanlon's eyes.

"I'm out."

261

"What?"

"You heard me, Kevin. I'm out," Leonardi said again, only with more conviction.

Scanlon looked at his friend and shook his head. He couldn't believe what was coming out of his friend's mouth.

"Are you fucking crazy? You can't just get out!" Scanlon declared loudly.

"You took an oath. You were sworn in. I highly recommended you to the 'angels.' You were checked out and approved by everyone," the Wayne County prosecutor reminded his friend.

" You can't get out!"

Leonardi looked at his friend across the table and said the same statement again.

"You don't understand, Kevin. I'm out. I'm done. I don't want any part of this. It's against everything I stand for. I cannot support and be part of a group that goes around...."

"Shhhh!" Scanlon stopped him.

A moment of silence.

"That goes around doing that," he whispered loudly.

"What the fuck did you think you were joining up with? The fucking Rotary Club? I told you what was going on and what we were all about, especially after you came to me complaining about the fucked up judicial system and all of the shit you were eating in Mount Clemens!" Scanlon replied, looking around to make sure no one else was within earshot of his statement.

"You didn't tell me that."

"Fuck you, Jeff. You knew damned well what you were affiliating yourself with. You knew damned well what you were doing!"

There was a cold moment of silence.

"Well, I didn't think I would have a problem with it. Well, now I do. I don't want to be a part of some group of zealots that go around...."

"Shhhh!" Scanlon said again. This time the anger was starting to form and become very noticeable in his deep blue eyes.

"Do you know what you're fucking saying, Jeff? You just can't walk away. You just can't submit your resignation to the 'angels' and expect them to let you go with a smile. That doesn't happen."

Scanlon was now trying hard to control his anger.

"As a matter of fact...it NEVER happens. They're not going to let you walk away with a smile and forget that you ever joined up with us. They're not going to let that happen. Besides, you'll make me look like an asshole for highly recommending you."

The waitress suddenly appeared at the table with their lunch orders. She placed the Rueben sandwich in front of Leonardi, then loudly put the BLT sandwich plate in front of Scanlon. At that moment, the tension between them became too intense that neither one of them had much of an appetite.

Leonardi looked around before reasserting his position.

"I can't do this, Kevin. I'm not going to be a part of this. My conscience won't let me," he pleaded.

Leonardi's eyes were starting to well up, and he was now struggling to control his emotions.

"How can I face my family and go to church and pray in front of God while I'm voting for some exonerated criminal that escaped justice to receive 'mortal redemption,'" he reasoned.

"You're a fucking asshole!" Scanlon angrily declared, now too upset to even eat his lunch.

"You knew what we were all about. There should not have been any surprises here. You wanted to be a part of this. You just can't wake up one morning and decide that you don't want to be a part of this anymore. It doesn't work that way."

"And what are you all going to do? We live in a free society, Kevin. You can't force someone to be a part of something. What kind of organization is this? The Mafia?"

A long moment of silence absorbed the booth they were both sitting in as neither one touched their food. The waitress then approached the table.

"Is everything okay?"

"I'll take this to go, please. I have to run," Scanlon told the waitress.

Another moment of silence.

"You need to think about this, Jeff. As I've told you before, you just can't walk away!"

There were now tears welling up in Leonardi's eyes as he wiped his right eye with his sleeve.

"I told you, Kevin. I can't do this. I've been struggling with this for the last two weeks. I can't sleep. I can't eat. I can't concentrate. I can't talk to anyone about this. I have all this guilt built up inside me, and I can't do anything about it. I can't even talk to you!"

"So what do you want me to do? Hug and kiss you for walking away? Don't you understand what you're bringing on to yourself and your family?"

"What?"

There was a long moment of silence as the waitress brought Scanlon's BLT sandwich in a silver foil container, wrapped in a plastic bag. He then pulled out his wallet and put a twenty-dollar bill on the table. He glared at Leonardi as he mentally formulated his words, ensuring that his friend understood his dangerous predicament.

"Think long and hard about what you're doing, Jeffrey," as he pointed his right index finger at his friend.

"You have absolutely no fucking idea what you're doing. You took an oath. You swore on the bible. You are committed to us for life. There is no quitting. There is no turning back."

264

Scanlon glared at his friend one last time, as Leonardi's eyes were now soaked with tears. He stood there staring at him for several long seconds. He then grabbed his lunch-to-go and abruptly walked out of the restaurant.

Jeff Leonardi sat there in silence, staring at his Rueben sandwich. He wasn't hungry. He was too distraught even to eat. Butterflies were going through his stomach, and he was feeling nauseous. He felt so conflicted over this, and he knew that he had no choice but to do the right thing.

But judging from Scanlon's reaction, he now established his worse fears in resigning from the Malizia Society of Detroit. He now confirmed his deepest concerns if he walked away from the Archangels.

Jeffrey Leonardi suddenly realized that his life was now in danger.

# CHAPTER THIRTY-TWO
## SUMMER BBQ – 2021

The block party on Yale Street that afternoon was just starting on that bright, warm Independence Day. It was a long-standing neighborhood tradition, where everyone gathered together once a year to push their grills, lawn chairs, and bean bag toss sets in the middle of the street to celebrate.

Our house at 20336 Yale Street in St Clair Shores was in the middle of the block, so everyone seemed to gravitate in front of my house and block my garage and driveway. Every year, it was the only occasion when we all parked our cars the next block over on Princeton, as wooden horses and bright orange traffic cones blocked local vehicles from entering or leaving our street.

We had lived in our house since Laura, and I got married eighteen years ago. My daughters and I always looked forward to celebrating the July Fourth Yale Street Block Party. Unlike other teenagers, my girls had always looked forward to gathering with our neighbors and bringing potluck dishes of potato salad, bean and taco dip, and BBQ hamburgers and hot dogs in the middle of the street. My neighbor across the way, Rich Walker, always took responsibility for the music, and his large, four-foot amplifiers usually began blasting out seventies tunes very early on block party morning.

It was the only occasion when everyone walked beyond the end of their driveways to get to know their neighbors every year. The block party was very popular to all of us who lived on Yale Street and to the entire city of St. Clair Shores. Residents from other nearby blocks participated in our annual festivities. The local police cars stood guard at the entrances from Princeton Street to Harper Avenue. Our block party was the highlight of every summer, as we all looked forward to the celebration and catching up with our neighbors. My girls usually put together some concocted dessert recipes that they saw on the Food Channel. At the same time, I made my famous pasta salad. I made sure that I was always generous in including the garbanzo beans, black olives, and the tri-color ziti that blended nicely with my zesty Italian dressing.

We usually all pitched in ten bucks a piece to buy a generous supply of hot dogs and hamburgers. At the same time, several other neighbors took charge of picking up and tapping the Old-Style beer kegs. With all of the music, food, and lawn games abundantly scattered across everyone's front lawns, the celebrations usually continued until one o'clock in the morning.

Of course, the local fireworks show usually started at dusk, as several of the neighbors would climb up on their roofs to watch the fireworks display. Many of the neighbors blew off M-80's, bottle rockets, and black cat firecrackers throughout the block, sometimes blowing them off throughout the late evening and into the early morning hours. I always crossed my fingers, praying that none of these amateur pyrotechnics would carelessly blow off their hands or fingers off, as some of the dangerous explosives and bottle rockets were quite extensive. But all of that aside, our neighborhood's annual summer block party was always a grand celebration.

My daughters and I pushed our Weber grill and patio furniture onto the middle of the street when it became officially blocked off, and I was getting our area ready to celebrate. As I was about to start up my gas grill, I noticed several of my other neighbors starting to push out their BBQs out in the middle of the street as well.

One of them was Jeff Leonardi, who lived three houses away from me. He and his boys were setting up their wooden picnic table in the middle of the street as his oldest son, Anthony, walked over to our house to chat with my daughter.

While they were talking, Jeff walked over and greeted me with a firm handshake and man-hug, which I thought was unusual. The man had been my neighbor for several years, and other than an occasional wave when he saw my unmarked patrol car cruising down the street, he was seldom ever sociable. I can't count how many times I would see him cutting his grass or shoveling his snow when he would only wave at me, then look the other way.

"Hey Mike, how's it going?"

"Great, Jeff. How's your family?"

"Doing great, Mike. Our boys have us involved in traveling little league baseball, so my wife and I are running around from one side of the city to another," he lamented.

"Wow, sounds like you're having a busy summer," I observed.

I knew he was an attorney in Mount Clemens. I would occasionally see him and his family at St. Monica's Parish on Sundays. But other than the occasional hand wave, Jeff Leonardi never made an effort to get very friendly with either my late wife or me. I remember several of my neighbors attending my late wife's wake and funeral at Calcaterra Funeral Home, but he wasn't one of them. He always seemed rather cold and distant and often kept to himself.

We made more small talk while I stood in from of my BBQ grill, anxiously waiting for him to walk away so that I could start grilling. At that moment, he suddenly became very serious.

"Mike, do you think we could get together later and talk? There are some things that I need to discuss with you?"

I looked at him rather suspiciously. Although it wasn't unusual for a local neighbor or friend to ask me some questions because they knew that I was a detective, I was still taken aback. Since it was the Fourth of July and that we were all celebrating, the last thing I wanted to do was discuss police business. The only tasks that I had in mind at that moment were to eat, drink, and forget about the day-to-day problems of being a police detective. Having a serious discussion about anything with one of my not-so-friendly neighbors was the last thing I wanted to do on that summer holiday.

"Can we do it another day, Jeff? I wasn't planning to...."

"Oh, no, no, no...of course, we can talk another day. I know this is a holiday and all. I'm sure you're not eager to discuss any serious police business today."

"Great, Jeff. Let's talk tomorrow," I eagerly agreed.

He smiled at me, then motioned his older son to come and help him with taking out more of his elaborate patio furniture.

As the day went on, we all enjoyed more BBQ goodies and socialized with some of my other neighbors. I was sitting in the middle of the street on one of my cushioned lawn chairs, consuming my third Corona beer. As we all kept talking and enjoying each other's company, I noticed Leonardi continuously making eye contact with me, as if he was utterly consumed and troubled with his problems. He wasn't talking or socializing a lot with the other neighbors, as his wife Denise was on the other side of their wooden picnic table chatting with the other neighbors. I could tell that this man was troubled, and I started to get very concerned. The last thing that I needed was one of my neighbors going 'postal' in the middle of our block party.

At dusk, the fireworks started, and several of the local boys climbed onto Richie Walker's roof across the street. I glanced over at Leonardi, who was sitting alone on a lawn chair holding a styrofoam cup filled with beer. He was oblivious to the surrounding celebrations, and I began feeling very guilty for not talking to him earlier. I decided to finally approach him.

"Hey, Jeff...can you come with me to my garage? I need you to help me grab some stuff," I shouted in front of his wife so that she wouldn't get too suspicious.

"Sure," he eagerly said, as he immediately popped up from his lawn chair and followed me into my garage.

With the fireworks going off, he followed me inside, and we stood next to my classic car, a 1969 Chevrolet Camaro, covered up with old blankets and a dark canvas.

"You look troubled, Jeff. What's on your mind?"

He looked at me as if a bolt of fear had suddenly overcome his face.

"Mike, my life is in danger."

I looked at him for a few silent seconds.

"In danger? How?"

"I've gotten myself involved in something that I probably shouldn't have gotten involved with," he said slowly, as his eyes began welling up with tears.

More minutes of silence.

"It's a local group, and they call themselves the Archangels."

At that moment, all the bells and whistles started going off in my head. I recalled my conversations with Justine Cahill regarding the non-for-profit group she was investigating and the information she had discovered concerning that clandestine organization.

"Are these the guys with the black bowler hats?" I asked.

"Yes," as his face lit up. "You know about them?"

"Vaguely. They're a group of well-dressed do-gooders who get together at the Roma Café every three months. They anonymously send out a lot of dough to needy organizations, from what I've heard."

Leonardi looked at me as if he was struggling to tell me more.

"That isn't all that they do."

"Really?"

Another silent moment.

"I was asked to join them a few months ago, and after attending one of their meetings, I realized that I had made a mistake."

More silent moments.

"A mistake? How so?" I curiously asked.

At that moment, my oldest daughter, Adrianna, came barging into the garage.

"Daddy...come and watch the fireworks with us. The grand finale is coming soon. We always watch that together as she put her arms around my waist, begging me to follow her.

"Okay, honey...I'll be right with you in a minute," as I kissed her forehead, motioning her to exit the garage so that I could finish talking to Leonardi.

After a few more minutes, Jeff Leonardi continued:

"These guys are like modern-day executioners, Mike. They're putting out contracts on criminals who aren't getting convicted in the courts."

At that moment, I began putting two and two together, realizing that these guys were the ones who were responsible for some of the unsolved murders that had been recently occurring in the city.

"I was sworn to secrecy, Mike...and now, I can't get away from them. These guys are nuts, Mike, they're fucking nuts," as he was starting to get highly emotional.

"Nobody walks away from these fucking guys, Mike. Nobody!" he whispered loudly; his face now saturated with tears.

My impatient daughter then came storming back into the garage.

"Come on, Daddy...they're starting!"

At that moment, I realized that we had abruptly ended our very private conversation.

"I'll be right there," I replied. I then looked at Leonardi.

"Call me at my office tomorrow, Jeff," as I pulled out my wallet and handed him one of my business cards.

"Come down to the Third Precinct tomorrow, and we can finish this conversation."

He looked at me as he was struggling to dry his eyes with his T-shirt. He then gave another uncomfortable man-hug, and we both proceeded to rejoin the celebrations. As I stood on the edge of my driveway with my daughter, my mind was utterly consumed with what Leonardi had just disclosed.

These were the guys in the black bowler hats. They were the ones who had been making some of these alleged convicts disappear, as the whole Detroit Police Department has been scratching their heads, trying to figure out who was behind these covert homicides.

I went into my office at the Third Precinct the following day, expecting to receive a phone call from Leonardi.

He never called.

# CHAPTER THIRTY-THREE
## THE MOUNT CLEMENS PARKING GARAGE

Jeff Leonardi casually kissed his wife and sons goodbye that morning as he grabbed his Brooks Brothers suit coat and proceeded to leave his house for work. As he sat there in traffic, his mind was consumed with the matters he had discussed with his neighbor, Mike Palazzola, the previous evening.

Leonardi knew that he had jeopardized his life by joining the Malizia Society of Detroit. He still remembered the anger in Kevin Scanlon's eyes, knowing that he had put himself and his family in danger. He had blindly joined this covert organization, feeling troubled about the local corruption that had been going on, not only in Macomb County but throughout the city as well. But Leonardi had no realization of what he was getting himself into. He was sanctioning murder. He was supporting an eye for an eye. He was breaking God's most sacred commandment.

Leonardi wasn't comfortable playing God with the lives of others who had successfully beaten their murder charges in court. What gave him that right? Who gave the right to the Archangels to replace the scales of justice with their verdicts, their rulings, and their own judgments?

Who in the hell did these men think they were? Who gave them the right to distribute their brand of justice to those who were considered innocent until proven guilty beyond a reasonable doubt?

He battled the traffic on Cass Avenue for over twenty minutes until he pulled his Mercedes into the parking garage on Crocker Boulevard where he usually parked.

He then turned off the ignition.

Suddenly, a well-dressed stranger wearing a black bowler hat opened his car door.

'Michael The Black Angel' forcibly entered the back seat of Leonardi's Mercedes. Without initially saying a word, the black angel put the barrel of his gun up against the back of Jeff Leonardi's head.

'Today is a good day to die," he softly said to the former prosecutor. He then ordered him to take out his weapon in the glove box.

With fear in his eyes, the Mount Clemens attorney unlocked his console glove box and pulled out his Baretta M9 semi-automatic pistol, which he normally kept locked in his car for protection.

He inserted the gun clip and turned off the safety. His eyes were now saturated with tears as he glared at himself in his rear-view mirror for several long minutes. His once dark raven hair was now turning gray. There were dark circles under his eyes, and he noticed the deep etching of wrinkled skin taking over his once youthful, forty-eight-year-old face. Leonardi noticed that he now looked like a very old man, as the personal, private stresses that he had been enduring were now beginning to age him quickly. As he gazed at himself in his rear-view mirror, he looked like he had aged twenty years. His recent anxieties were well displayed all over his rapidly aging face.

"If you're not going to do this, I will," the black angel said.

Jeff Leonardi took one long last look at himself. He then put his Baretta pistol under his chin and pulled the trigger.

His blood splattered all over his front seat and the inside roof of his car. The black angel had been splattered with Leonardi's blood all over his face and hands.

The black angel, 'Michael,' then took off his black bowler hat and covered Leonardi's face with it as if he had only fallen asleep.

The deep, dark secrets of the Malizia Society were still safe indeed.

# Chapter Thirty-Four

The traffic on Ten Mile Road was bustling that late evening, as Judge Ryan O'Conner made a left-hand turn onto the restaurant parking lot. The East Pointe Café was one of those popular Greek restaurants known for its delicious gyros sandwiches, famous baklava, and other Greek deserts.

It was a warm, mild evening as O'Connor pulled his 2017 Ford Escape into a parking space in the back of the parking lot. He was more than fifteen minutes late. The judge had received a phone call earlier that day from retired Judge William Ellis. He made it apparent that a 'sit-down' meeting was necessary. He asked two other Archangels to meet up at the restaurant, and the four of them agreed to meet at the Greek cafe. It was a late-night establishment where they could meet discretely without any interruptions.

The elderly judge had been tipped off to some vital information. Information that could be detrimental to the Malizia Society.

It was almost nine-thirty, and O'Conner had just finished having dinner with his family that evening. He made an excuse to his wife that he had a necessary meeting to attend and knew that he would be out until late.

Wearing a black Polo shirt, tan khaki shorts, and white Nike shoes, O'Conner looked like he was going out for drinks at the Detroit Yacht Club instead of a discrete meeting at some small, obscure coffee shop. He locked his car and quickly walked into the restaurant, looking for his Archangel companions. He immediately noticed Judge Ellis, Kevin Scanlon, and Paul Calcaterra sitting in a small booth in the corner when he entered.

Ellis waived down the chairman, and he immediately walked over to the back corner of the café.

"Hey, Bill," as they all rose and took turns hugging and kissing each other on the cheek. It was their usual means of respect to one another, as the four of them were all esteemed, bound members of a secret society family.

As they all sat down and settled in, a Latino waitress approached the booth where they were all sitting.

"Coffee, Judge?"

"Thanks, Esmeralda, but I'll take a Diet Coke," replied O'Conner.

The chairman noticed the others drinking coffee while Scanlon was enjoying a glass of Pinot Noir.

"You're ready to party, I see," O'Conner smiled at Scanlon.

The Wayne County prosecutor half-smiled back while nervously glancing at the other two brother members.

"You may need a drink after you hear what Judge Ellis has to say," he commented.

O'Conner looked at Ellis, immediately noticing that he had a grim expression on his face.

The waitress brought O'Conner his beverage, and they all settled into their booth as the waitress gave them menus.

"You guys having dinner? I just ate."

"No, Ryan, I'm not that hungry," Calcaterra answered.

The other two shook their heads.

"Leave the menus, honey. We may order something later," Scanlon mentioned to the waitress.

"Okay." The waitress looked at the four of them and immediately knew they didn't want to be disturbed. The four of them had several evening get-togethers at the restaurant before. She was

276

very familiar with their desire to be left alone while they discussed important business.

O'Conner unwrapped his drink straw and quickly took a sip of his Diet Coke, as the other three looked at the chairman without expression.

"Well," O'Connor said. "This better be good," as he studied his three brother Archangels sitting there without expression.

The four of them had met at the East Pointe Café on several occasions to make important Malizia Society decisions that couldn't wait until the next quarterly meeting. All of those meetings required the need to make an important decision after considerable discussion between the four of them.

All of those meetings usually required a decision of mortal redemption.

"It is," Scanlon replied.

The other two Archangels looked at Judge Ellis, who looked as though he had been given six months to live.

"So," O'Conner pressed them. "What's up?"

Judge Ellis swallowed hard, gazing at the three of them.

"We have a rat in our club."

A moment of silence, as O'Conner was initially shocked.

"A rat? What are you talking about?"

"We have a rat in our club, Ryan. My contact at the federal building overheard one of the FBI agents discussing with another agent, making sure that one of our members was properly wired up for our next meeting at the Roma Café on September 29th."

O'Conner looked shocked as he gazed at the elder statesman.

"A rat? Who?"

Another silent moment, as if Judge Ellis was purposely building up the suspense around the table.

"Campana," he softly replied.

"Campana? Are you fucking kidding me?"

"No. The Feds got to him. He was busted two years ago on a Ponzi scheme that he was running out of his investment office, and he cut a deal with the Feds to avoid a long prison sentence."

The other Archangels looked at each other as a grim expression had fallen onto all of them, trying to process this shocking news.

"That son-of-a-bitch!" O'Conner responded, fidgeting with the plastic straw wrapper, twirling it around his finger.

"How the hell did this happen?" he inquired.

"Very easy," Ellis replied. "He was living too fucking large. He bought a large yacht in Florida two years ago, and the stupid bastard paid cash for it. This large purchase got the attention of the IRS, who conducted an audit of the investment firm and discovered the Ponzi scheme. They started bugging his cell phone and figured out that he was one of us."

"Oh shit!"

There were several more moments of silence as the four of them looked at each other in disbelief.

"Are you sure?"

"Definitely. My source found this out because the agents were planning their surveillance at the Roma Café at our next meeting, and she is in charge of assigning the agents."

"Who is she?" Calcaterra asked.

Ellis shook his head.

"I'm not at liberty to say who it is. Let's just say that this woman is a reliable source and has tipped me off on what's been going on with the FBI over at the federal building for years," the retired judge responded.

O'Conner shook his head again.

"This is unbelievable. We have been able to skirt the Feds from investigating and infiltrating

278

our society for almost one hundred years. Now, how the fuck did they get to Campana."

"We all know that Campana has a big fucking mouth and lives a 'spaccone' lifestyle. We just never realized that he was doing something illegal," Calcaterra observed.

Ryan O'Conner glared at Scanlon across the table.

"Didn't you bring that bastard into our club? Aren't you guys supposed to be best friends or something?"

"Well yeah, but I never thought he could ever be a rat?"

Ellis rolled in eyes in the air.

"But you had to know about his lifestyle before you brought him in. You were never suspicious?"

"Hell no. As a matter of fact, I invested over one hundred thousand dollars of my own money into a retirement portfolio with Campana several years ago. I never had a problem with him. I just figured that he was doing very well."

"Well, you can kiss that money goodbye," Ellis commented.

O'Conner shook his head again in disbelief as the four of them were silent at the table. Ellis was slowly sipping his black coffee while Scanlon had polished off his glass of wine.

"So?" Calcaterra asked.

"So what?" Scanlon replied.

"What are we going to do?"

"What the fuck do you think we're going to do? He's gotta fucking go," Ellis demanded.

Another pause.

"Slow down here," O'Conner warned.

"If we take this guy out, the Feds are going to immediately get suspicious, and they're going to move in on us. They will know that we know about them and their federal probe. The FBI will then grab each of us and try to get us all to rat each other out to salvage their investigation. They've done that shit before," the chairman rationalized.

"But we have no choice. This guy can't be allowed even to be near us if he's wearing a goddamn wire. We've gotta take him out," Ellis replied.

The four of them sat there in silence for what seemed like a long period of time. Nobody had any rational solutions for this very real problem. The Archangels had encountered many issues with other members in the past, especially when it concerned their devout oath of secrecy. They always knew that if the thirteen members of the Malizia Society were to continue to be successful, their ultimate discretion was paramount. They had always dealt with these problems in the past, and there was only one way to handle them.

Mortal redemption must immediately be sentenced against anyone who broke their silence.

And like Thomas Blakely, Jeff Leonardi, Daniel Breazie, and Justine Cahill, those sentences of mortal redemption had to be fast and swift.

"We have to do this, Ryan. He's gotta fucking go," Scanlon stated, even though he was supporting a death sentence to his once best friend and fraternity brother.

Ryan O'Conner sat there for a moment, quietly staring at his soft drink while still fidgeting with his paper straw wrapper. He then pulled out his cellular phone and checked his calendar.

"September 29th falls on a Wednesday," he said.

"That gives us a little over a month to figure out a viable solution here. If we have one of our black angels take him out, it will tip off the Feds."

Scanlon then mentioned an option.

"Couldn't we make it look like an accident?" he suggested.

"How?" Calcaterra asked.

"Maybe his brakes might suddenly fail. Maybe he could get hit by a car walking down the street,"

O'Conner laughed.

"If Campana is working for the Feds, they're going to make sure that nothing will ever happen to their golden goose. I guarantee you that they have him under twenty-four-hour surveillance right now. They're going to make sure nothing happens to him," the chairman stated.

A pause.

"At least until the Feds get their indictments."

The four of them sat there in more silence as Scanlon called over the waitress.

"I'll have a gyros sandwich, please. Extra creamy garlic sauce, easy on the onions," he ordered.

"With fries?"

"No, throw in a fruit plate."

Calcaterra then volunteered his meal order as well.

"Okay, give me a BLT club sandwich."

"Fries with that?"

"Yeah, sure."

As the waitress left, and Ellis gave a disturbing look to Scanlon and Calcaterra.

"How can you fucking guys eat right now?"

"I haven't eaten," Scanlon answered, not feeling ashamed of his appetite.

The four of them sat at that table while they pondered their problem. No one, especially William Ellis, could ever recall a situation where the Feds had ever infiltrated their organization. If there were ever threats to the secrecy of their association's manifesto, those threats were dealt with quickly and swiftly. No Archangel has ever been investigated by the FBI.

"Look," Chairman O'Conner finally rationalized.

"We need to play it cool here. For starters, we can't sentence any more redemptions to anyone until we deal with Campana. Until then, we have to play it cool."

"And allow that rat bastard to wear a fucking wire to our meetings?" Scanlon asked.

"Look, if Campana has been working for the FBI for the last two years, and if he were all wired up, they would have come in and busted us already," O'Connor reasoned while sipping his Diet Coke.

"They obviously don't have enough direct evidence or information to indict us right now," the chairman reasoned.

"We need to play it cool."

Another silent moment.

"So, you're saying no more redemptions?" Ellis asked.

"At least not for now."

The four of them were all quiet for a few more long seconds. At that point, the waitress had brought over their late-night dinners to Scanlon and Calcaterra.

"We need to all play stupid right now and pretend that we don't know anything about this. We will keep this confidential, and no one here will mention another word to anyone about Campana or his situation."

The other three looked at the chairman.

"We will be mild-mannered, respectable, community philanthropists that only give away money to those in need."

A pause.

'There will be no mention of redemption on anyone, and we will conduct ourselves as though we were reporting our activities to the Detroit News."

"Really?" Scanlon asked.

"Yes," Ellis replied.

"We've done this before. Whenever the heat started coming down on us over the years, we backed off on the contracts until it was safe to conduct them again."

Scanlon now had garlic cream cheese on the side of his mouth as he was enjoying his late-night dinner, while Calcaterra had quickly devoured his BLT sandwich.

The four of them continued to sit there, now nodding their heads in agreement.

They now had a plan. They knew that their justice manifesto had to be temporarily put on hold until Michael Campana had been dealt with.

"So," O'Conner smiled, now trying to change the subject. "How about those Tigers?"

"Fuck them," Scanlon said. "They lost again to the Houston Astros. They've got no big hitters and no bullpen."

O'Connor pulled out a fifty-dollar bill from his wade of cash and placed it on the table.

"I need to get back home, gentlemen," as he rose from the booth and shook hands with the other members.

He waved to Esmeralda, the waitress, as he walked out of the front door and directly to his car in the back of the parking lot.

O'Conner was doing his best to play it cool as he pulled out of the parking lot, but deep down, he was bothered and extremely worried.

He knew that a federal investigation into the Malizia Society would destroy the organization, his judicial career, and his life. Everything that he had worked so hard for, everything that he had strived to keep secret and out of the public eye, was now about to be compromised. Ryan O'Conner's whole life and career would be absolutely annihilated if the FBI were to acquire any information on the Archangels.

How much information did the FBI really have? How much detail did the Feds have on their mortal redemptions? How much information did

283

Michael Campana give to the federal agents? How should he react?

As he was driving east down Ten Mile Road, the judge entertained the thought of exposing Campana at the next meeting, then assassinating him right there in front of everyone.

Then what?

It would have to be a mass suicide, with each one of the Archangels being killed and destroyed at the end of their final meeting at the Roma Café on September 29th.

He wanted to expose Michael Campana as the true rat that he really was. The Feds would then never be able to affiliate his good family name to murder. There would be no one, including Campana, around to testify. There would be no one left of the Archangels for the Federal Bureau of Investigation to indict.

Everyone would be dead. Everyone would be gone.

Perhaps, he thought to himself, that was the real solution. The Malizia Society of Detroit would be ultimately destroyed by the murder of all of its members after dinner, then ending with his own suicide. He was not about to let this worthwhile organization, a family legacy since his great-grandfather had established it in 1927, go down and be destroyed in shame by federal investigators. He would do whatever he had to do to protect the Malizia Society of Detroit and its worthwhile reputation.

Judge Ryan O'Conner smiled to himself.

He knew that he would be bringing his loaded Baretta pistol to the next meeting.

# CHAPTER THIRTY-FIVE
SUNDAY MASS – AUGUST 2021

The bright sunlight of that early Sunday morning was blinding as I parked my car across from the St. Monica Parish rectory. The summer morning felt like it would be the start of a hot, muggy day, as my two girls got out and waited for me to exit my SUV and lock the car door.

Since my late wife's passing, I had made a habit of getting my daughters up every Sunday morning to go with me to Sunday mass at eight o'clock. Since Laura had passed away, I had taken the responsibility of raising my two girls as Catholics. I had promised her that I would do so, even though I wasn't very religious at the time. Over the years, I felt a calm come over me while spending that one hour at holy mass every Sunday, and it helped me heal while experiencing my wife's untimely death.

St. Monica's was a gothic, old Catholic church on Detroit's west side, and I always felt a special connection there. Laura and I had gotten married at this church and baptized both of our daughters. They made all of their sacraments there at the time, and we all felt an extraordinary connection to that church, especially after having Laura's funeral mass.

On that early Sunday morning, my mind was cluttered, and I felt I had a lot to pray about. The recent deaths of those children several months ago and the means of their killer being murdered had left me feeling a tremendous amount of guilt. I needed to somehow get all of these guilty feelings out of my system and praying over them at Sunday mass was the only way I knew how.

But why was the death of those killers making me feel so damned guilty? They had gotten the vengeance that they deserved, and it was probably the Malizia Society that made sure justice was served. So why the guilt and all of the inner anger?

As a detective with the Detroit Police Department, it wasn't unusual that I felt a tremendous amount of responsibility to protect the people of my precinct and my city. But lately, my guilt feelings have been working overtime. Some victims were ruthlessly being murdered. Some murderers were escaping justice in one form or another and released back out on the streets.

And then some criminals were being strangled and killed for revenge. There was street justice for those accused killers who were tried in our esteemed justice system by very smart and experienced prosecutors who couldn't get a solid conviction against them.

Street justice.... vengeance....and retribution.

As an experienced detective, I had seen and heard it all. They say that vengeance is the act of killing, injuring, or harming someone because they have harmed you in some form or another.

In this case, vengeance and retribution is the act of instilling justice for those who have harmed society as a whole and have not paid for their heinous crimes. Street justice is the act of acquiring vengeance by one's act of retribution by seeking justice against those who have been personally harmed.

As an experienced law enforcement officer, I have developed my own definition of vengeance, retribution, and street justice. I could count how many times I wanted to point my Glock 17 pistol against the head of those monstrous criminals whom I knew, deep down, would never receive the justice that they so greatly deserved. In my mind, street justice was more than just an eye for an eye. An act of vengeance is a form of not only making some demonic criminals pay for their crimes but protecting society from making sure that the killer didn't harm anyone else in the community again.

For those reasons, I've learned to pray. I've learned to seek God, to seek that almighty being to save my soul from the temptation of acquiring vengeance to those monsters who so greatly deserve it. Every Christian knows that the old testament of an eye for an eye is not within the true codicils of the bible or God's teachings. Every God-fearing man knows that taking one's life as redemption for the loss of another is not within the Catholic Church doctrines.

We pray to learn forgiveness. We pray to learn compassion. We pray to grant mercy to those who have harmed others in ways that our deepest nightmares could never imagine. I can't count the sleepless nights I have experienced from the brutal crime scenes that I've had to endure, created by monsters who have no right to walk this earth.

The mass began promptly at eight o'clock that morning, with Father O'Neill asking those in attendance to pray for their sins. It was a preamble to every mass I had attended since being a young boy at St. Angela's Parish in East Detroit. My brothers and I would fidget around in the church pews and make silly faces to each other while the priest celebrated holy mass every Sunday. My mother often gave us dirty looks, sometimes pinching us to keep quiet since she couldn't crack us in public. Back then, the words 'praying for our sins' meant very little. As little boys, our sins were as trivial as telling a lie, stealing a pack of gum from the party store, or swearing like a truck driver in front of our little friends.

But as an adult, as an experienced Detroit Police detective, those sins have been greatly expanded. Those sins could now encompass stealing cash from a crime scene before the other policemen had the chance to notice. Or they were beating up a perpetrator with the butt of a gun until you got the truth out of them. Those sins could also include severe acts of vengeance.

287

Vengeance that no other human being, according to God, has the right to inflict on another individual.

On that morning, my mind was elsewhere. The phrase 'pray for our sins' had taken my mind to another realm. My head was in another place, and every word that the mass celebrant said wasn't even registering in my mind. I thought about all of the sins I had committed, and I then realized that my soul was as tainted as those I trusted to protect society from. Those sins, in my mind, at that moment could never be forgiven. My once clean and pure soul was now as dark and as corrupted as every single criminal who had broken the Lord's most coveted commandment.

I walked up to the front of the church to accept communion, and there were tears in my eyes. I had been praying and reflecting on all of my sins. I knew that wasn't a chance in hell that I could ever be forgiven for the flagrant trespasses I had committed during my career.

"The Body of Christ," as Fr. O'Neill placed the host in my mouth.

"Amen," I whispered loudly, knowing that I was truly not worthy to accept communion on that morning. I went back to my pew and began sobbing to myself, feeling incredibly guilty for all of my sins.

"What's wrong, Daddy?" my youngest daughter Adrianna asked as I buried my face in my hands while trying to say a prayer.

As I looked at her, I felt my face turn red, trying in vain to hide my tears. I shook my head and smiled at her, then kissed her on her forehead.

"Don't worry, Daddy," Adrianna whispered, trying to console me at that moment.

"Mommy is looking down on us, and she's smiling."

I smiled back at her, then hugged her as we all sat at that pew in church, waiting for the mass to end.

At the end of the service, I walked up to the candles displayed in the front of the church. I gave a dollar bill to each of my daughters, and we all lit a candle for my late wife and said another quick prayer. As I looked toward the east side of the church, I noticed two or three people lining up for confession. I thought for a moment and told my girls to wait for me outside.

I walked over to the other side of St. Monica's Church and stood in line for five minutes or so until it was my turn to enter the confessional.

"In the name of the Father, the Son, and Holy Spirit," starting my prayer.

"Bless me, Father, for I have sinned."

A long silent moment.

"I have taken the Lord's name in vain countless of times," I started to confess.

"I have been dishonest to my daughters and myself, many, many times."

Another silent moment.

"I have wished death to those sinners who have broken the Lord's most coveted commandment."

More silence.

"Go on, my brother," the priest from the other side of the confessional said.

At that moment, I broke down and began crying. I started sobbing so loudly that it was embarrassing, having to confess to those sins to whom I was responsible for protecting our society from being perpetrated.

"Go on, my brother...it's okay."

At that moment, I couldn't continue. I felt as though my body and soul were dripping and soaked with guilt.

"I'm sorry, Father, I can't do this," I hastily said as I quickly exited the confessional.

I dried my tears with the sleeve of my jacket, having made the sign of the cross after dipping my hand in holy water. I then looked up at that large, life-size wooden crucifix hanging in front of the church.

I stared at that cross for ten long seconds.

I had now come to the eventual conclusion that had been gripping my tainted soul for so long, for so many sleepless nights. It was an assumption that I hoped I would never come to:

I realized at that moment that all of my mortal sins would never be forgiven.

# CHAPTER THIRTY-SIX
A DAY OF RECKONING –SEPTEMBER 29, 2021

It was a calm, fall evening as the cars were starting to encircle the restaurant on Riopelle Street. The Roma Café was busy as usual, as customers were finding their parking spaces before entering that restaurant on that warm Thursday evening.

As the restaurant patrons entered the café, several men wearing dark suits and black bowler hats entered the banquet room for their quarterly Archangels meeting. They were entering the front door two and three at a time and were being led to the back banquet room at the rear of the restaurant.

Two black Crown Victoria vehicles were also parked in proximity to the restaurant, filled with federal agents. There was also a white utility van parked several hundred yards away across from the restaurant, marked 'Season Comfort' displayed on both sides of the vehicle. Inside, two federal agents were listening on their remote radios, prepared to hear whatever information that would be revealed by their wired-up informant, Michael Campana.

Because of the recent newspaper reports and with the several recent murders of felonious criminals, the Federal Bureau of Investigation had decided that the faithful day had finally arrived. The FBI would make their move that evening and arrest the members of the Malizia Society once they declared murder contracts on those convicts whom they wished to instill justice.

Kevin Scanlon was early that evening. He took his time parking his late-model Mercedes along Riopelle Street. He casually walked to the restaurant with his black bowler hat in his hand.

He stopped at the restaurant entrance and hastily put on his hat. As he entered, the restaurant hostess immediately knew who he was and what his business purpose required that evening.

"You're an Archangel. You're here for the meeting," the hostess said.

"Eh...yes, I am."

"Follow me to the backroom, please."

Kevin Scanlon looked at his watch, noticing that he was indeed early. The meeting didn't start until 7:00. He walked towards the back room, along a darkened hallway past the restrooms. Two men were already seated at the long table with ornate chinaware, crystal wine glasses, and fancy silverware.

As he entered the meeting chamber, the Archangels chairman, Judge O'Conner, shook hands with several other arriving members. He was carefully guarding his Baretta pistol, which was holstered and hidden underneath his suit coat on his right side. He had made sure before entering the meeting that the safety was off so that he could quickly draw his weapon.

. The chairman then took his place at the head of the table, shaking the hands of each esteemed member that was present.

"Kevin Scanlon, so nice to see you," the judge said, as they gave each other an emotional, vigorous man-hug. They smiled at each other, even though they had met over a month before at their clandestine meeting on Ten Mile Road. They were both wearing their black bowler hats.

The other members soon filed into the antiquated meeting room through the restaurant's rear door. Judge William Ellis and Pastor Jonathon Albright came in. They both went around the room, shaking hands and passing out man-hugs to Scanlon and O'Conner, as others started to arrive.

Judge Ellis, being the elder statesman of the group, glanced at the board chairman and nodded. They both mentally noted that their specific plan of mortal redemption for several selected candidates had been deleted from the meeting's agenda that evening.

Thomas Cleary entered wearing a dark, Canali pin-striped suit and black bowler hat, looking as dapper as ever.

"Good evening, Gentlemen," he exclaimed, shaking hands with the other two gentlemen present before settling himself next to Scanlon.

The four men sat down at the long table and continued to make conversation as the other men started to arrive for the meeting. They all greeted each other, giving man hugs and customary kisses to those who seemed amicable enough to do so.

A waitress came into the room and brought red and white wine to the long table. Each of the 'Archangels' started filling their glasses and enjoying their camaraderie.

Michael Campana parked his black, late model Maserati alongside Riopelle Street, parking almost a block away from the federal agents. He sat in his car for several long minutes until he heard a voice come over his hidden hearing aide, implanted deep into his left ear.

"Red Robin, are you there? Can you hear me?" the voice inquired in his earpiece. It was an FBI agent.

"Loud and clear, Blue Finch," Campana responded.

Red Robin and Blue Finch were the code names for Campana and the federal agents who had him wired up and were observing his every word. He quickly exited his vehicle, walking right past the unmarked Crown Victoria vehicles parked alongside the restaurant.

Campana entered the restaurant, wearing his dark suit, black tie, and black bowler hat. He greeted several archangels already seated at the long table in the backroom as other members approached Campana and gave him the traditional man-hug.

Judge Ryan O'Conner immediately noticed Michael Campana, who was now smiling with the other members while shaking hands with each one of them.

*You fucking rat*, he was thinking to himself, as he was making direct eye contact with him. The chairman gave Campana a very dirty look. Ryan O'Conner was having a difficult time hiding his contempt.

At that moment, Judge O'Conner went to the men's restroom, stopping briefly in the restaurant kitchen to greet one of the kitchen chefs.

Then at seven o'clock, O'Conner called the meeting to order.

"The Chairman will call this meeting to order," O'Conner said as he rose from the head of the table with his hands folded. He then temporarily removed his hat. Everyone put their right hands over their breast and said the 'Pledge of Allegiance,' facing the American flag displayed at the far corner of the room. He then asked Pastor Albright to say the prayer before dinner.

"Oh dear Lord," he began. "We ask that you bless this bountiful food and wine that we are all about to enjoy. We ask that you bless our brotherhood of Archangels, the love and camaraderie that we all share, and to bless us one and all with good health and prosperity to every one of us here this evening," Albright loudly said with his hands folded.

"We also ask that you grant us your will, along with the swords of the Archangels of Michael, Gabriel, and Raphael. Guide us in our decisions for the mortal redemption against the dark souls of evil. We ask that we may be guided in your humble

294

wisdom towards our battles with the malevolence of Satan. In Jesus' name, we pray...."

All answered, "Amen."

At that moment, the food entrées began being served, as everyone, still wearing their black bowler hats, placed their napkins across their laps while preparing to enjoy their dinner.

At that moment, the Chairman rose again and made an introduction:

"My dear brothers, it is my pleasure to introduce to you our new Archangel brother, David Marrocco. As you may have heard, he is currently a practicing attorney in Birmingham and an assistant prosecuting attorney with Oakland County for several years. It is a pleasure and an honor to have him here at our meeting this evening."

Marrocco stood up and nodded his head in acknowledgment to everyone there present. They all gave him brief applause. Then each member started standing up one by one and introducing themselves.

"As I mentioned, my name is Ryan O'Conner, and I am the board chairman here this evening. I am a circuit court judge, and I've been an Archangel since 1997. My great-grandfather, Anthony Siracusa, was the founding member."

And then, the next member stood up and introduced himself until finally, the very last member came up and disclosed his name and occupation.

"My name is Kevin Scanlon, and I am also a prosecutor with Wayne County. I've been an Archangel since 2017,"

Marrocco was well aware of who Scanlon was. They had become good friends recently and had been recruited by Scanlon to become a newly initiated Archangel.

Several waitresses entered the room and began serving their meal.

Their entrées for dinner that evening included minestrone soup, Caesar chicken salad, fried calamari, farfalle pasta with vodka sauce, rib-eye steaks with baked potato, and a medley of vegetables espresso coffee, and tiramisu deserts. Their extravagant dinner concluded by nine o'clock.

Then the Chairman called to order the meeting again, and everyone discussed a charitable outdoor carnival that the Archangels were sponsoring for a local handicapped facility in Macomb County. After other matters were discussed, that portion of the meeting was concluded.

"Gentlemen," the Chairman then said, "I ask that you put your hand on our bible and repeat the vows which we are all about to take this evening."

The chamber doors were closed and locked. There was no one else in the room as a large, antique bible was withdrawn and placed at the front of the table. The chairman put his right hand on the bible, while Brother Thomas Cleary, who was seated to his left, put his left hand on the bible. The members then removed their black hats and held hands, forming a circle around the table. They all then recited the Archangel's solemn oath of secrecy together loudly with their bowler hats placed neatly in front of each member at the table.

"We, as devout lifetime members of the Malizia Society of Detroit, will not divulge nor disclose, nor ever betray the actions and directives of this society upon our souls to all the Archangels in heaven, all of the heavenly saints, and to the Lord our God. We do solemnly swear this upon our hearts and souls. In Jesus's name, we pray."

"Amen."

Everyone sat back down again and, putting their hats back on, tended to the real business that was now at hand.

As everyone was sitting back down at the table, Chairman Ryan O'Conner withdrew his Baretta pistol and promptly aimed it at Michael Campana.

"My brothers, before we continue this meeting," O'Conner said, "I would like to introduce to you a brother traitor sitting among us."

All of the Archangels were shocked, as it was so unlike their chairman to suddenly withdraw his pistol in the middle of a Malizia meeting.

"Ryan," Thomas Cleary immediately exclaimed loudly. "What the fuck are you doing?"

O'Conner smiled at the head of the table.

"Well, Mr. Campana, why don't you stand up and tell us about your recent activities with the FBI," O'Conner demanded.

Michael Campana had a shocked look on his face and began turning red. At that moment, he was soaked with embarrassment and wanted to crawl under the table.

"STAND UP, YOU RAT FUCK!" O'Conner demanded, his Baretta pointed squarely at the traitor Archangel.

"Explain to everyone here about the wire you're wearing and the information that you have divulged to the federal agents, who have been stalking our meetings for the last several months."

At that moment, Campana began to stand, his hands in the air and legs shaking with nervousness. At that moment, he looked as though he had urinated all over himself, as his body was wracked with fear.

Chairman Ryan O'Conner walked over to Michael Campana, his pistol still withdrawn, and pointed squarely at the Archangels traitor.

"There is a Judas among us, my brothers. We have a traitor who has been informing the FBI of our mortal redemptions, and he is looking to convict all of us while trying to save himself."

Federal Agent David Arnett, one of the FBI agents in the stakeout, was in the utility van listening to everything transpiring at the Archangels meeting. Both he and another agent had been sitting in the truck listening to everything occurring at the meeting. Arnett was suddenly in shock.

"How the fuck did they figure out that Campana was wired?" he said to the other agent listening to the surveillance.

"How could they know?" he shouted.

A moment of silence as they both listened. He then pulled out his flip phone radio and called the other two agents sitting in the two unmarked cars parked adjacent to the Roma Café.

"Are you guys getting all of this?" he said over a flip-phone radio to another federal agent.

"Should we move in now? It looks like he's been discovered!" said the voice on the other end.

Federal Agent Arnett continued to listen to what was going on at the meeting.

"Let's give it a few minutes," he said over the radio. "I don't think we should rush in just yet."

Back at the banquet room, Judge Ellis continued to sit at the table towards the back of the room. He was discretely smiling to himself, knowing that Ryan O'Conner didn't have the balls to murder Michael Campana right there in the middle of the Archangels meeting.

Tom Cleary gazed at Ellis as a look of fear was starting to come over him. Judge Ellis glanced back at Cleary while looking at Calcaterra. Ellis shook his head and smiled at both of them. He was confident that O'Conner was only looking to embarrass Campana and throw him out of the meeting. O'Conner, he rationalized to himself, was not crazy enough to kill Campana execution-style, right there in front of everyone else at the meeting.

All eyes were now fixated on Ryan O'Conner; his Baretta weapon still pointed at Campana's head.

"Our dearest brother here has been operating a Ponzi scheme in his office and has been discovered and busted by the FBI. So he has traded in his oath of secrecy to our membership in return for a favorable plea deal with the Feds. We are all sitting here as sacrificial lambs, my brothers. Our dear brother Campana wishes to sacrifice all of us to save himself."

At that moment, O'Conner continued to jam the gun up against Campana's head as though he were ready to pistol-whip with the butt of his gun.

"Okay," Judge Ellis said out loud to O'Conner, still standing next to Campana with his gun next to the traitor's head.

"We've made our point to this fucking traitor," Ellis said out loud.

In the meantime, the waitresses and busboys were in the kitchen sorting out the dirty dishes from the banquet room. They were loading them up on a pull cart to bring them to the dishwasher. Several waitresses and waiters were busing the tables and bringing the dirty dishes to the kitchen. They all immediately noticed a distinctive odor coming from the back of the kitchen.

"What is that smell?" one of the waitresses asked the busboy who was assisting her. They both stopped for a moment to study the odor.

It was the distinct smell of gas.

Kevin Scanlon, who had left the meeting room before the confrontation with Campana, was looking to get a refill of his Jack-on-the-Rocks., He had temporarily left the meeting to walk over to the bar in the front of the restaurant, waiting for the bartender to refill his drink.

The head chef, Enrico Ventimiglia, was alerted by several of the wait staff of the prominent scent from the back of the kitchen, near the industrial stove. He noticed one of the assistant line chefs walking over to the stove near the rear of the kitchen. He was about to turn on the automatic lighter and begin to sauté something in a large pan.

All of a sudden, there was a thunderous sound of a gunshot that reverberated throughout the entire restaurant.

Ventimiglia was unexpectedly distracted by the loud noise coming from the closed meeting room, sounding like a very loud firecracker. As he approached the closed meeting room to see what was happening, the line chef was getting ready to turn on the stove.

Upon hearing the loud gunshot noise, the federal agents outside dropped their listening devices and grabbed their holstered guns. They now knew that Campana was in grave danger. They quickly exited their vehicles and began to converge onto the restaurant.

While getting his drink, Kevin Scanlon suddenly froze in his tracks, knowing that a firearm in the back room had abruptly been discharged. He had no idea what was going on or what had happened.

Simultaneously, the assistant line chef turned on the automatic pilot light that ignited the burners to the gas stove.

Suddenly, there was a loud, horrific explosion.

# CHAPTER THIRTY-SEVEN
## A DETROIT TRAGEDY

I was finishing dinner at home, eating with my daughters, when my cell phone first went off. It was just past nine o'clock, and my daughters were helping me do the dishes at the time, and I didn't hear my cell phone go off since it was on vibrate.

"Daddy, your phone is going off," my daughter Adrianna said as she was loading the dishwasher. At that moment, I looked at my phone display and realized it was my partner.

"Hello?"

"Mikie? It's Johnny. You need to come down and help me out here?"

"Help you out? Where are you?"

A moment of silence.

"Didn't you hear? There was a huge explosion at the Roma Café. The whole restaurant is in flames. There are a shit load of casualties. We need your help."

As he was talking, I changed the channel of the TV, and there was a news bulletin from Channel Six Eyewitness News:

*"This is Joanne Spada, Channel Six Eyewitness News. There has been a huge explosion at the Roma Café on Riopelle Street in the Eastern Market. There are more than a dozen fire trucks and patrol cars here at the restaurant, as the EMS trucks and ambulances are now starting to pull to the burning structure. We are still trying to get information on the number of restaurant patrons here having dinner when the restaurant exploded. Several firefighters have been seen pulling bodies out of the back of the restaurant where the banquet hall was located. We were told by one of the managers, who didn't want to appear on camera, that there was a meeting going on when the explosion occurred. We will have more details in the next thirty minutes. Stay tuned."*

I wasted no time bolting out of the door with my jacket, my badge, and my gun. When I arrived at the Eastern Market, I had to put my sirens on for the patrolmen who were doing traffic control to let me park my patrol car closer to the fire. As I got out, I ran as close as I could get to Riopelle Street.

There were a countless number of EMS trucks and fire engines parked within proximity of the fire. Several firefighters were busy extending heavy hoses from the nearby fire hydrants to the back of the restaurant, where the fire had started. Several news crews were assembled around Riopelle Street, trying to get as close as possible to where all of the action was, as the reporters on the scene were scrambling to get information on the fire.

I overheard one of the eyewitnesses being interviewed by a reporter saying that the explosion was so violent and loud that the nearby houses and buildings experienced broken windows and glass shattering everywhere on the streets.

After several minutes of trying to get as close as possible to the fire, I found my partner, John Valentino, trying to assist some of the paramedics in stabilizing several victims who had been escorted outside of the burning structure.

"Johnny, Johnny!" I yelled his name out several times until he heard me.

"Mikie! Help me get some of these victims out of the building!"

I took my jacket off and threw it onto the sidewalk, and ran into the front of the restaurant, which was engulfed with smoke. I had my cellphone with me, so I turned on my flashlight app and saw several people trying to negotiate their way out of the front door.

As the flames were still engulfing the burnt structure, I looked around the front of the vestibule on the east side of the building. At that point, I saw a man lying

302

in front of the restaurant by the bar. His face was blackened and bloodied, and his white shirt was torn. I shined my flashlight on his face.

It was Kevin Scanlon. I came to find out later that he had gone to the bar while the Archangels meeting was going on in the back room at the moment of the explosion. His face was covered in crimson red, and his hair had been charred from the sparks and smoke of the fire. Scanlon looked as though he had a head injury of some kind. I found out later that the force of the explosion caused a fury of broken bottles and glass at the front of the bar, and he was struck by several of the glass bottles.

I picked him up by his arms and threw them over my shoulder, trying to escort him out of the front door. At that moment, Valentino saw me trying to escort Scanlon out of the building, and he grabbed his other arm. At that point, we both were able to walk him towards the ambulance that was stationed nearby. I quickly called for the assistance of another firefighter, who was helping the other firefighter in trying to put out the blaze. The three of us then managed to drag out Scanlon, whose body now seemed lifeless as he was carried out and onto an awaiting stretcher. He was then placed on a gurney and quickly loaded onto Detroit EMS Truck. At the same time, a paramedic worked on his vitals and administered oxygen.

"How does he look?" I then asked one of the paramedics.

"Not good. He has a faint pulse and has lost a lot of blood."

Kevin Scanlon had suffered from broken glass injuries, burns and smoke inhalation. He was barely breathing when I found him at the bar area by the door. Valentino and I then went to help a few other policemen, assisting other paramedics, and began pulling bodies out of the burning building.

By that time, several more news trucks started showing up at the scene. The back of the restaurant was still engulfed in flames, and the brave firefighters kept trying to enter the banquet hall area and the kitchen where the fire had started. I assisted some firefighters in carrying out several injured patrons, bringing them to the ambulance trucks in close proximity. After two hours, the firefighters were able to get the intense fire under control. Several bodies started being recovered from the fire scene, as the building had been so inflamed that many of the firemen couldn't assess how many more people were inside.

I had later found out that there was also a homicide at the restaurant, only minutes before the explosion. Because the FBI was staking out the Roma Café and the Archangels meeting going on inside, there was a confrontation between the Archangels Chairman Ryan O'Conner and Michael Campana, the member wearing a wire at the meeting. The Feds confirmed that there was indeed a gunshot.

It wasn't until several hours later, well past midnight, that the firemen and EMTs were able to re-enter the building. It was after 2:00 am when the flames were completely extinguished, and a crime scene tape had been circled around the burnt-down structure. Twelve bodies were immediately recovered but were pronounced dead on arrival at the hospital. Eight more bodies were pulled from the burning building but died at the scene from their burn injuries. The final three bodies were not immediately recovered until all the flaming debris was removed the next morning. Those three bodies had been charred beyond recognition. They were surrounding the back of the restaurant where the banquet hall was located. There were twenty-three fatalities in all, with one injured firefighter and another officer in critical condition.

One of those bodies that were withdrawn was the body of investment broker Michael Campana. Besides his body being burned beyond recognition, the coroner at the autopsy had confirmed that he had been shot in the head within seconds of the fire explosion.

"How the hell did this fire get started?" I asked Fire Chief Jordan Casmirski as he was assessing the damaged structure.

"It was definitely a gas fire, coming from the kitchen. It probably came from either the stove or the open area," he hypothesized.

"But I'm still not sure how it happened. The kitchen had been recently remodeled. There was new kitchen equipment installed, including a new industrial stove and new Baker's Pride ovens.

He paused for a moment.

"Unless someone turned the gas on and left it on to run for a long period of time, there is no way that this explosion should have happened."

Joanne Spada began her news feed for Channel Eight Eyewitness news broadcast. She began reporting on the restaurant explosion and the number of fatalities inside. She started getting emotional when she mentioned the number of deaths incurred from the restaurant explosion.

"*Firefighters and police here at this burning restaurant are trying to figure out how such a massive explosion could have occurred here at the Roma Café. I spoke to one of the fire chiefs here at the scene. He suspected that a gas explosion probably triggered this massive fire, which destroyed this landmark, one hundred and twenty-seven-year-old structure. Unfortunately, there was a banquet room conducting a meeting when this fire started. This is where the majority of the fire fatalities occurred. All of the injured have been taken to Detroit Mercy Hospital. We will try to have more for you, and we get more information from this tragic scene,*" she emotionally announced.

305

She then wiped the tears from her eyes as she tried to complete her newscast:

"*One of the victims, we have verified, is Wayne County Prosecutor Kevin Scanlon, who was at the restaurant and was suffering from burn injuries and smoke inhalation. He has been transported to Detroit Mercy as well and is in very critical condition,*" she ended.

"*This is Joanne Spada, live at Riopelle Street at the Eastern Market, Eyewitness News.*"

I then noticed the news reporter walk over to her news truck and, tearfully, tried to lite up a cigarette. One of the firefighters quickly stopped her, chastising her for not realizing that there was still traces of gas lingering in the area. It was almost three o'clock in the morning when several of us went to the emergency room at the Detroit Mercy Hospital to support those injured policemen and the families who had gathered there. Third Precinct Commander Anthony Ambrose showed up with a few of the 'Ivory Tower' top brass. Detroit Police Superintendent Joseph Piotrowski and several other police officers met the other precinct commanders at the door. He gave them a briefing of the number of deaths and injuries that were incurred in the explosion. One of the 'Ivory Tower' top brass inquired about Kevin Scanlon and his condition.

"He's fighting for his life. Scanlon endured several glass cut wounds to his head and torso, and he lost a significant amount of blood."

"It's not good," Commander Ambrose interjected.

At that point, several other people from the media started walking into the waiting room of the Detroit Mercy Hospital emergency department. They began asking questions about several of the victims who were meeting at the Roma Café. Someone had mentioned that the meeting that was going on in the back of the restaurant were the guys who gathered periodically to meet there, the ones with the 'black hats.'

At that moment, I felt the hairs stand up in the back of my neck. This would explain why Kevin Scanlon was at the restaurant. He was obviously there to meet up with the Archangels. Besides the several fatalities of wait staff and kitchen employees of the Roma Café, all of the patrons who were meeting in the banquet room in the back restaurant were killed in that fire explosion.

Except for Kevin Scanlon, I suddenly realized that all the Malizia Society of Detroit members were now dead.

# CHAPTER THIRTY-EIGHT
### A VISIT TO THE HOSPITAL – OCTOBER 2021

The Detroit-Mercy Medical Hospital parking lot on Conner Avenue was packed with cars on that Thursday afternoon. I pulled up my Crown Victoria sedan, looking for a parking space near the front entrance door.

It had been almost a month since that devastating fire at the Roma Café. There were twenty-three casualties in all, with several waiters, waitresses and kitchen chefs among the deaths. All of the Archangels, except for Scanlon, did not survive that fire catastrophe. The news coverage of the fire disaster was headline news for several days afterwards, not only in the Detroit area but nationwide. Although there was mention of the dignitaries and political VIP's that were attending that meeting in the rear banquet room of the restaurant, no one mentioned anything about a gathering of Archangels, or the Malizia Society of Detroit.

Even with the FBI and other federal agents stalking the meeting, there was no mention of why there were several federal agents at that restaurant fire. Even though a few of them, including David Arnett, suffered some minor injuries, no one either in the media or at the Detroit PD publicized the ongoing investigation that was occurring at the time of the explosion.

The cause of the fire still remained a mystery, even though it was a foregone conclusion that someone had turned on the gas and left it on in the restaurant kitchen. But there were still questions as to whether the Roma Café explosion was an accident, negligence, or a deadly, planned incineration.

That autumn day, I noticed another Detroit P.D. squad car parked illegally in front, taking up two handicapped parking spaces close by. The autumn rain had let up that afternoon, as there were large puddles of water scattered everywhere around the parking lot. There was still a very light drizzle as I parked on the far side of the parking lot and walked through the rain, slightly sprinkling up to the front door entrance.

"Must be nice to be a high-class detective. I see you get a handicapped, double-parking spot." I mentioned to my partner as I walked in from the damp parking area.

I had asked John Valentino to meet me at the hospital, as I wanted to make a special visit to one of the surviving victims of the Roma Café fire. I was not on any investigation, and I certainly wasn't obligated to make this special hospital visit. But we both had a lot of unanswered questions in our heads, and we both realized that the best way to get some of them answered was to pay a special visit to Detroit Mercy Hospital.

"It was raining harder before you got here. I didn't want to get my brand-new K-mart $39.95 corduroy jacket all wet," Detective Valentino replied.

"I get it. Probably because it's so cheap, you're afraid it's going to shrink while you're wearing it?"

"Yeah," Valentino laughed, "that's it."

The two of us entered the hospital through the front door and into the large reception area filled with patients, doctors, nurses, and other hospital staff.

The aroma of the Starbucks kiosk was mesmerizing, as the coffee smell dominated the hospital atrium as there was a long line of medical staff lined up to get their caffeine fix that afternoon. The two of us casually walked over the elevator after asking for directions to the burn unit from a senior citizen operating the information desk.

When the two of us arrived on the seventh floor, we asked a nurse working at the nurse's floor station desk for the patient's room number we were there to visit.

"Good afternoon, may I help you?" the nurse politely asked.

"Room number for Kevin Scanlon, please."

"Visiting hours don't start until 5:00," the middle-aged nurse with gray hair replied.

Valentino then showed her his Detroit police badge.

"Room 7106," she answered.

As we walked down the hall to the burn unit, several unoccupied hospital beds and IV machines were scattered along the hallway walls. There was a distinctive odor, resembling the smell of urine, as we entered the hospital room where Scanlon was recovering.

I knocked on the room door and noticed a curtain pulled halfway around Scanlon's hospital bed. A nurse was changing his dressings when we entered, and we didn't want to interrupt.

"Is it okay if we come in?"

The nurse looked at us, surprised that we were bold enough to enter his hospital room during non-visiting hours.

"Visiting hours are not until five o'clock," she reminded us again.

"Police business," I boldly answered.

She glared at the two of us.

"You've got five minutes," the older nurse replied.

She begrudgingly pulled back the curtain surrounding Scanlon's bed and quickly left the room. There was another empty hospital bed next to his, along with an empty chair.

Kevin Scanlon looked like he was half asleep and barely noticed that he had any visitors. I walked closer to his bed and put my hand on his left hand, which was attached to an IV machine.

"Kevin, how are you feeling?" I quietly asked him, trying to get his attention.

He looked up at both of us, and his eyes widened.

"Hello, detectives," he answered with a half-smile, obviously trying to absorb the intense pain that he was still feeling.

Scanlon recognized the two of us as Valentino stood at the foot of his hospital bed while I pulled up a chair.

"So, how are you feeling?" I asked again.

"Like a burnt piece of toast," he replied.

There was a large white bandage around his head, and I could see the extensive burn injuries on his face and both of his arms. Several machines were hooked up to his body as the heart monitor was quietly recording his pulse rate.

"Mind if we ask you some questions?" I eagerly asked.

He looked at me, realizing that we were both pretty ballsy, barging into his hospital room while he was recovering.

"What's the matter, Palazzola? Are you afraid that I'm going to croak before you get some answers out of me?"

"No, Kevin. We just have a lot of questions that we need some answers to."

"Like what?"

"Like, what were you doing at the Roma Café that night?"

He looked at me, smiled, then coughed a few times. At that moment, there was a large styrofoam cup filled with water with a straw placed on his serving tray. I grabbed it and put the straw next to Scanlon's mouth.

He took a few sips, then silently glared at me.

"Well?" I asked him again.

"What the fuck do you think we were doing there?" he sarcastically replied in a soft voice.

"Let me guess," Valentino exclaimed.

"Your son's first communion party?"

311

Scanlon smiled, knowing that we all knew why he was assembled with twelve of his other Archangels associates.

Another silent moment.

"They're all dead, Kevin. You know this, right?"

He looked at me as his eyes now were getting moistened with tears.

There were several more silent moments.

"So, you want me to give you my statement? Is that what you fucking guys want?" he said in a soft, raspy voice as he had a difficult time speaking.

I then decided to level with him.

"You know that the Archangels were getting investigated, and the FBI was involved. They even had one of the members wired up at the time of the explosion. They've got a lot of information on the Archangels and who was involved."

Scanlon smiled at me after coughing a few more times.

"So I guess they'll be passing out indictments at Mount Olivet Cemetery," he sardonically replied.

"Kevin, we're here, unofficially, to talk to you about the Archangels. We're here to assist you before the Feds send you an indictment as well. They know that you're involved."

Scanlon smiled at me, winking his eye.

"Then I guess we both have problems now," he paused. "Don't we, Mikie?"

At that moment, my partner looked over at me, not understanding Scanlon's last statement.

There were more silent minutes as the three of us looked at each other.

"We all have secrets, Mikie," Scanlon said.

More silence.

"Some of those secrets go with us to our graves."

Scanlon then looked at me intently.

"You have nothing to worry about, Palazzola. I don't rat on my friends," he said, breathing intermittently between coughs.

"Alive or dead," he added.

At that moment, a nurse came into the hospital room.

"You both need to leave," the older nurse demanded.

At that point, I got up from my chair and placed my right hand over Scanlon's hand. He grasped it and looked at me for several long seconds. It was as if he was trying to shake my hand as if we were making some kind of solemn pact.

Valentino and I then both left the hospital room and walked towards the elevator. As we entered its opened doors, I knew that my partner was going to interrogate me.

"What the fuck was Scanlon talking about?"

"What do you mean?"

"You know what I mean, stop the bullshit," he loudly declared while we were alone in the elevator.

"Were you involved with these fucking guys?"

A long moment of silence as I tried to ignore his question. I knew that, even in the privacy of that hospital elevator, there were cameras that had been installed, recording everything that was going on. I looked at him, and then I glanced at the camera, letting him know that everything was being recorded.

At that moment, the elevator doors opened, and we exited into the lobby and out the front door.

As we walked to the parking lot, I was several feet ahead of my partner as he was going towards his parked squad car.

"Mikie?" I heard him yell out my name.

I walked over to Valentino as he was standing next to his police vehicle.

"I know why you asked me to come here to the hospital with you. You wanted a witness in case he said anything that would incriminate you."

He paused for a few seconds.

"You knew that I would have your back," he said.

I looked at him and smiled.

"Whatever it is that you're doing, you know that I will never say anything," he declared.

I then gave him an intense man-hug, as if we were both trying to keep ourselves from getting emotional.

No matter what the two of us had gone through over the last few years, I knew that my partner, Johnny Valentino, would always look out for me. Johnny was a great partner and an even greater friend. We had been through so much ever since the 'Water Pistol Murders' two years ago. He knew that I had his back, especially after all of the accusatory investigations that had gone on by the Detroit PD, trying to tie him up with those murders. We had developed a special bond as police partners and best friends, and I knew that I could count on him for absolutely anything.

*Anything.*

"Talk to you later, pallie," I said to him as I walked over to my unmarked squad car. I pulled out of that parking lot, feeling better and less nervous about Scanlon and those deceased Archangels.

The Wayne County Prosecutor Kevin Scanlon died from his third-degree burns and smoke inhalation injuries four days later.

I woke up early on that snowy morning from an agitated night of wrestling with my demons. My losing sleep and becoming a chronic insomniac was becoming a nightly ritual. I was sleeping less and less, and my nightmares were getting more intense since learning about the deaths of those members of the Malizia Society.

It was four o'clock in the morning, and my house was dark and silent. I tried making as little noise as possible, as both of my daughters were sound asleep. I turned on the coffee pot and popped in a Keurig coffee pod. Within minutes, I was sitting in front of my Christmas tree, all lit up in the dark, trying to enjoy a morning cup of coffee after an almost sleepless evening.

At that moment, my mind was on a lot of things. I was thinking about the deceased Kevin Scanlon and the Malizia Society of Archangels after the horrific fire at the Roma Café. I was thinking about all of the many years of vengeance murders that the Malizia Society had so successfully performed for almost one hundred years. I thought about all of those people, twenty-three people in all, that had died in that accidental fire. I thought about Scanlon, who had passed away in that hospital room, refusing to give any information to the federal investigators, despite being on his death bed.

I thought about Thomas Blakely and how he wished to take revenge against the Archangels for putting a contract out on his felonious grandson.

I thought about Michael Campana and how he was wired up and covertly reporting to the Federal Bureau of Investigation regarding all the Archangels covert activities.

I thought about Jeff Leonardi, who tried to save himself after naively getting involved with a clandestine secret society that was way over his head.

And then I thought about poor Justine. I should have done a better job protecting her. Maybe if we had that deep, intimate relationship that she was looking for, she would have allowed me to be more caring and defending her. Maybe she would still be alive today.

With the society now destroyed, there was almost no possibility of the Malizia Society of Detroit to ever resurrect itself, with the death of all of its members. After ninety-four years in existence, the chamber of judges, lawyers, doctors, businessmen, teachers, prosecutors, clergy, and other upstanding community members would no longer stand guard in the Motor City. There was no longer an elite squad of hitmen who could invoke their rightful justice of those heinous perpetrators who escaped the lawful scales of justice.

The Detroit Fire Marshals had come up with an initial report on the cause of that Roma Café fire explosion. Their findings believed that it was a gas-leak-related fire perpetuating from the new industrial stove. Since the stove was still under warranty, acquired by the restaurant several months prior, that equipment having a random gas leak seemed unusual.

During an interview with several kitchen survivors, one of the busboys saw a well-dressed man with a black bowler hat near the gas stove. He was obviously from the Archangels meeting.

How the gas from that stove was turned on and left open was still very much a mystery.

But for all intents and purposes, the Malizia Society of Detroit was now dead.

I sat in front of my Christmas tree, watching the white lights blinking on and off. I gazed at the various boxes of gifts and presents that had been placed under the tree. I then studied the Nativity that Adrianna had so carefully placed on the glass table next to the Christmas tree. That Nativity set consisted of thirteen ceramic pieces that my late wife, Laura, had carefully crafted and hand-painted for our Christmas decorations. I studied each one of those Nativity pieces.

My yellow Labrador, Ginger, snuggled up next to me while I sat on my couch, blankly staring at my Christmas tree. She was now almost ten years old and had been next to me as a faithful partner for her entire life since she was a puppy. Ginger grieved with me when I lost my wife, looked after my two young daughters, and kept me company every morning and every night. She looked at me with her big brown eyes, and she immediately knew that I was distraught.

It was Christmas, and I was a broken man, ridden with anger, guilt, and a long string of sleepless nights. Twelve of those Archangels had initially died in that restaurant fire, and I had arrived too late to save anyone of them. I was suffering from survivor's remorse, even though I was not a society member.

Only Kevin Scanlon initially survived, eventually dying in his hospital bed a month later from that fire. He lingered near death from his burn wounds. He was eventually visited by the FBI and the other federal agents. Scanlon kept his word and never said anything to anyone about his involvement.

Or mine.

I sat in front of that Christmas tree for over an hour, in total darkness and silence. I needed to clear my head. I needed to talk to someone about what was going on.

Justine was dead, so that I couldn't talk to her. Her pushy investigative duties put her in the line of fire with the Archangels, and she was eventually found dead in her car, strangled to death, holding her steering wheel. I couldn't save her.

My partner, Johnny Valentino, was still in a fragile state of mind, so I didn't want to trouble him with my problems. Besides, he was still fighting to keep his sobriety. Now that he was back home with his wife and family, the last thing he needed was to hear about my problems and the reality of the Archangels. Even though he came with me to the hospital to visit Scanlon, I suspected that he figured out what was going on.

Johnny Valentino knew the score. But I knew that anything I said to him could make him an accomplice, and that was the last thing that he needed.

I took a shower and got dressed. Then at quarter after seven, I went back to the only place where I thought I would find some inner peace and solitude.

St. Monica's Catholic Church had their usual daily mass at seven-thirty, so I thought I would attend mass that morning. I wondered if my going to daily mass on Christmas Eve would count for my holy day of obligation.

The church was mostly empty, as Father O'Neill recited a quick service and homily. I sat at my favorite pew in the back of the church, and I continued to stare at the large, wooden crucifix.

There were now tears in my eyes, as all of my intense demons were continuously playing in the back of my mind.

I continued to tell myself that I was destined for hell.

After receiving communion, I went back to my pew and said a few prayers. I then pulled out my gold medallion necklace and kissed my medal of Saint Michael.

I thought that perhaps since it was Christmas Eve, I would take another crack at giving my confession to Father O'Neill. After several other worshippers went into the cubicle, it was now my turn.

"Bless me, Father, for I have sinned. It has been a very long time since my last confession. I have since lied, stolen, and taken the Lord's name in vain...."

"Mike? Mike Palazzola? Is that you?"

A long moment of silence. He must have seen me going up to communion.

"Yes, Father."

"After your last attempt at coming to confession a few months ago, I've been hoping that you would come back."

"I've been pretty busy, Father."

Another silent moment.

"Mike? I can tell that you are extremely troubled. Is there something wrong that perhaps the Lord can help you with?"

"Well, yes, Father. There is."

I paused.

"I've been very troubled."

"What about?" the pastor asked.

I was then silent, as the words couldn't come out of my mouth. I then held my breath for a moment, then let the words come out.

"I have committed the vilest of sins, against God's most sacred commandment, Father. I have committed the worst sin of all."

A long silence.

"Several times," I added.

Another silent moment.

"Why are you confessing this to me, Mike?" the priest suddenly asked.

A silent moment. Then he said something that completely shocked me.

"Shouldn't you be at the police station making your confession?"

*Huh? What the fuck?*

I suddenly became ashamed, enraged, angry, furious, and embarrassed, all at the same time.

Who the hell was this 'Man of God', making a judgment call on me while I bore my soul in his confessional? How did this man have the right to judge me and talk to me as though I were the 'Son of Satan?' It had taken so much out of me to bring myself to verbally acknowledge what I had been doing wrong over the last two years.

During an earlier period of my life, I was exhausted with frustration and grief. I was tired of watching so many convicted felons and perpetrators walking away, practically unscathed by the justice system, only to go back on the streets to kill again. I was now wracked with guilt.

"You know, Father O'Neill, this wasn't a very good idea. I came here to seek forgiveness and to bare my soul in front of the Lord."

"Look, Mike...if you want redemption and forgiveness, go to the authorities and face the music. Coming in this confessional and confessing to those kinds of sins does not impress God or me."

The pastor was now chastising me in a loud voice.

"Go to the authorities, and make your confession there, Mike. I can't help you here."

I then got enraged, quickly rising from the kneeler.

'FUCK YOU," I loudly said to the pastor in his confessional.

"WHAT THE HELL WAS I THINKING?" I directly yelled to that hypocritical fucking priest.

As I quickly exited the confessional, several other worshippers stood in line and prayed in the nearby pews. I was sure that they all had heard me screaming in the confessional.

I then stormed out of St. Monica's Church, totally regretful of my attempt at confessing my sins. I got into my car and drove around the city for almost two hours. I was so distraught and angry. I felt as though I had no other place to go on that Christmas Eve.

I then decided to go to Partridge Creek Mall off of Hall Road and attempt to do some Christmas shopping that I needed for my daughters. I hoped it would take my mind off of everything. I walked into the Abercrombie and Fitch store and dropped almost a thousand bucks on clothes for my daughters. I then went to Nordstrom and purchased some bottles of perfume for my girls.

By then, it was almost two o'clock, and I realized that there was one more place that I could go to find my redemption and some private peace on that Christmas Eve.

I drove to White Chapel Cemetery after stopping off at the florist to pick up some flowers, then parking my car near the back of the parking lot. I opened the trunk of my car and took something out, then put it in one of those empty Nordstrom shopping bags. Walking into the cemetery, I found the grave that I was looking for.

There on that marble gravestone was my wife's tombstone with the inscription:

**Laura Ann Palazzola**
**Wife, Mother, and Beloved Angel**

As I stood in front of her grave, my eyes became very moistened by all of the emotion that I was suddenly feeling on that day. I thought about our life together, our children, and my attempt to be a single father to our two beautiful daughters.

I thought about all the right things and the wrong things that I had done with my life since her passing. I thought about the Malizia Society and how they all had died trying to fix the incredible wrongs of the legal system by sentencing those criminals who escaped the rightful judgment of the courts.

I thought about my responsibility to the Archangels. I thought about how I was playing God by taking out criminals' lives for the sake of 'mortal redemption.'

I felt used. I felt dirty. I felt like a ragged toy soldier who was used as a tool to assist the Archangels in granting those malicious criminals their final judgment.

Judge Ryan O'Conner approached me two years ago to assist the Malizia Society in achieving their mortal acts of redemption. They needed another 'black angel,' as he had phrased it. There were two other black angels at the time, and they needed a third.

I had helped them find their paths to death. I had assisted those malicious felons in giving them the brand of justice that they so greatly deserved. Even though I was well compensated with an obscene amount of money, I felt incredibly guilty.

I had sold my heart, and I had realized that I had sacrificed my tainted soul in the process.

*I was a 'black angel.' I was one of them.*

After almost twenty minutes of solemnly standing in front of her grave, I said one last prayer out loud.

"Merry Christmas in heaven, honey. If you get a chance to talk to God, please ask him to forgive me."

I placed the bouquet of red roses in front of her grave marker.

I then opened up a Nordstrom's shopping bag then pulled out something that had been in my trunk. It was an essential item that I had purchased so many times before on the internet.

It was an acquired item that I always ensured I had before maliciously breaking God's most sacred of His Ten Commandments. It was the Lord's most revered, most holy decree that I had broken several times over the last two years.

Over and over again.

I took the item out of the bag and gingerly placed it on her grave.

It was my black bowler hat.

# WHY WE WRITE
## A PERSONAL ESSAY

For those of us who are bold enough to put words down on a white piece of paper, we call ourselves writers. We write for relaxation. We write for profit. We write for creativity. We write for fun.

But in reality, there begs one difficult question that is so often asked:

Why do we write?

As novelists, poets and authors, there are many reasons why we push ourselves to string some words together and express ourselves on a blank piece of paper. We normally do this using a laptop, a computer, an ancient Underwood typewriter, perhaps.

And if none of those are available, even a number two lead pencil will do.

Of course, there are many subjects that we as writers pursue in our expressions for the literary word. Some of those subjects delve into mystery, fiction, non-fiction, history, language, music, romance, and those other cultural topics we writers tend to express ourselves. But for some of us, there is one haunting, *common thread* that we as novelists and poets all seem to battle and combat within ourselves in one form or another.

For some of us, that *common thread* is called *demons*.

We all have them, some of us more than others. We all know of others in our lives who have them. We all have loved ones who battle their demons every day, every evening, sometimes every waking moment. Day in and day out.

*Demons.*

The definition of such horrific, imaginary beings comes from the dictionary as supernatural, unseen, invisible beings, typically associated with dark horrendous evil, prevailing historically in religion, occultism, literature, history,  thriller fiction, magic, folklore, and mythology. They are a large part of the media, comic books, video games, movies, and of course, cable television. In ancient and medieval times, a demon was considered a harmful spiritual entity that could cause demonic possession, calling for a religious exorcism performed by the Catholic Church. In Western occultism and during the Renaissance period, a demon was a spiritual entity conjured and sometimes controlled. The supposed existence of demons remains an important concept in many modern religions and numerous occultist traditions. Demons are feared because of their alleged powers to possess living creatures.

Demons come in many shapes and sizes and are created from a long intimate history of our own life's pains and particular disappointments. They may come from a traumatic experience during childhood, or a violent incident from our past, perhaps. Or a failed relationship, a broken marriage, a haunting image of someone whom we truly loved with our whole heart, who only managed to terrorize, hurt, and disappoint us. Or someone who has passed on to another world, crying out for our help within the abyss of some dark, distant purgatory.

Or perhaps...the promised afterlife.

And for many of us, those demons come to visit when we close our eyes. Our failures, our broken dreams, our traumatic experiences all come to call on us deep down inside; when the lights are dark, the shades are down, and the world around us is completely silent. We all struggle with those internal monsters, a constant battle to keep our sanity and our wit's end. We constantly struggle to maintain a sense of normalcy, as our internal monsters work on our inner psyche, pushing us to points of despair, depression, anxiety, or some constant internal strife.

These satanic, invisible, evil spirits can sometimes possess us, taking over our rational thought processes and turning them into self-doubting weapons of inner destruction. And as we all know...that internal destruction can be extremely dangerous. They are dangerous to our loved ones. They are dangerous to our families and friends. But most of all, our personal demons are extremely dangerous to us.

As writers, we sometimes compose words on a blank page to rectify those thoughts that are unwelcome to our minds. We write to express ourselves, trying to release the negative energy pent up inside our brains and in our souls. We put words down on paper, attempting to create a story that will satisfy those demonic thoughts tightly crammed into our heads. We create fictitious characters who are able to commit evil crimes between two bound covers of leather that we, as civilized human beings, cannot realistically do in real life nor in the real world. We generate storylines and compose poetic stanzas, telling a tale of fragility in determining right from wrong, good from evil, black and white.

We, as writers, no matter how good our stories are, are published in some medium and all end up the same way once they are finished. We are back to the same place....struggling to eradicate our imaginary demigods.

We can all think of several famous writers that come to mind who have tried to battle their internal demons on their own and have lost in doing so. Writers like John Berryman, Jack London, Virginia Woolf, Anne Sexton, Edgar Allen Poe, and of course, Ernest Hemingway....all ended their lives by dying from their own hands.

All destroyed....by their horrific demons.

And there once was another famous Chicago writer, with whom I share a surname, named Eugene Izzi. He was found hanging from a sixteenth-story window of his Michigan Avenue office. A rope was tied around his neck and attached to one of the legs of his office desk. He staged his own death, making it look as though it was an actual murder. He had a small can of maze, a loaded gun, and a set of brass knuckles in his coat pocket when the Chicago PD found him on December 7, 1996. His suicide, although well-staged, included an unpublished draft of an upcoming book with a well-written description of his own final murder scene documenting his actual death. That writer had published a long list of well-documented inner demons.

These famous, talented authors battled depression, bipolar disorder, mental illness, schizophrenia, and intense inner anxiety using alcoholism, drug use, and other destructive addictions to help them cope.

All of this, from their personal inner torments.

And so, as struggling writers, with day jobs as teachers, lawyers, accountants, dentists, chefs, doctors, waiters, factory workers, managers, salespeople, administrators, and the like, there remains one fundamental question:

*Why do we write?*

To express ourselves. Perhaps.

To tell a good story. Maybe.

But deep down inside all of us, there are those lingering terrors that just never seem to go away. And latently, deep down within our souls, lies the real reason for our writing.

We write to cope. We write to communicate. But most of all, we write to release the demonic images that can dangerously overtake us in the form of a liquor bottle, a bag of white powder, or a small vial of pills.

As writers, especially those who struggle with our demons, we fight a losing battle coping with those psychological monsters. For some writers, on some days, every day is a struggle. For some of us, every evening is an attestation of completing another day without hurting ourselves or someone else.

And so....we compose words and sentences on a blank computer screen. For every word, for every sentence, for every paragraph we put down on paper, we continue to temporarily push those evil monsters away.

Far, far away....for now.

And as we put all of those words together, streaming them into a storyline, we have successfully drawn out the emotions of our readers, our adorning book fans who enjoy the string of words and sentences that our private demons force us to create and put together.

Our phrases, our sentences, our storylines make others laugh. Our words make others cry. Our stories make others think about subjects or topics they would never have imagined or even considered. Our fictitious tales, paperback novels, and electronic books on Kindle bring out the emotions of our readers that no other medium can ever do, at no other time or place. Our leather-bound novels can bring entertainment, contentment, and even joy, to those who appreciate our written words.

Written words, which most often originate from our diabolical personal demons.

And so, as an author, my advice to anyone who is awakened in the middle of the night, who has experienced a nightmare or a terrible dream....

To any person who has had a personal visit from their satanic demons. Or to a fellow insomniac, who may have trouble going back to sleep in the middle of the night.

My advice to them is to get up, get out of bed, and walk over to the window. Pull up the shades and look up at the dark, starry sky.

At that moment, know that you are not alone.

Somewhere out there, there is an author or a poet, battling their private monsters in front of their laptop computer, converting their psychological conflicts into storylines of fiction, mystery, enjoyment, and personal prose.

Somewhere in the darkness, beyond their particular demons, someone is striving to put their dreams or nightmares into words of healing and comfort.

Somewhere in the middle of the night, someone is transforming their cries of malice and evil into some written form of profound, literary joy.

Somewhere beyond the dark evening sky, someone is writing a great story.

And this....is why we write.


*November 25, 2021*

# MORE GREAT BOOKS BY CRIME NOVELIST EDWARD IZZI:

Of Bread & Wine (2018)

A Rose from The Executioner (2019)

Demons of Divine Wrath (2019)

Quando Dormo (When I Sleep) (2020)

El Camino Drive (2020)

When A Rook Takes The Queen (2021)

The Buzz Boys (2021)

They Only Wear Black Hats (2021)

## New Book Releases Coming Soon:

Evil Acts of Contrition (Spring, 2022)

Never Catch A Firefly (Fall, 2022)

His novels and writings are available at www.edwardizzi.com, Amazon, Barnes & Noble, and other fine bookstores.

Made in United States
North Haven, CT
29 January 2024

48071177R10198